# Nevertell

## KATHARINE ORTON

WALKER BOOKS

*For Matt, who always kept me going,*
*and for Isaac and his moth friend*

First U.S. edition 2020
First published by Walker Books (U.K.) 2019

Library of Congress Catalog Card Number pending
ISBN 978-1-5362-0712-5

20 21 22 23 24 25 LBM 10 9 8 7 6 5 4 3 2 1

Printed in Melrose Park, IL, U.S.A.

This book was typeset in Stempel Schneidler.
The illustrations were created digitally.

Walker Books US
a division of
Candlewick Press
99 Dover Street
Somerville, Massachusetts 02144

www.walkerbooksus.com

A JUNIOR LIBRARY GUILD SELECTION

# 1

In the depths of Siberia, in the harshest cold, an eleven-year-old girl dressed in gray overalls crossed the assembly square on the way to her prison quarters. She walked alone. She blew on her hands for warmth and left her breath behind her. It made white whirligigs through air laced with ice.

Lina neared the barbed-wire prison fence. There, she stopped. The wind played in the tufts of her sand-colored hair; her eyes glinted like varnished wood. If she'd been a fox, her ears would've been pricked. Voices? Out here? At this hour of dusk?

This wasn't good. Besides her, the only other prisoners who would be lingering about now were the ruthless kind. Thugs. Robbers. The ones that would hold a blade to your throat and strip you of everything you owned, soon as look at you. Boots, overalls, and all. They'd leave you to freeze.

That's if they didn't do you in first.

Lina glanced around. On one side stretched the back of the barracks complex: the sleeping quarters. Half a winter's worth of snow towered next to her on the other side. Prisoners shoveled it off the path and dumped it every morning as their first job of the day, before they set out to work in the mine. It was gray-brown at its base and peaked white at the top—the closest thing to a mountain Lina had ever seen.

Every winter of her life since she could walk, she'd trudged back and forth in its shadow. Tonight, as if things weren't bad enough, it had voices leaking through it. Voices she now recognized.

It had to be mad Old Gleb, Alexei the Butcher—and someone else. Probably Vadim.

The thought of Vadim sent a shudder through her. At sixteen, he already had the tattoos of the criminal underworld. He had quick eyes and no patience for work—as if he felt he had somewhere else to be. Lina had seen it before, all too often. Denial. It made people hard to predict—which also made them dangerous.

"And supplies? We'll need more food than this, Vadim Ivanov, O great and sage leader. Much more, if we're to—"

"Shut your mouth, Gleb." That was Alexei's voice: deep—and blunt as a shovel. Enormous, dark-haired

Alexei, always with his eyebrows knitted and always with coldness in his pale glare. He was Vadim's muscle—twice Vadim's age and double his size, known to act first and let others do the thinking later.

"Quiet, both of you." Vadim. "The kid will be here. Katya said this is the way she always comes. The best place for 'a quiet word,' away from the guards, she said."

Lina gasped. Katya was her mother's name. They were talking about *her*. Why would her mother tell them, of all people, where to find her? Lina was confused for a moment—but only a moment. Her mother was brave. And smart. Lina trusted her. If Mama had told this group where to find her, there must have been a very good reason.

Still, Lina hesitated. These men were dangerous. Maybe they'd only *overheard* her mother saying she'd be here. Maybe they were planning something . . . Lina began to back away.

"*Shh.* What was that?"

Heavy, crunching footsteps sounded, and Alexei loomed around the snowbank. Fear set in Lina's bones.

Alexei reached out. To grab her. Lina sprang into action. She ducked under his arms at the last second and scrambled to get away. Too late. Alexei's ice-cold hands clamped down in an instant. Lina was small for her age, and he lifted her up like a bundle of twigs and whisked her behind the snowbank.

Vadim narrowed his eyes when he saw her and smiled. To the other two, he said: "See. I told you the kid would come."

"Let me go," Lina said through clenched teeth. But Alexei held her fast. No escape. She could kick, however. She drove her heel hard into his shin. He grunted in pain, though his grip didn't falter.

"Oh, for goodness' sake," said Old Gleb. "Look at him. How is he going to help us? He's so small, he'll barely be able to carry his own supplies! Hardly any muscle on him at all. And listen. He sounds just like a girl."

"Idiot!" said Alexei. "She *is* a girl."

Lina smirked. "I'm stronger than I look. And I have more meat on my bones than you, old man." Hurt flashed in Old Gleb's eyes. Lina bit her bottom lip. Starvation wasn't something to joke about in a forced labor camp—and Old Gleb was painfully thin. Almost what people here called a *goner*. "And anyway," she barked, recovering. "What do you want? Why are you looking for me? Shouldn't you be getting your rations, quick, before someone else eats them?"

Vadim sneered. He was good-looking in a certain light. Not when he sneered, though—then he looked ugly and cruel. "Rations are exactly what we're after, but not the measly ones served up here. Can you be trusted to keep a secret, as Katya insists? You understand there's no going back if I tell you this, don't you?"

Lina tried to shrug the chills out of her spine and stand tall. "I can be trusted. Can *you*?"

Alexei and Old Gleb glanced at each other. Old Gleb's cheeks puffed with a barely contained laugh. "Well, Vadim Ivanov, O great and sage leader. She'll be good entertainment on the other side of the wire, at the very least."

Lina's eyes grew wide and round. "You're planning to cross the wire? To escape! Are you mad?" Hardly anyone got past the outer fence. Those who did . . . If the cold didn't get them, or the lack of food, then the wolves would. Or, if you believed that sort of thing, the spirits.

Even so, awe rang in her voice. She gazed at the sliver of horizon, just visible through the wire and beyond the outer fence. By some trick of the fading light, when she squinted, she could see tiny, dark shapes out there, slanted and bracing against the wind.

She imagined she was one.

"Surely, we'd die," she said.

Vadim didn't appear to see any folly in his idea, however. Not judging by that stare. His eyes seemed to search inside her, as if trying to strike a deal with her soul.

Lina stared back just as hard. Vadim may *think* he's clever, but could his plan, whatever it was, really be good *enough*? In two days' time, Lina would be twelve. She didn't intend to celebrate by freezing to death in the Siberian frost. No way.

Then again, how many hundreds of hours had she

spent dreaming of going beyond the wire? Not just to the mine, where the prisoners hacked out precious metal every day. Beyond even that. She fixed her gaze on the horizon, and a smile crept over her face.

She'd go to Moscow. Find her grandmother. Her mother's stories of this amazing woman were one thing. But to actually find her, to finally meet her, to be with her . . . Lina had to come too.

Vadim smiled as if he read the resolve in Lina's eyes. "Good," he said.

A strong wind whipped through the wire fence with a howl, flinging ice crystals that scratched at their faces like needle-sharp claws. The rising storm would only get worse.

"Better find your mother," Vadim said to Lina with another nasty sneer, "and put on your warmest boots. But first, we need you to do something for us."

# 2

I f I say no?" Lina asked Vadim cautiously. It wouldn't
be wise to look too keen. Not right away.

Old Gleb hooted with laughter and slapped his
thigh.

Alexei wasn't as impressed. He shook her. "Stay here
then, runt, and see where it gets you. You'll only slow us
down anyway."

Vadim held up his hand. "That was Alexei's lack of
patience talking. Alexei?" Alexei grunted and let her go.
The sudden release made her arms tingle. She rubbed
them as Vadim spoke again. "What Alexei means is that,
of course, if you and your mother choose to stay, there's
nothing *I* can do. But think of this: freedom. I know it's
what you want, Lina. It's what we all want. But we need
you to do something for us first, to prove you'll be useful

to us beyond the wire, as your mother claims. Or will you, perhaps, be more trouble than you're worth?"

"No, I can help," piped up Lina. So much for not looking too keen. "Whatever it is, I can do it. Try me."

Vadim raised an eyebrow. "Food," he said. "We need food if we're going to survive out there."

And now Lina understood what they wanted from her and why her mother had told them to meet her here in the dark. She was one of Commandant Zima's greenhouse assistants—although *assistant* implied he worked too, instead of just barking his orders at them. Some—like Vadim—presumed this meant she had the favor of the camp's chief officer. It meant nothing. Lina had seen the commandant turn on the people he apparently favored. Working in his greenhouse *did* spare her the toil of the mine, though, and she was lucky she'd inherited her grandfather's talent for gardening. But it meant being under the commandant's nose. Always. And Commandant Zima hated people. He didn't care about the plants either—not the way she did, about nurturing them or helping them grow. The only thing he cared about was the prestige they would bring him at the annual officers' banquet.

Lina feared Zima as much as everyone else. Anyone with any sense would.

She couldn't let her fear get in the way, though. "Listen. I can get you supplies. Vegetables—from the greenhouse. I've got a key, remember."

Alexei grunted. "A handful of rotten onions. We don't need that rubbish."

Vadim glowered at Alexei. "I've told you. We need *everything* we can get."

"Honestly," said Old Gleb, smiling and wiping his eye. "A greenhouse. In *this!*" He gestured at the snow. "That commandant is truly unhinged."

Alexei snorted. "Says you. You believe in children's fairy tales. Sorcerers and spirits who roam around with ghost hounds, capturing men's souls."

Old Gleb set his teeth in a grimace. "Don't," he whispered, barely moving his jaw. "It's dangerous to even speak their names. They—"

Vadim glowered at Gleb this time, then turned back to Lina. "Are you brave enough to do it, Lina? Commandant Zima cares more about those plants in his precious greenhouse than any human being. Even you."

Lina scowled at "even you." She'd heard the rumors. Everyone had. But her mother refused to say who her father was—and Lina couldn't believe that it was the commandant.

"I *can* get you supplies," Lina said. "Much more than just rotten onions." She shot a pointed look at Alexei as she said it. "I grew most of it myself. If it's good enough for the commandant's banquet, it'll be good enough for all of you."

"I knew you'd be able to help us," Vadim said. He

looked self-satisfied, as if everything was happening according to his plan. Lina didn't like it. Not one bit.

A sudden gust of wind from the rising storm started a mini avalanche from the top of the snowbank, and the tumbledown lumps pattered at their feet. Lina shifted out of the way.

"It's settled, then," said Vadim. "We'll meet back here come the dead of night, when everyone is asleep."

Lina felt her stomach twist, though she couldn't tell if it was with fear or excitement. This was actually happening. She really was going beyond the wire.

# 3

It was dusk by the time Lina emerged from behind the snowbank. Only the violet-white glare from the snow still battled against the settling gloom. She glanced over her shoulder, but the others were still hiding. Vadim didn't want them to raise suspicion by arriving at the mess hall in a group, so they would take off once she was out of sight.

Years of trudging had worn patches out of the path, so she navigated the ridges. Today's faint sole scuffs marked the journey of other prisoners to and from their day's work at the mine, over-trodden in places by the cut of the guards' hard-heeled boots.

Normally Lina would go back to her quarters before dinner to put on cleaner overalls. Her mother, Katya, always arrived at the mess hall early from the camp hospital and collected her rations for her, so she wouldn't lose them. But she'd wasted enough time already tonight, and a sense of urgency now drove her. She desperately needed to talk to her mother about what had happened with Vadim and the others.

However, when she sat down at the long wooden bench, worn smooth by elbows and hands, her mother said: "You should've gotten changed as usual, Lina. Someone might notice."

Lina stared at her in surprise. "Mama," she whispered. Her mind was full of the escape. They were going beyond the wire. Really. "I—"

"Don't," said her mother. "Not here. Save it till we're back at our quarters. It's safer to talk there." She looked at Lina for the first time since she'd taken her seat and nodded toward one of the guards patrolling the benches.

Lina understood. The guards were always close by in here. Always listening. The fact that Vadim and the others had dragged her behind a snowbank just to let her in on the plan said it all.

"Here," said her mother, looking away. "Eat up." She pushed a bowl along the bench. A hunk of black bread was poking out of the top. "I've soaked the bread for you. It's like trying to gnaw on a rock today."

"Thank you, Mama." The soup looked watered-down, even by the usual standards, and it smelled putrid—but that may have just been the lingering stench of the mess hall. Lina felt sick with nerves, but she was hungry too. She took several fast slurps of soup.

"Perhaps they've decided that slow starvation isn't working," said her mother, "so now they're going to try choking us with the bread."

Katya radiated tension tonight—which wasn't surprising, given their plan to escape—but Lina felt it was more than that. Perhaps there'd been patients at the hospital who were beyond her help: goners, or even people who'd died. No doubt it reminded her of Lina's grandfather and his slow spiral into illness inside the camp—no, *because* of the camp.

Lina wished she'd known him.

When someone died at the hospital, which was all too frequently, her mother's rage grew so volatile it could spill onto anything and anyone at any moment and turn to a blistering wrath. On days like these, she could play a ruthless game of poker. She almost always won, even against the guards. The prisoners all despised the guards—none more so than Lina's mother. But there were benefits for those willing to play them: more food rations and extra clothes to begin with, as well as other coveted goods. In the camp's world of forbidden card games, there were just two types of people. Those who played and those who didn't.

Between the benches and the stalking guards in their woolen winter uniforms, many dirt-streaked prisoners still lined up for their evening rations. As always, there were three lines. One for those who'd earned the largest portion through their work in the mine. This line was the shortest—and no wonder: The targets set by the officers were all but impossible. The second one was for a moderate portion. The third was for everyone else. This was the longest line—for "starvation rations." No one lasted long on those alone.

As Lina watched, Vadim and Alexei crossed the hall and joined the short line. There were other ways to get a full meal, of course. Their ways—like bribing and bullying. They didn't call Alexei "the Butcher" for nothing, and everyone knew about Vadim's criminal connections on the outside.

Old Gleb, the last to arrive, skulked to the end of the longest line. Clearly hanging around with those thugs didn't bring the payoff he might've hoped for.

Lina scanned the hall and soaked in its sounds as her bread soaked up soup. A hundred different conversations murmured on in a hundred different tongues. Russian. Hungarian. English. Japanese. It amazed her how people from every corner of Russia—and beyond—had ended up in the same place, all together, their stories becoming entwined with hers.

Prisoners collected their portions. The lines shuffled on. The crisscross of bodies opened a space in front of her, and for an instant, Lina caught sight of her best friend,

Bogdan Buyan, the only other person her age in the whole camp. She glimpsed him just before his line moved forward and more adults got in the way. She bit her lip. Looked like starvation rations for him again.

"Less daydreaming, more eating," said her mother. "It looks odd otherwise."

Lina came back to herself and her soup. Little was more urgent for a hungry prisoner than eating. To ignore food after a long day was to basically admit you were up to something.

Act normal, Vadim had said. She owed it to her mother too. She shoveled in her soup as fast as she could. Besides, she'd need strength for what would come.

4

When she'd finished eating and the prisoners began to be dismissed, Lina and her mother shared a look—they both knew it was time for Lina to carry out her part of the plan. With a solemn nod from her mother, Lina left her side and made her way toward the greenhouse. A lump sat in her throat, like dry black bread that hadn't been soaked—impossible to swallow.

She'd grown to love the greenhouse. She'd worked hard tending the soil with her fellow prisoners, whispering encouragement to every buried seed until they dared poke their curious green heads out of the earth to look at her. And now here she was, about to destroy it all.

It was strange, but every plant she touched seemed to grow a little bit quicker and hardier than everyone else's.

Was *that* why the commandant sometimes spoke kindly to her, why every now and then he let her eat the odd vegetable that she'd grown? Because of her skill?

The wind grew in strength and bitterness every time it blew. This storm would be big. No doubts there. Its howls made her think of something living, like an invisible beast gathering its senses after sleep. Perhaps Old Gleb's stories—about evil spirits, about ghost hounds—weren't so crazy after all. Not that she could ever say so. Superstition like that was viewed as mental weakness in Soviet Russia. Even the most harmless fairy tales were banned from schools.

Lina reached the greenhouse—a long plastic-and-wood structure the length of a small shower block—glanced around, and let herself in. She had the only other key besides the commandant's: another reason for some of the others' gossip about favoritism. Lina scowled just thinking about it. She shook the thought off and glanced around once more as she shut the door behind her. To be out after curfew like this was dangerous. If she was caught, she would be questioned. She could be shot. Just because a guard felt like it.

Inside, she breathed the rich scent of earth. The familiar smell was usually calming, but this time, her heart kept pounding. This time was different. Soon, nothing would be the same again.

Leaves rustled eerily from long, dark rows that

stretched out into gloom. Drafts always found their way in, as long as the wind outside had enough force. Tonight, it banged and roared against the panes. Even so, it was warmer inside here than anywhere else in the camp. Commandant Zima had had extra wood-burning stoves brought in by train and installed for heat. Not for the prisoners—but for the plants.

Lina took a grubby sack the size of a pillowcase from a stash by the door. She could always find uses for them—though she'd never expected it would be this. A painful twinge of guilt made her eyes sting when she thought of stealing Zima's vegetables. The commandant was unkind. More than unkind. But he trusted her. Lina hated to break trust—no matter whose it was.

There were also the rumors. The ones that he was her father.

Lina had never asked him, and he'd never mentioned it. But there were times he'd shown patience while she was learning about the plants. He'd genuinely seemed to want to get to know her, asking which vegetables she liked the best and saving the weeding of those for her. But then he would seem to remember himself, and who he was, and the next time they met he'd be even nastier. Did that mean he wasn't her father? Lina had no idea. She owed him nothing. *And they're all relying on me to do this,* Lina thought. *Vadim. Mama. Everyone.* Lina set her jaw and shook out the sack, scanning the rows for the best place to start.

The commandant had not allowed her grandfather to set foot in the greenhouse, despite his having once been a gardener renowned throughout Moscow. "Punishment." For what? No doubt just to be cruel. Commandant Zima had sent him to work in the mine instead, where the dust had slowly choked his lungs. Lina hated that the commandant was sometimes kind to her when he was so ruthless with everyone else.

It was too late to meet her grandfather—he had died before she was born. Not her grandmother, though. She was still free and living in Moscow, as far as they knew. She had been away when her husband, son, and daughter had been arrested, so she hadn't been able to protect them. Apparently, the woman was both tiny and formidable. Lina doubted she was formidable enough to intimidate the secret police, but either way, her grandmother could easily still be somewhere in Moscow.

But with no idea of how to get there, could Lina and Katya really make it? They didn't even know exactly where in Siberia the camp was. Moscow could be hundreds of miles away—or several thousand—for all they knew.

And they had to escape from the camp first. Would they even manage that? The others had to believe they could make it out, or they wouldn't try—would they? She trusted her mother's judgment. After all, Katya was famous in her poker circles for taking risks and still winning. Perhaps her luck, her "magic touch," was all they needed.

Lina brushed a tomato plant with her fingers and breathed in the pungent leaf smell. She felt the familiar, subtle tingling in her fingers—like pins and needles. When she looked down, she was *sure* some of the leaves had unfurled. It wasn't the first time she'd noticed this, but Lina was still shocked. Things like that didn't—*couldn't*—happen. It had to have been a trick of the light, she told herself, as she always did.

Or fear, confusing her senses. She *did* feel strange—it was probably nerves. She pulled her hand back into a fist.

The wind howled and her stomach twisted each time as she reminded herself why she was there. What she had to do. Lina sighed. This was the only place she'd ever felt warmth, and now she was tearing it apart.

# 5

She'd done this all wrong.

Now Lina had a sack full of stolen vegetables and nowhere to hide them but beneath her flimsy overalls. The lump in her throat had gone, replaced by waves of sickness. From the nearby tower, she could hear the guards' chatter carried on bursts of merciless wind. She eyed the assembly square, too frightened to cross.

She ducked around the corner to her friend's quarters instead.

Bogdan slept by the window—a simple opening covered by whatever the prisoners could find: mostly planks of wood and rags. Lina heaved herself and the sack onto the sill and peered inside. "Hey, Bogey."

It was gloomy in there, but Lina could just make out a dozen or more people-size lumps under sackcloth, all pressed in tight together. It smelled awful. "Bogey!" she hissed again.

Lina would've called him Bogdasha—a proper Russian nickname—but having survived a childhood in besieged Leningrad during the Second World War, and with a mother who was a Soviet diplomat and had Western connections, he'd rejected a classic Russian nickname. He said he liked Bogey best. "It's what Western pilots call something unidentified," he'd said mysteriously. "Could be a 'friendly.' But could be a missile . . . "

There was also the bogeyman, which he'd relished telling her about. "A fearsome spirit who comes for people when they're bad," he'd explained, a light like fire flickering in his eyes. "Same kind of thing as Baba Yaga. Just not an old woman—and without the walking house."

She'd later discovered that *bogey* could mean a piece of snot, too. Bogdan just ignored that.

He sat bolt upright when he heard his name. "Lina. That you?"

"Who else?" She swung her legs over the sill, accidentally kicking a wooden plank.

Someone groaned.

"What you up to? You got beans?"

"Yup." Lina often swiped a few for Bogdan—the blighted ones that Zima wanted weeded out and composted. When Bogdan had arrived ten months ago—no family, no friends, no one—he'd been strong. Maybe that was the reason he'd ended up here instead of a children's home—he'd looked a lot older then. Lina never met people her own age. Now, after all that time spent in the mine, Bogdan needed all the nourishment he could get.

"Listen," she said. "I've got more than usual today. You'll need to string them out. This'll be the last bunch for . . . a while."

Bogdan chuckled. "He-he. 'String them out.' That's funny." He coughed. It sounded like his lungs were churning gravel. When he spoke again, his tone had darkened. "Zima getting ready for his party, is he?"

The officers' banquet would be in a week or so. The commandant was providing all the vegetables, while another brought eggs—and another meat. One apparently knew where to get his hands on a calf's brain, which they would eat broiled and buttered. A truly forbidden czarist feast.

It was all Commandant Zima had talked about for weeks, and now, thanks to Lina stealing his best vegetables, he was going to lose face, badly. In front of everyone. Another wave of sickness rolled through Lina's body. If he caught her after what she'd done to his plants . . . Would the chance that she was his daughter make any difference? Lina doubted it.

A swell of sadness tightened her chest. *Shouldn't a father care more about his child than his reputation? Did that mean he wasn't* . . . ? She shook her head and pushed the thoughts down, just like she always did. Now wasn't the time to dwell on it.

"Not quite," she said, handing Bogdan some of the green beans. In a low whisper, she added, "There's not going to be a party."

Bogdan took the beans and gnawed on one immediately. "What're you going on about?" he said between bites.

"Listen." She wondered how she could phrase this without raising too much suspicion from anyone who might be eavesdropping. "I won't *be* here tomorrow."

Bogdan knitted his eyebrows. "Go on."

"I . . ." She hesitated, lowering her voice even more. "I'm going *beyond the wire*. With Mama, Vadim, and some others—"

"Vadim!" shrilled Bogdan. One of the sleeping bundles—an older boy named Keskil, it looked like—grumbled and turned over.

Fear squeezed Lina's throat. She'd said far too much already.

"Lina, Vadim is no good. You can't trust him."

Lina crossed her arms. "Yeah? Says who?" She knew Bogdan was right, though. There was no way she could trust Vadim.

"Don't do it, Lina. Please. It's not worth it." Bogdan stuffed the beans into his sock and began to lie down. "Can't look out for you if you go, can I? You don't see me

24

running off with some criminal . . ." He wrung his hands for comfort.

Lina's heart ached to see her closest friend that way. When Bogdan had first arrived, Lina had stalked him for days, eager to be friends with the only other kid her age, but first trying to work out if he could be trusted. What she'd seen had baffled her.

Bogdan had wandered through camp, every so often peering out from under his heavy black lashes, before pulling a slip of paper from a secret pocket, sketching on it with the stub of a pencil, and quickly hiding it away again. What was he doing? She had to know. She'd sneaked up on him while he was sketching and scared him half to death. He'd been mapping the camp.

Lina had been stunned. She'd never seen a map before. Mapmaking was considered espionage. The guards would've shot him for it. She'd decided right then to be Bogdan's somebody, to protect him. And he was her somebody too. "Somebodies" were important. She had seen people with nobody to look out for them get picked off—by the guards or by vultures like Vadim—and she didn't want that to happen to Bogdan.

The paper and pencil got stolen, of course—which was probably for the best.

And now? Now she was deserting him.

Before she knew what she was doing, she jumped down next to him and grabbed his face with such force that he tried to recoil but couldn't. He stared up at her with near-black, startled eyes. "Bogey," she said. "I'll come back for you. If there's any way . . ."

Bogdan succeeded in pulling away this time. He frowned and closed his eyes. "You need to worry about yourself, out there with Vadim. Not me."

"Fine." Lina turned. Her ribs felt crushed and her throat knotted up tight, but she wouldn't let him see that she was smarting from his words. She never would've expected that they'd part this way. Not her and Bogey.

She had one leg on the windowsill when she heard a rustle. She felt Bogdan's thin arms coil around her shoulders to embrace her. She rested her head against his. When he uncoiled himself, he gave her a slap on the back. It would've been hearty, if he wasn't so weak. "Take good care of yourself, my friend," he said.

Outside again, Lina blinked away her tears before they had a chance to freeze her eyelashes together. The wind raged. It beat itself against the walls of the prison complex, making an eerie animal wail through the holes in the wire fence.

Lina cuddled the lumpy sack of vegetables. For the second time that night, she thought of Old Gleb's stories of ghost hounds.

6

There was no other choice. Now Lina had to brave the square.

She stuffed the sack of vegetables under her overalls again. It was a pitiful hiding place. Anyone who saw her would know instantly that she was up to something. The vegetables made all kinds of misshapen lumps under her shirt, and they kept shifting around inside the sack so that they were impossible to hold on to.

Barrages of savage wind stung her eyes and made her ears ache. It had started to sleet. The sky was dark, and buttery light flickered from the nearest guard tower. Shadows flitted about inside, stretching long, pale arms across the snow. Lina shuddered.

She braced herself and marched across the square. She didn't think, didn't stop, didn't look around, not once—

not until she'd safely reached the door of her quarters. Snatches of voices ebbed on the air, and an oil lamp on its last dregs flickered and flashed from inside. Those who shared her quarters clearly hadn't bedded down yet.

She couldn't take the sack inside if everyone was still awake. Lina glanced up and down the deserted path, squinting out into the darkness filled with sleet and ice pellets that stung when they struck her. In the end, she tucked her vegetable sack around the side of the building and covered it over as well as she could with old snow. It was the best she could do.

Inside, Lina discovered why no one was in bed yet. An argument over sleeping space had started up. No change there. She slipped past sharp elbows and raised voices toward her mother's spot. Lina just missed a poke in the eye by a misdirected finger belonging to a woman named Elena, then dodged a shoulder barge by Yulia, meant for Elena.

Some of the women here were imprisoned because their husbands had been arrested—and vice versa. Whole families could be thrown into places like this on the back of one arrest—mostly for sabotage. Ultimately, *sabotage* could mean whatever the authorities wanted it to.

It's what had happened to Bogdan's family. His parents had been sent to another camp, far away, and he'd come here. It's what had happened to her own family, except they'd all been kept together, at least in the beginning. Katya had been only a few years older than

Lina when she was arrested, along with her brother and their father—Lina's grandfather—on some silly charge. Many hundreds had been sentenced to forced labor in the camps—maybe thousands. Maybe more. It was impossible for them to know the true number arrested in the purges of the "Great Leader," Joseph Stalin.

"Hey, Lina." That was Zoya, who looked like a bag of sticks. "Do us all a favor and stay small, will you? None of this growing that children do. We're running out of room here—the ladies are at each other's throats."

Seeing Zoya so thin gave Lina a guilty lurch. She had a sack of vegetables stashed outside, after all. She hated how this place forced people to think only of their own daily survival, but what could she do? Those vegetables were for the escape.

Soon she'd be out of here for good. Could she send back extra food, perhaps? Provisions, to keep them all going? No. Of course not. It would never make it past the guards.

"Cut it out, Zoya," said Lina, with a laugh that she hoped didn't sound too nervous. Zoya wouldn't have to worry as much about space after tonight. Not that Lina could tell her so.

"Yes. Cut it out, Zoya." Katya didn't sound as amused. Zoya withered under her glare. Lina barely had a chance to pity Zoya before her mother grabbed her arm from behind and yanked her—firmly but not unkindly—into the corner.

"Did you get them?" asked her mother in a whisper, looking Lina up and down. She must have meant the vegetables.

Lina nodded. "They're outside. Hidden."

"Good." Her mother's shoulders relaxed a little—but only a little. "There's something for you under there," she said, gesturing toward the sackcloth blankets where they usually slept. "Go and take a look. But make sure nobody sees."

Lina's throat tightened as she knelt down next to the makeshift beds. She fumbled around under the material. It scratched and pulled at the dry skin on her hands.

Her fingers stumbled over something hard. What was it?

Facing away from the rest of the room, Lina pulled back the covers. A warm winter jacket—just her size. And something else. A pair of boots.

"How did you . . . ?" Lina stopped herself. It was best not to ask where contraband came from. Katya could've won them in a card game. Equally, a lot of things became ownerless at the camp hospital—when the owner stopped needing them, that is.

"Don't put them on yet. Wait until everyone settles down to sleep," said her mother in a hushed tone. "But take a look inside the left boot now."

Lina reached deep inside the fur trim and found something lumpy and hard.

What she pulled out looked like a beaded necklace with a pendant attached—except, instead of a pendant, it was some sort of gnarled old piece of wood or stone. It was rough, pockmarked, and warm. It shimmered in the dim light—like the snow did, sometimes, in moonlight. She'd never known a stone to do that before.

"It was your grandfather's," said Katya over Lina's shoulder. "I've kept it at the hospital since he died."

Lina turned the stone over in her palm and traced its little hollows with her finger. "Why at the hospital?" she said, still studying it.

"It's too precious to keep here. Someone would have taken it, and then I'd have had to get angry. Anyway, it's served more people at the hospital through the years than it would've done as someone's personal trinket." Katya raised one eyebrow as she studied the room behind them, no doubt checking that no one was listening. The argument between Elena and Yulia had wound down, and now the tears flowed, bringing with them tight hugs and lots of hard back patting.

All at once, Lina's mother moved around her and drew her in, cupping the necklace inside Lina's palms and squeezing hard. "Lina, whatever happens to me, you have to promise you'll keep going until you find your grandmother. Do you still remember the address I taught you?"

*16 Gorky Street, Apartment 4.*

"Of course," said Lina. When she was small, Lina had

committed the address of her mother's childhood home to memory. She'd learned it by heart long before her mother had taught her to read and write a little—her way of reaching out beyond the prison fences to her family, far away.

"The last we ever saw of her was at our home in Moscow, so she could be there, or . . ." Katya trailed off, mumbling. "All these years I've hoped for a miracle, but there's no way she could possibly find us here. I should've known that. It's up to me to get us out." Lina's mother let go of her hands. "Listen, Lina. Everyone who's in on this plan has a part to play. Vadim thinks he's the brains." She rolled her eyes. "Really it's his connections on the outside that are most useful. Alexei is the brawn. Old Gleb is a survivor—he knows about the wilderness: finding food and building shelters."

"And I've got the food," Lina said.

Her mother nodded, but she looked distracted and drew Lina in again. "As an extra precaution, I told them your grandmother would reward them as long as they brought you safely to her. She has great power, Lina, like I've always told you—she can give them whatever they need: money, protection . . . As I've said, we all have a part to play. Me?" Katya took the necklace, looped it over Lina's head, and tucked it underneath her overalls. "I'm the distraction while you escape."

"What?" Lina could feel panic rising up her legs. They suddenly felt like stone.

"I've arranged a poker game—tonight in the guard tower. With Danill and a few of the others."

"*Mamochka!* You'll come, though—afterward?" asked Lina, gripping her mother's hands and struggling to fight back pricking tears. "You will, won't you?"

"I hope to. Once I'm sure they're engrossed in the game, I'll slip out and follow your tracks. The storm will make it hard, but if I haven't found you by morning, I've agreed on another meeting spot with Vadim. If I've made it, I'll see you there. If I haven't, you'll need to keep your wits. Trust Old Gleb—and your gut. This"—Katya tapped the stone on the necklace through Lina's overalls— "will help."

Then she sighed and squeezed Lina's shoulder.

Lina couldn't begin to disguise the bewilderment on her face now. All those "ifs" had sent her thoughts into a spin. Breathing was suddenly hard. "Can't you just come with us, Mamochka? We can take a chance that the guards won't be looking . . ." Lina knew that would never work, even as she said it.

Katya shook her head sadly. After a pause, she said, "I'm sorry you're only finding all this out now, Lina. I felt it was safer that you didn't know anything—not until the last minute. That way, if the guards had found out . . ." Katya trailed off. She didn't need to finish her sentence. If they'd found out, Lina would've been innocent. Less likely to be punished.

Lina nodded, but the heavy, cold feeling had reached her chest. Her lungs.

"What if something goes wrong, Mamochka, and you don't make it?"

Her mother shrugged. "Then it goes wrong—and you carry on to Moscow to find your grandmother, like you promised. Life's a gamble, my little one. At the moment, these are the best odds we have. Lina, breathe."

Lina gasped for a real breath, then another and another. She concentrated hard to make each one slower, quieter. Calmer. Staring into her mother's steady eyes helped. Lina realized she'd been shaking. With focus, the trembling started to subside.

There was no point in arguing. Her mother had made up her mind, and no amount of debate would shift her.

Katya quickly got ready to leave, yanking on her own coveted fur-lined boots. She kept them either on or nearby, and anyone who'd ever tried to take them had been given a black eye for their trouble. Her mother planted a warm, hard kiss on Lina's head. "Take off when the lights are out," she whispered. "Good luck, Lina. We may never find another group with these skills and connections who is even willing to try an escape. And if luck's on my side, I'll be with you tomorrow—and we'll both be free."

Lina watched her mother go, fighting every urge to throw herself at her ankles, and cling and cling until

Katya stopped and stayed and held her back just as tight. Just as Lina needed her to. But that was not to be.

※

Lina waited in the dark as the women around her settled down to sleep. Their blanketed bodies made a landscape of rolling hills and valleys that soon she'd need to cross. Every so often, when she thought they must surely all be asleep, one would wriggle, turn, or sit up to adjust herself before lying back down. To stay patient, Lina tried to imagine her mother's progress across the icy path to the guard tower, then up into the warmth of that little armed lookout box—to greet her enemies as friends.

Lina waited until the oil lamp sent out only pulses of weak blue light, and Zoya snored. Soon the thudding of Lina's own heart was the loudest sound she could hear. Only then, with trembling, clumsy fingers, did she put on her brand-new jacket and boots and creep to the door.

Hard, icy pellets still fell from the sky outside and tumbled in the wind like river rocks. Lina thought the storm might help them escape—cover their scent so the dogs couldn't track them. Make them harder to see—and therefore harder to shoot.

Or it could hinder them badly. Blind them. Drive them in circles. Freeze them.

What had she gotten herself into? She wished more than anything that Mama was with her. Still, she had to be brave. She'd promised she would be. And besides, nothing could ever be worse than this place.

Around the corner, she dug through fresh snow on top of old and sighed with relief when the shape of the vegetable sack showed through. It was still there, thankfully, as she'd left it.

Lina wedged the sack firmly inside her new jacket—tucked under her armpit. It was much better hidden in there than under her overalls, and she could pin it against her body. It was strange, but the stone necklace against her chest felt hotter by the second. She did up the jacket and set out.

Straight into the path of Commandant Zima.

# 7

Commandant Zima reached for his pistol. Lina froze. Would he do it? Pull the trigger? She winced, expecting the bang at any second. Instead, silence.

The commandant, recognizing Lina, put the pistol back in his belt. He looked disappointed that it was only her—not a "troublemaker."

"Little Lina," he said, unsmiling. "You startled me. What are you doing out here?"

She opened her mouth to make up something—anything—but the commandant interrupted, answering his own question. "Looking for your mama, I expect." As he strode toward her across the cleared path, Lina listened to his black leather boots crush the grit to dust. She tried not to flinch at the sound. What mood would he be in this evening?

He looked her up and down with narrowed eyes. "What's this?" he asked. "A new coat?" He reached out to feel the collar. Lina didn't dare move—or breathe. "Good quality," he said, clearly impressed. "Which poor wretch did Katya extort this from?" Lina stayed as still as she could. Would he confiscate the jacket—and discover the hidden vegetable sack? Or let it pass?

A burst of raucous laughter hit them with the wind—a woman's voice mingled in. It came from the guard tower.

Commandant Zima nodded toward it. "She's up there, you know," he said. "Poker again." His gaze lingered a little too long on the tower, and a certain look came over his face, a look that often appeared when he spoke about her mother. A little sad. A little pained. It only lasted an instant. "Let them have their fun," he said, shrugging. "I'll be waiting for them after the game."

Lina felt herself bristle like an animal. What could she do? There was no way she could warn her mother. She just had to hope her mother could slip past him.

He glanced back at Lina. A thin smile crept across his pale lips. "Oh. Don't look so worried. I won't go too hard on her, not on your mama. But I'm the commandant here, little Lina. I have my job to do." He turned his attention back to the jacket. "Looks thick," he said, reaching out to pat the sides.

Lina took a step back. "It is," she said. "And warm." The vegetable sack shifted. It was slipping from under her arm. She squeezed it against her, hard. She had the sack by no more than a corner.

And it was still slipping.

All Lina could do was grit her teeth as the last piece of material escaped from the grip of her underarm. The sack slipped and then stopped suddenly—restricted by the slightly tighter hem. She hoped Commandant Zima hadn't seen it move beneath the thick layers of her jacket or heard the vegetables shift.

Zima closed his outstretched fingers into fists and slowly placed the fists behind his back. "You can keep the jacket, little Lina. As I'm in a generous mood. You'll remember that I did you this favor, won't you?"

Lina nodded quickly. "Yes, Commandant."

"But there's a condition," he added. Of course there was. He went on, "If any of the degenerates around here try to take it, you must tell me immediately. It's been a while since I made an example."

Lina knew all about his "examples." She wouldn't wish that on anyone—not even on the likes of Vadim. She didn't care what the gossips said—this man wasn't her father. He couldn't be. Everything in Lina recoiled from the idea.

The commandant stepped around her and strode on. She let her breath escape in a low hiss, but the release of air from her lungs started the vegetables off moving again. She had to get around the corner before they fell out all over the square.

"Lina?" It was the commandant again. His voice cut through the gloom behind her. She tensed. If she turned around now, she risked spilling his precious vegetables all over the dirt at his boots.

"Yes, Commandant?" she answered, without turning.

"You know where she is now, don't you?"

"Yes, Commandant."

"So where are you going?"

Lina pressed the jacket tight against her, still staring straight ahead. "I don't know, Commandant."

"Get back to your quarters. I want you fresh for working in the greenhouse tomorrow. Everything has to be perfect for the banquet."

"Yes, Commandant." Lina dared a quick glance over her shoulder.

He gave her a confused scowl, pulled up his collar against the howling wind, and strode into the darkness—just as the vegetable sack slipped out from under her coat and thudded into the snow. Green beans and onions rolled everywhere.

Lina let out a long sigh of relief.

# 8

After hurriedly picking up the vegetables, Lina tucked them under her jacket again, roughly this time, and waddled to the snowbank where she was supposed to meet Vadim's gang. To see her, anyone might think she was desperate for the toilet. She dived behind the snowbank and looked around, but Vadim and the others weren't there.

What was going on? This was definitely where they were supposed to meet. Had Vadim and his gang been caught? Or had the whole thing been a way to set her and her mother up? A cruel trick to get her to betray Commandant Zima and seal her own fate? Zima rewarded tattletales, and the thugs were often used in this way to police the other prisoners. Sometimes they would play games too, to take down those the other inmates thought of as favorites.

She should have listened to Bogdan. To her own gut instinct. She shouldn't have trusted Vadim.

Out of the corner of her eye, she saw something move in the darkness. The movement was small, but it was amplified by the bulge of a tear. A slip of a figure hurried between the snow and the wire. Something skeletal. Barely there.

"Psst," it said, waving an arm. "This way."

Old Gleb.

Lina had never been so relieved in all her life. She hurried toward him.

There she found the other two as well, hidden behind more snow and crouched by a low hole in the wire fence. The fence stretched over ten feet tall and ran the entire way around the camp. It had little barbs all over it that looked like hundreds of spiders crawling along a web. Even the horizontal lengths of wire resembled spider silk, now that the frost made them iridescent in the moonlight.

All three men were bundled up in woolen jackets, with long-eared *ushankas* on their heads and thick felt boots on their feet—probably stolen from other poor prisoners, who'd now be left with nothing. She thought of Zoya, Bogdan, and all the others. If only they could *all* escape. If only no one had to be left behind.

"What do you think you're doing, throwing those around?" snarled Alexei with a nod toward the vegetable sack stuffed beneath her jacket.

Lina's relief at finding them gave way to anger. It carried on the swell of her adrenaline—which made her brave. "Do you ever cheer up, Alexei?" she snapped. "I mean, do you always have to be so miserable?"

Old Gleb spluttered through bone-thin fingers. Lina knew instantly that she'd gone too far. No one ever spoke to Alexei the Butcher that way. He had a reputation as a killer, after all, that he regularly lived up to.

Alexei loomed over her. "You've got a big mouth for a little girl," he said.

The wind clawed at Lina's exposed cheeks and stole her breath. It barely ruffled Alexei's hair. It was the glint of moonlight that made her look down. Alexei was holding a large hunting blade.

"What have you got that for?" she asked, taken aback.

Vadim stepped between them. "Enough," he said. "We need to get moving before the real storm hits. And first we need to cross the breach."

Lina's insides felt like they'd turned to water. She couldn't believe she was about to cross the breach: a ten-meter-wide gap between the wire fence they stood next to and a second, outer fence made of crisscrossed wood. The second fence was even higher, and climbing it would leave them exposed. It was ramshackle, however—badly looked after. If they hit the right spot, they might find a hole big enough to clamber through, or Alexei, at least, might be able to pull some of it apart to make a gap.

The big problem was the breach itself. No prisoners were ever allowed inside it. If the guards caught anyone there, they would shoot them on sight.

Fresh powdered snow already half filled the small hole in the wire. Perhaps it was an old escape route the guards had never found. Perhaps Alexei had cut it with his knife—although that blade was made for flesh, not metal. Alexei scooped some of the snow away, threw two large sacks through, and then squeezed out after them.

Old Gleb was next. "At least the guard dogs have been fed today," he said to Lina grimly.

He was right. Yesterday several older prisoners had died of pneumonia in the ward next to her mother's. It didn't bear thinking about, what those dogs were fed.

Old Gleb slipped through the hole with ease.

Vadim turned to Lina, who still clutched the sack of vegetables against her chest beneath her jacket. "You next," he said. "We need to cross the breach as quickly as possible to avoid being seen. Stay close to the others so you don't get separated on the other side. We wouldn't want our rations to get lost with you, would we?"

His words made Lina's stomach turn. She pulled the vegetable sack out from under her jacket and crouched down to peer through the hole. Bright snow spiraled against blackness on the other side. She couldn't even see the outer fence.

The hole was already filling up again. With a deep breath, she pushed the sack through and followed close behind.

# 9

The full force of the wind hit her. Lina's head spun. Snowflakes—pulled and pummeled into long, snaking streaks—whorled and whizzed all around. Staring at them spinning in a black sky made her lurch with dizziness. The coldness reached its fingers inside her skull.

Lina staggered backward. In her spin, she caught sight of the bright guard tower, the shadows moving around inside. Right now, that was where her mother was. Would Lina ever see her again? The thought was so crushing that she almost turned back immediately. But Lina remembered her promise—to look for her grandmother in Moscow, whether her mother made it out or not. She didn't want to remember her mama as a flickering shadow, though—as snatches of laughter.

A phantom. She wanted the real thing. Warm and fierce, with her smell of wool and pine.

Vadim grasped Lina around the shoulders. "Keep moving," he hissed in her ear. "Katya can only do so much . . ."

Lina flushed. Her mother had risked everything to make sure Lina made it out. She couldn't let her down. She had to go on, no matter what. The wind. The snow. The darkness. Freedom—it had all overwhelmed her. She'd let Vadim's warning about not getting separated slip right out of her head. *Stupid.* She couldn't afford to get distracted like that.

Vadim shoved her forward. They ran on together, Lina not daring to look back again in case she tempted fate and someone saw her. She felt more exposed—as if she was being watched—than ever before. At any moment, she expected bullets to start whizzing past. That's if they missed the first time.

Old Gleb and Alexei swam back into view. They were crouched next to the outer fence's hodgepodge of wood. "Come on, come on!" urged Gleb. He shone a flashlight onto the fence. Alexei grasped a plank and strained—his fingers turning a ghostly white with the effort. The plank gave way with a splintering sound.

He yanked on another piece, which bent in two rather than snapping. It must've been damp. Rotten. He made a gap wide enough for Old Gleb to slip through, taking the flashlight with him. Lina wasn't about to get left behind. Not here in the breach. She dived in too, the bad wood catching on her clothes and crumbling off in chunks. Vadim followed immediately—and then Alexei himself did. Giant Alexei—through a tiny gap. It took all of them to pull him out the other side.

Once through and on his feet, Alexei snatched the flashlight from Old Gleb. All together, they ran. In the jerking light, a treeless white wasteland stretched out—odd lumps were scattered around that might conceal dead wood or juts of rock. Lina hated not knowing what she might step on—that at any moment something hidden could trip her up. As if to prove her fears were founded, her foot plunged through ice. The freezing mudwater flooding her boot made her gasp. She gritted her teeth and tried to ignore the pain.

The feeling she'd had in the breach, the sense of being watched, hadn't gone away. In fact, it had gotten even stronger. It was almost unbearable.

The stone hanging from its necklace sent out a pulse of startling heat. What was happening? This second shock, together with her fear, was too much. She couldn't go on. "Stop. Something's wrong—really wrong."

Alexei, who'd overtaken her at quite a pace, turned and fixed the weak beam of the flashlight on her. His glare betrayed his fury but also his fear.

"What is it?" snapped Vadim, next to her ear. "Do you want us to leave you here?"

"I can't explain," said Lina. "But we've been followed." Could it be her mother? So soon?

"It can't be Katya," said Vadim, following the same train of thought. "Not yet." His breath was ragged from running, but he was trying to steady it.

The stone sent out pulses of heat that stung her skin, just as it had done earlier.

Right before she had crossed paths with Commandant Zima.

This time, Alexei seemed to read her mind. "Guards?" he said darkly.

Old Gleb wrung his hands. "It's the spirits of this place. They *know*. We're in trouble."

The driving wind died away. In an instant, Lina's battered ears could hear every shuffle the others made. Beyond their panting breath, which sent up plumes of shuddering fog, Lina heard the crunching of snow. It could only be footsteps. She glanced around at the others. They'd all heard it. Everyone was still now, listening. Alexei passed the flashlight to Old Gleb, who covered it with his hand, so all Lina could see were dim shapes.

Vadim still stood close behind Lina, his face pressed to her ear. "Did anyone see you when you came to us?" he whispered. "Any of the guards?" His breath felt hot and wet on her face.

Lina didn't answer. She couldn't. She was remembering the sound Commandant Zima's boots had made earlier as he paced toward her across the grit path.

Old Gleb's hands started trembling over the flashlight. "We have to run," he said. "I won't stand here like this, waiting for death."

"No," said Alexei in a low voice. "Sounds like just one. We'll ambush him. Leave a diversion for the dogs, if any others come."

Lina heard metal scrape leather and knew Alexei had pulled out his hunting blade.

The crunching of footsteps got closer. She stared into the darkness where they'd just been, seeing nothing but patterns made by the falling snow. Lina itched to see more. Not even the light from the guard tower was visible now.

In the darkness, something moved. A spectral shape against the snow. The figure stopped, and so did the footsteps. He'd seen them—or perhaps sensed them. Lina felt Alexei tense, ready to attack.

The figure surged toward them. Alexei lunged forward too.

"Stop!" cried Lina.

Startled, the others turned to stare at her—even Alexei.

The figure kept coming. But he was slight and scruffy and short—not tall and broad like Commandant Zima. Lina gasped. She knew just who it was.

Bogdan. Her best friend.

# 10

B ogey?" she said.

"Lina? That you?" came his small voice, in between quick, shallow breaths. "Thought I'd lost you. I can't see much."

Old Gleb groaned—a mixture of relief and dismay. A bluish beam of light cut through the dark. He had uncovered the flashlight again. In front of them was indeed Bogdan. Alexei looked back at Vadim. They exchanged a glance over Lina's shoulder that worried her. She saw Alexei tighten his grip on the knife.

She had to step in. Quick.

"You leave him alone," she said, glaring at Alexei. "Bogey won't tell, I swear."

"You're right about that," said Bogdan. "Because I'm coming too. Couldn't let you take this risk on your own, could I?" he added to Lina, eyeing the others—Vadim in particular.

"What?" Lina was aghast. He *couldn't* come. His boots were little more than rags, and they were full of holes. His jacket was standard issue, and that was old and worn out too. Already he shook with cold. The storm would freeze him solid.

"You can't," she said. "Bogey. Go back."

Bogdan laughed. "You think I'm going through that again, Lina?" he said through chattering teeth. "I was lucky enough to make it out. I'm not about to break back *in*."

Lina smiled and couldn't stop. In truth, she was so relieved to see him.

Bogdan grinned back with just one corner of his mouth: his signature smile.

Maybe they could both make it out here in the snow, Lina thought. Besides, did Bogdan really stand a better chance at the camp alone, working more and eating less each day?

"Everyone else has a purpose here," said Vadim to Bogdan. "What can *you* offer us?"

"Maps," said Bogdan. "Some on paper. Some up here." He tapped the side of his head.

Lina couldn't see Vadim, but she imagined him sneering again. He frightened her. Vadim was a rarity at the camp. His links to organized crime meant that, unlike most of the prisoners, he probably *had* done something terrible to end up there. He wouldn't hesitate to have Alexei hurt Bogey if he thought he might mess up his escape plan.

"Maps would be useful," said Gleb, glancing between Alexei and Vadim, his face gaunt and his eyes huge in the weak flashlight. "I mean, I can navigate, no problem, but to be able to cross-check . . ."

Alexei gripped Bogdan's arm. "Maps or no maps, we have to move. Now. Listen!" The wind had lulled, but now it picked up again with new and brutal force. From somewhere behind them came a howl that curdled Lina's blood. Not the wind, this time. It sounded more like dogs.

One howl joined another. And another. A whole pack of them—rallying one another to join the hunt. Were they dogs? Or wolves?

Either way, no doubt *they* were the pack's prey.

Old Gleb's face loomed toward Lina out of the snow-peppered darkness. "It's them," he said, wild-eyed. His gaze darted this way and that—he didn't seem to know where to look. "It's not those stupid guard dogs—it can't be. It's the ghost hounds. I knew they would come." His voice grew louder and more panicked. "You still think it's a joke, do you, Vadim Ivanov, O great and—?"

"Get a grip on yourself, Gleb," hissed Vadim. "Or shall we leave you as bait for your 'ghost hounds'?"

Old Gleb made a strangled sound. Lina's heart went out to him.

"Just try it, Vadim." Lina raised her voice above the roaring wind. "Think you can build shelters without him? Find your way?" She shrugged Vadim off and took Gleb's hand. He looked down as if only just remembering her. "Come on, old man," she said. "Nothing can track us in this if we keep moving. Let the ghost hounds try."

Finally they were all agreed on something. They ran with all of their strength.

The wind lashed at Lina. It tore the air away before she had a chance to breathe it. Her left side started to twang. It was what her mother called a "stitch"—when your muscles didn't get enough oxygen to work. If the pain kept spreading, she wouldn't be able to go on running for much longer.

The hunting pack's barks sounded strong. Full of stamina. Old Gleb was right about one thing: These weren't the fierce but feeble creatures that guarded the camp—animals that could only charge for short bursts. These were something else. Would a normal wolf even want to hunt in this storm?

Lina's stitch spread until the only thing she could think of was the pain. It mingled with the searing heat from the stone pressed against her chest.

As she slowed, Bogdan came up alongside her—Bogdan with his wheezy lungs from working in the mine. She couldn't see much of him in the dark—only hear his struggle to breathe in tired gasps.

An ear-piercing howl cut through the darkness. It sent a shiver through Lina's blood. A chorus of other howls joined in. And then, all at once, they fell silent.

The group kept running in the darkness until Vadim shouted for them to stop. Lina collapsed to the ground in a heap, gasping for breath. Her stomach cramped and all her muscles ached.

Everyone listened for the animals, but there was no more noise from them. Just the roaring wind, rising and falling—and the ethereal swishing of diamond dust as it whipped across plains of snow.

A hand gripped Lina's shoulder. Bogdan crouched over her, urgently catching his breath. The loud churning noise that came from deep in his chest scared Lina. She'd never gotten used to it.

She reached up to cover his ice-cold fingers with a gloved hand. Her mind was on other things. There'd been a sound before the final chorus of howls. A high-pitched screech. A whistle, perhaps.

Had somebody called off the pursuit?

A long time went by while everyone recovered themselves. Nobody spoke. Each of them listened. For all they knew, the wolves—or whatever they were—could still be out there, hunting them. Nevertheless, the storm was now ferocious, and the temperature of the wind had plummeted. It would be impossible to keep going.

They found snowdrifts with the flashlight and dug

shelters with their hands—under Gleb's instruction. They started low and dug a tunnel upward into the drift. The angle would help keep warmth in, apparently. Then they scooped out a hollow that could fit one or two people inside, as long as they crouched or lay flat. Unless someone spotted the tunnel opening, the shelter would look just like a normal heap of snow after a storm.

It was so dark they did most of the work blind, but for the weak blue flashlight beam. Alexei shoved the flashlight toward Lina for her to hold while he worked on scooping out snow. It was lightweight and had writing scratched on the side: PROPERTY OF CAMP NINE HOSPITAL. DO NOT REMOVE. Her mother's handiwork.

Lina's heart stung. Even if her mother made it out, would she ever find them?

Lina and Bogdan took a shelter together, while the others made their own. It wasn't exactly warm inside, but at least they were out of that freezing wind.

Once Bogdan had clambered in too, Lina stuffed the vegetable sack down by their feet. She could barely shift it anymore. Her whole body ached. All she wanted now was to sleep. No one had tried to take the sack from her—that was a good thing. If she could keep charge of their food rations, it would be one more reason for the others not to leave her and Bogdan stranded. Before her mother joined them, that is.

She curled up next to Bogdan on a small, thin blanket

Vadim had given them. It covered part of the snow floor, at least, which had been trodden down smooth and compacted into ice. Bogdan was shivering uncontrollably. Shivers wracked her too, but not as badly. She wriggled out of her jacket and laid it over them both.

The stone against Lina's chest grew warm, but not as sharply as it had done before. It settled at a consistent warmth that seemed to reach her blood and carry around her body. It thawed her bones from the inside. And with it pressed between their hearts, Bogdan's shivering soon subsided too. Was this what her mother had meant when she said it was precious and would help Lina?

They slept—Lina in fits and starts. Nightmares of being buried deep underground chased her into the waking world—where each time she'd forget where she was—and then followed her back into sleep again. And so too did the howls of the hunting pack.

# 11

Something was in the snow shelter with them.

Lina sat up in an instant, her hands balled into fists. "Wha-wha?" Her words wouldn't come—fright had chased them away.

But she could relax: It was only Old Gleb. He grinned, showing the gaps in his teeth. "Up you get, kids." His crackly voice sounded businesslike but warm—one a father might use to wake his own children. For the first time, Lina wondered what Old Gleb's life had been like before the prison camp. Unlike her, he'd grown up beyond the wire. No doubt he'd had a livelihood once. Perhaps even a wife. And children?

He hadn't always been this wiry, malnourished man with licks of gray in his matted hair and half the screws loose in his brain. That was a strange thought.

She twisted a fist into her eye and shook Bogdan with her other hand. He hadn't moved a muscle since Old Gleb barged in. In fact, since the shivering had stopped, he hadn't moved all night. She shook him harder, relieved when he finally stirred and started coughing.

"Come on, up, up, up," said Gleb. "Our dear *mother hen*, Alexei, is preparing breakfast." He caught the look on Lina's face and his grin vanished. "Sorry, kid. No sign of Katya yet."

All of Lina's fears for her mother gushed through her again, like a river channeling a thaw.

Gleb squeezed her shoulder and ducked back out of the small exit tunnel. Daylight filtered in after him and splayed across the lumpy ice ceiling.

Lina sighed heavily and dislodged the vegetable sack from the snow wall. Bogdan caught her arm before she could leave. "Wait. What *is* that?" He pointed to where the stone—the source of their warmth through the night—lay under her overalls.

"This?" Lina pulled the necklace over her head and held it in her palm between them. Its string was threaded with tiny wooden beads, all odd sizes, some with fragments of chipped paint in reds, purples, and blues. It looked old. The stone itself was pale brown and woody—perhaps not a stone at all. It had cooled overnight, but it wasn't as cold as it should have been. Not like a normal stone. "I don't know. My mamochka gave it to me before I left. It gets warmer when I'm cold. And to warn me about stuff. It told me you were there last night, you know. Otherwise . . ." Lina trailed off. Without the warning pulse from the stone, there was no doubt she'd have kept on running, with no idea that Bogdan had followed them—and he would have been lost. Frozen stiff. Or found by someone other than her. Is that what had happened to her mother?

"Looks like a shriveled old wasp nest," said Bogdan, sniffing and looking at the stone.

Lina could see what he meant. She peered into the stone's tiny dark holes. It did look like something could be inside it—though not wasps. Not unless they were miniature ones.

Something besides heat seemed to emanate from it, but Lina couldn't say exactly what. It was the way you could tell the difference between something dead and something alive, without having to see it move. Lina knew about this from the plants inside the greenhouse. They were obviously *living*. Just in a different way from her. A slower, more subtle way that she could feel in her fingers whenever she stood near them—a kind of thickness to the air, an electric tension. It was the same with the stone.

"So you'd never seen it before?" said Bogdan. "Ever? You reckon your mama had it all this time, then?"

Lina didn't answer. A memory was unfurling at the back of her mind. It was from a particularly cold winter when she was little. She'd gotten ill. Really ill. So ill they'd sent her to the hospital, which everyone in the prison camp knew was a last resort. Her mother had layered blankets on top of her and stuffed something warm under her mattress. "Shh. Don't tell," she'd said to Lina.

Instead of answering Bogdan's question, Lina put the necklace back on and tucked it safely inside her overalls again.

Bogdan seemed to understand that she didn't want to talk about it anymore. "I've got something too," he said. His eyes flashed and one corner of his mouth curled upward in the start of an involuntary grin. "I wasn't lying last night, about the maps." He ferreted around inside his boot and pulled out a bundle of parchments, which he unfolded and laid flat between them.

"Bogey!" Lina couldn't believe it. "More of them? I thought they were stolen."

"My one of the camp was," said Bogdan. "Not these. These are some of my papa's drafts. Look—there's one of Leningrad, where I'm from, and one of Moscow. Your grandmother's there, isn't she? We can find where she lives, easy. You know her address, right? And these two are other parts of Siberia." He pointed to them as he explained. Each one was etched with roads, rivers, monuments, mountains—and the finest curled writing Lina had ever seen. It must've been Bogdan's father's. He was a mapmaker from Tuva. The maps were so beautiful she couldn't believe they were just drafts.

It must have been wonderful to grow up with a father, as Bogdan had. To know he was a decent person.

Lina shook her head in disbelief at the maps. "If the guards at the camp had found these . . ."

"Not a problem now, is it? Lina, I'm going to make a map of our journey. It's just what *he*—*Papa*—would do, if he were here. Do you know how important this could be? Civilian maps of these areas are unheard of. When I find him again, he'll be so amazed. I've started already—see?" The parchment Bogdan pointed at now had a square sketched onto it, representing the camp, a winding route and a rough drawing of paths and tunnels with the words CAMP'S MINE underneath. Somehow he must've made it on his trips back and forth when working there.

She had to hand it to him. He was definitely determined. And stubborn. Maybe that was why they were friends.

Lina pulled her jacket on while Bogdan collected his maps. She eyed his flimsy clothes. Should she swap jackets with him? She had the stone for warmth, after all . . .

Bogdan crawled out of the shelter before she could make up her mind. He would never *ask* her for it, she knew. In these conditions, it would be like asking someone in the sea for their life jacket. So it was up to her to offer it—and even then he might refuse to take it.

Outside, Alexei carved up stale black bread with his knife. They must have pillaged it from one of the kitchen workers, Lina guessed. There would be even less to go around at the camp today.

Alexei grunted and jabbed the knife toward Lina's vegetable sack. She took that to mean he wanted some.

"Good morning to you too, Alexei," she said, flashing Bogdan a grin. She felt a safe enough distance away, and with enough people in between them, to give him a gentle taunt. After rummaging about, she pulled out two small onions, frozen solid, and rolled them over to Alexei. He carved them up too and handed out the breakfast: a slice each of black bread topped with a chunk of the frozen raw onion.

Lina looked at her and Bogdan's portions. They had easily half the amount the others did. "Hey!" she protested. "Why do we get less?" The men totally ignored her. Lina scowled but, still, she wasn't too bothered. It was the same as, if not better than, they'd get at the camp.

"We'll head to the meeting point with Katya after this," said Vadim. Lina's stomach turned at the mention of her mother's name. How she hoped she'd be there. Then Vadim added, "Gleb and I have discussed it. We think the mine is a mile or two that way, so we'll need to be careful as we pass."

Lina choked on her onion and bread. "What?" she said. "You mean we went through all that last night, and we're not even past the *mine*?" Most of the camp prisoners — like Bogdan — went to work there every day, escorted by armed guards first thing, and brought back again by them later. They didn't want to get spotted by *that* procession.

For the first time ever, Vadim actually looked sheepish and as young as his sixteen years, despite the tattoos. He flushed and glanced away. "I thought we'd make more headway on the first night," he mumbled. "The storm was worse than I anticipated."

"*Someone* slowed us down," barked Alexei, glaring at Bogdan. His pale-blue eyes flashed like sheer ice.

If there'd been an edge of self-consciousness to Vadim's tone before, he was back to his usual self in an instant. "Why *did* you follow us?" he asked, narrowing his eyes at Bogdan in that way that made him look like he was working out a complicated sum. Lina thought she actually preferred Alexei's brutishness to Vadim's slipperiness. At least Alexei was up-front.

Bogdan sat up straight. "I couldn't let Lina go alone," he said loudly. "She's my best friend."

"I see." Vadim turned back to Lina. "Well. He can't go back now because he'll give us away. Maybe he'll last the day, in those clothes. Maybe he'll even last another night. Either way, it makes no difference to me—but he's not having any of our food. You'll have to share yours or let him starve." He smiled.

That explained their half rations, then.

"He'll be fine," said Lina through a mouthful of bread,

acting casual. "You'll see." She slapped Bogdan's shoulder.

Bogdan glared at Vadim defiantly and took a big, loud bite of his share of onion. "I've made it through worse than this," he said once he'd swallowed it.

Vadim only sneered.

They'd show him, Lina thought, but her gut turned. However much she and Bogdan bluffed, what Vadim said was true. Bogdan's clothes would be useless out in this exposed wilderness. Again she had the nagging feeling that keeping her jacket *and* the stone was wrong. But would the stone be enough on its own to keep her from freezing? It wasn't like she could turn it on and off at will. As far as she could tell, *it* decided when to heat up and cool down. Her head felt clouded and confused.

Behind Alexei, Old Gleb bumbled about, humming to himself as he filled a small pot with snow. He took out some matches — he was going to melt snow for them to drink.

"Where are we going to, anyway?" asked Lina warily. "I assume you've planned that far, Vadim Ivanov, O great and sage leader?"

Hearing his own familiar jibe, Old Gleb glanced up from his work, then spluttered a laugh into his chest.

Vadim went pink.

Suddenly Lina could see why Gleb did it. Baiting Vadim was fun.

"We're meeting my associates at an abandoned peasant

house," Vadim said gruffly. "They're bringing supplies. Clothes. New identities. So we can 'disappear.'"

"Where is it?" asked Bogdan.

"West of here. We should reach it in three weeks, at a good pace."

"Three weeks!" Lina couldn't believe it. Even if Alexei's sack contained nothing but bread, and even with all her vegetables, they had nowhere near enough food to keep them all going for three weeks. And who were these "associates" of Vadim's? No doubt members of his criminal gang. Could they even be trusted to turn up?

Opposite her, Alexei cleaned the stench of onion off his hunting blade with the snow, drying both sides on sackcloth before slipping it back in its sheath. What choice did they have but to go along with Vadim's plan?

# 12

Lina would be twelve tomorrow. Today was her first day of freedom, her chance to start a new life in Moscow—just as she'd always dreamed. She should've been happy. Overjoyed. Except that Moscow was likely thousands of miles away across frozen tundra, and they were going to run out of food long before then.

It felt stupid now, but in her most private daydreams, pieced together from photographs and stories of other people's lives, Lina had imagined herself into an apartment overlooking her grandfather's famous gardens in Moscow—the luscious fruits, the exquisite Georgian palms. They would be her gardens too, where she would carry on his work.

She could picture the communal kitchen of her made-up building the most clearly. The food. The warmth.

She'd share vast meals with her neighbors there—produced, as if by magic, from a small but hardy Soviet stove, because people could do all sorts of things when they pulled together. She may have spent her life in a forced labor camp because of their Great Leader's purges, but the Soviet ideal—of every person being equal, and each one working together for the greater good—still felt right to her.

Her grandmother was in the daydreams, of course. A typical silver-haired babushka at the center of it all, ladling out stew and barking cheerful orders. A small woman with a big heart, who'd stroll with her in the gardens and listen keenly as Lina spoke about plants.

Lina brushed tiny flecks of snow from her collar and looked at the frozen wasteland around her. Moscow felt a long way off. After last night's storm, deep snow covered everything, though on the horizon, its whiteness faded into shades of cream and gray. The sky itself stretched cloudless and pale, like a flawless frozen lake. It all felt upside down, as if the sky had switched places with the earth while they slept and now they were wading through yesterday's storm clouds.

In an odd way, they were. The contents of them, at least.

Now every trudge became a greater effort for Lina than the last. Even so, she had to keep going. Until they reached the meeting point, she wouldn't know if her mother had made it out last night. Whether she was even alive.

The less she thought about it, Lina decided, the better. Instead, she considered asking the boy of maps, Bogdan, how many miles away he reckoned Moscow was. Right away she knew that was a terrible idea. His answer could easily shatter the last of her hope. All her dreams were starting to look fragile and thin in this upturned place.

She glanced over at Bogdan a few paces in front, his shoulders hunched against the cold. *No matter what,* she thought, *at least I have Bogey.*

Now, in the kitchen scene she daydreamed about, she imagined Bogdan there too. Sitting next to her, digging in to the delicious stew and chatting between mouthfuls with a grin.

They trudged on until Vadim turned back and raised a finger to his lips. Lina shuddered to think that they were so close to the mine. It would be swarming with people by now. As if that wasn't bad enough, according to Vadim they would have to pass right by it if they were to make good time.

Vadim signaled for them to crawl, and they did. It would be safest that way. They might just be able to edge around behind the snowdrifts without being seen. The natural rise of the land should provide cover too.

Lina hoped so, at least.

Lina hadn't seen the mine in years—luckily for her. She held her breath as they passed over it. She was so close she could hear the guards below making casual chit chat over the prisoners' bent backs while they worked to clear the paths that had been buried by last night's snow.

Lina and the others kept low as they circumnavigated the lip of land overlooking the mine's entranceways.

Ahead of her, Gleb scooted along at a good pace. He was pretty nimble for an old man—surprisingly so, on all fours. Alexei, however? He wasn't exactly built for stealth. Those giant feet of his vibrated across the roof of the mine as if a bear were crossing. Any minute, he was going to get them all caught.

It got worse. As they passed over one of the mine's many busy entrances, Alexei barged a bank of snow with his elbow. It tumbled down toward the guards and prisoners. Lina and the others froze, listening. Forever seemed to go by before they heard it patter onto the ground— perhaps onto people's heads.

Lina remained still. So did the others. They all watched Vadim's face—whiter than usual, his neck tattoos prickled all over with goose bumps as he peered down. Finally he gave them the signal to carry on.

Lina let out her breath. "Does that idiot Alexei actually *want* to get us caught?" she hissed to Bogdan.

She risked peering over the edge herself.

A new wave of prisoners had arrived with picks slung over their shoulders. They were being funneled into a line by armed guards.

"Looks no different than any other day," Bogdan

mumbled next to Lina's ear. He was right. There was no clue to suggest that anyone knew about last night's breakout. Neither the guards nor the prisoners seemed to be behaving any differently.

But they must know. By now, they had to.

From the lip of land, Lina scanned their faces. In a way, all these people were her family. Was it fair that they should still be suffering while she was free? Lina tried to shrug the thought off. It was too painful to dwell on when there was nothing she could do to help them. And yet, the question of fairness sank its claws in and refused to let go so easily. She'd put her own survival above the lives of her comrades. There was no escaping that.

She shook herself, focused on moving and nothing more. She could push her thoughts out that way. For now. She hoped the chilly breeze would carry her guilt far away.

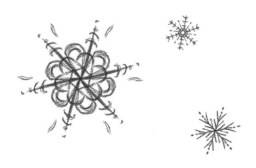

# 13

O nce Vadim felt they were far enough past the mine to stop crawling, all Lina could think about was her mother. When would they get to this meeting point? What if her mother hadn't made it out of the camp? What would Commandant Zima do to her if he caught her? He must've discovered the greenhouse by now—and Lina's absence. A chill ran through her.

High above, a falcon screeched. It was the largest Lina had ever seen. It circled them three times and flew off. Had it been sizing them up for a meal?

Next to her, Old Gleb spat. Lina hadn't noticed him sidle up. His saliva hissed into the snow like acid as he gave the distant mine a final glare.

"Know where to go, kid, to find this grandmother? *If* we make it past this abandoned house of Vadim's . . ." He glanced ahead at Vadim and Alexei walking side by side, heads bent close together as if plotting—again.

Lina found she could barely lift her spirits enough to open her mouth. "My grandmother might be in Moscow," she managed to say. "She doesn't know about me, though."

*Might be in Moscow. Doesn't know about me.* Her chances looked worse with every word. All she really had to go on were her mother's stories. A petite woman who came from the mountains of the Caucasus, she'd said. A woman who'd spent much of her time away from her family on some private, but no doubt important, business.

In truth, her mother had been cagey with certain details.

Still, the odds of finding her were better now than they would have been if Lina had remained at the camp. And at least she had her grandmother's old address committed to memory. A place to begin her search.

Old Gleb scowled. "What—no other family out there?"

Lina shook her head. "No. I was born in the camp. When my grandfather was arrested, so were my mama and uncle. But my grandfather and uncle are both dead now."

"Sorry, kid." Old Gleb gritted his teeth.

Lina squinted at the clouds. "Commandant Zima wouldn't allow my grandfather in the greenhouse, even though he was a skilled gardener. Kind of a botanist really. He got sick working in the mine and died before I was born, so I don't remember him. My uncle was shot in an argument with the guards when I was a baby. I don't remember him either."

Old Gleb nodded. "Commandant Zima is a cruel man."

Lina didn't answer. She retreated into her own thoughts. She found Gleb's new, sympathetic way of speaking to her unsettling, and she wished he'd go back to sarcastic wisecracks. Worse, though, was what he had said. Her mother had never named Commandant Zima as the one who had killed Lina's uncle. But it made sense.

That meant the commandant was responsible for two deaths in her family.

"What did he do to end up at the camp, anyway, your grandad?" asked Gleb.

Her cheeks flushed. "Nothing. He did everything he was supposed to do." It was true. According to her mother, Lina's grandfather had labored as hard as any Stakhanovite: role-model workers who always far surpassed their targets. He'd grown the most amazing gardens imaginable, ready for the grand opening of the All-Union Agricultural Exhibition—a vast park dedicated to the achievements of Russia and all of the countries that made up the Soviet Union. He had grown plants from his native Georgia that no one had even *seen* in Moscow.

"So what happened, then?" asked Gleb.

Lina gazed across the snow-covered plains. "My grandfather criticized the Great Leader. He claimed people were being sold a fairy-tale lie—about everything being perfect in the new society, while really others were starving, or worse. He was among friends. Except one of them wasn't a friend, because they must have told the authorities . . ."

Lina trailed off. There'd been something else that went against him during his "trial"—if you could call it that. Her mother had mentioned it to her once but refused to talk about it ever again. It was too dangerous. Like Old Gleb, it seemed her grandfather had believed in real magic. Spirits. Sorcery. He would tell his stories to some of the schoolchildren who came to visit his gardens. Fairy tales were not allowed in Soviet Russia. At least not the telling of them to children.

"That's our dear 'Comrade Stalin' and his 'merciful' secret police for you." Old Gleb spat again, then grabbed Lina's sleeve in a panic and spun right around. As if he feared that, even here, Stalin's secret police might overhear him.

Lina couldn't blame Old Gleb for his paranoia this time. Judging by how many of the prisoners were in the camp because of the secret police, they had to be pretty good at sneaking around.

"Anyway," Gleb went on in a hushed voice, "you don't have to convince me he didn't deserve it, kid. I make no judgment either way. I was a farmer, but officials from the city took everything. Bullies, they were. They accused me of hiding some grain. And you know what? I did—so my family wouldn't starve. I'd do it again too."

Lina stared at Gleb. He gazed off at the horizon with damp eyes, as if remembering that day. "Never mind," he said, wiping his tears on his sleeve. "When they took me to the camp, at least they spared my sons."

Was this what the escape had all been about for Old Gleb? The longing to see his sons again? Lina felt for him. She had been away from her mother for a matter of hours and she already missed her like mad. What must it be like to have not seen your own children in years? Or, like Bogdan, to have spent months away from your parents, not knowing if they're OK?

Lina touched Gleb's sleeve. "I hope you find them," she said quietly. "Your sons."

Gleb's mouth twitched in what looked like an attempted smile. He gave her a nod instead, before pacing off a little ways ahead, his shoulders hunched against the wind.

Bogdan had been quiet throughout this conversation, stopping every now and then to check his map. Now Lina realized he was shaking. His beige skin had gotten goose bumps in the freezing air, and his teeth chattered.

Both of Bogdan's parents were political prisoners in another, faraway camp. Lina knew he dreamed about seeing them again. At this rate, he wouldn't see the end of the day.

"Here," said Lina. "Bogey. Take this." She slipped off her jacket and offered it to him.

He stared. A mixture of relief, embarrassment, and even anger flashed in his eyes. At first, she thought he was going to say no. Instead, he said, "You sure?"

"'Course. Anyway"—she lowered her voice—"I've got the stone to keep me warm, don't I?"

Bogdan put the jacket on, and Lina took his old one. Hers was a bit short in the arms for Bogdan. It would do the trick, though.

"Where will you go, d'you think?" asked Lina, quickly changing the subject in case he tried to give the jacket back again. "Will you go back to Leningrad?" She winced a little, waiting for the answer. If he went to Leningrad, her vision of them in the same apartment block together would never come true.

Bogdan just shrugged. "Hmm. Maybe."

"Is it weird, me dreaming about a home I've never been to? Like Moscow?" Lina said. She didn't know what had made her say it, except that she trusted Bogdan more than anyone. "I mean, I've only ever known the camp, haven't I?"

"Yeah, but who'd want to stay there?" said Bogdan. "Anyway, it's not weird. I grew up in Leningrad, but I think about Tuva sometimes, where my papa was born. I've never been there, but I might like to go one day. I think about the Western friends my mama had too and wish I could see their countries. Seems strange to me, just staying in one place."

Lina nodded. "Think I sort of know what you mean."

A shadow fell over them. Lina glanced up in time to see the outline of a giant winged creature disappear behind the clouds. That strange falcon again.

Bogdan smoothed out the map against his palm with great care and went on. "Sometimes I think home is wherever you're happiest, mind you. Like with family." Lina rubbed her arms for warmth and looked at the snow. When she looked around again, he met her eye. "And friends," he said. "Obviously."

Lina felt a twinge of happiness, but it turned quickly to pain. "Bogey, what if Mamochka didn't make it out . . . ?"

Bogdan slapped Lina's shoulder. "She will have. If there's anyone alive who could do it, it's your mama."

"Thanks, Bogey."

"And listen," he said, resting his elbow on her shoulder, "we've got each other now. I mean, we're more or less family ourselves."

Before Lina could respond, the temperature of the stone hanging around her neck shot up. She yelped in pain and clawed at her chest.

"What is it? Lina?" Bogdan tugged at her arm. She barely felt him.

They all heard the next sound at the same moment—the howl of a wolf or hound, scenting its prey. It was joined by another, and another, and another.

# 14

A fifth howl joined the chorus. It was the hunting pack.

"Quick!" said Lina, recovering fastest. "Run!"

The mine with its snow-covered entrances was far behind them now, but the snow underfoot was still unpredictable. Last night's storm had sculpted a new landscape over the old: a false floor laced with tricks and traps. Sometimes it held up against the pounding of their feet. Other times their legs plunged right through it up to the knee.

The howls got louder at a shocking speed. Now Lina could hear the beasts snarling and panting right behind them. She risked stumbling to glance over her shoulder. Nothing. For miles. Nothing but her own breath.

It couldn't be.

The creatures were so close that Lina could hear their

claws tearing up sod and snow. But they were nowhere to be seen. It didn't make any sense. There was only one explanation: that Old Gleb's stories—about the ghost hounds—were true.

She pushed the panic down into her stomach, as far from her thoughts as possible. She could hear the hounds gaining on them. At this rate, they'd be caught in moments. She had to *think*.

Lina glanced left. There, a sheer ridge dropped away into who knew what? A bed of sharp rocks? A ravine? There was no other option.

"This way!" Lina grabbed Bogdan's coat sleeve and dragged him with her. She leaped without hesitating, and so did he. They plunged straight over the edge.

Her stomach lurched. Her feet pedaled air. She sailed above trees. Snow. Rocks.

Then she dropped. Bogdan did too. The ground rounded up to meet them like the curl of a giant's tongue. They crashed down its slope—steep but cushioned with pine needles and snow. Lina lost her grip on Bogdan as they tumbled and slid. Space opened up between them in a yawn. A sharp rock scraped Lina's palm, drawing blood.

She didn't have time to dwell on the pain. She was still falling fast. The slope—mottled brown with scratchy twigs and needles—was leveling out, but not fast enough. A pine forest loomed up ahead. Saplings slapped against her limbs, slowing her fall. Lina took one in the stomach.

The others came leaping after them. Lina heard their cries as they fell through the same hazards. The slope. The rocks. The saplings.

Finally at a stop, Lina lay in a ball, trying to draw breath. It wouldn't come. Her head swam. She had to breathe. She had to.

The stone on her necklace, which had been red-hot against her skin, subsided to its steady warmth. It was calming, the heat traveling inward toward her heart. Its pounding slowed. She managed to pull some air inside her, and as she did, the tightness in her throat gave way a little. Then a little more. She focused for as long as she could on breathing. Just to make sure she had it right before she checked around.

Her sack, once full of vegetables, now hung on the branch of a lone tree high up on the slope, like a white flag. Their food littered the ground. Nearby, Bogdan moaned and then raised his head. A gash in his hairline trickled blood.

The baying of the ghost hounds had faded away.

Lina sighed with relief. "You OK, Bogey?" Her wobbly voice surprised her.

Bogdan touched the cut on his head with an unsteady hand, testing its wetness, and studied the blood on his fingers. "Um. Think so." All around, the others were groaning and picking themselves up and checking themselves for injuries too.

Old Gleb limped over. He was staring at her.

The relief of their escape made Lina furious. She screwed up her face into a scowl—because if she didn't, she thought she might cry. "What is it now, old man?"

He stretched his mouth into a big, wide, toothy grin. His lip was split but, other than that and the limp, he looked unharmed. "Kid! Do you know what you've done?"

Alexei and Vadim stalked over then too. Alexei was clutching his arm at a funny angle against his body. It looked bad—perhaps even broken. Both of them wore dark expressions.

Not Old Gleb, though. He leaped forward and ruffled Lina's hair. "You've saved us, that's what. From the ghost hounds. From whatever *thing* is using them to come after us. Who knows—maybe it's even Baba Yaga herself. My child, you must be our lucky star."

Alexei slapped Old Gleb's hand out of Lina's hair. "Old fool," he roared at him. "You're not here to make *friends* with them."

Vadim's glare sucked the wind out of Alexei, and he said no more. Lina had never seen anyone of Alexei's size look so small, so suddenly.

# 15

The trees loomed tall and seemed to crowd in from all angles. The snow hadn't reached the floor in the denser parts of the forest, and shadows shouldered together. It smelled different, even right at the edge of the wood. A mixture of the pines' sap and a cold, earthy dampness. A jumble of growth and decay.

Some of the trees had ribbons and colored scraps tied around their trunks. Muddy white, yellows, and greens. Some were tied to their branches too, where they swayed a little on the breeze. Farther in, symbols had been painted directly onto the bark. They looked like eyes. Signs that others had been there before them. Traveling reindeer or horse herders, perhaps, or people from a nearby village.

"Spirit trees," said Gleb. He gestured at the ribbons,

the painted symbols. "Shamans have been here, see? This place connects the worlds—ours to the *other* realms."

"I'm sick of hearing your fairy tales," muttered Alexei. He stalked away from them, tore one of the sacred ribbons off a tree, and wrapped it awkwardly around his battered arm, struggling with his other hand and his teeth.

Lina scowled at him. To whoever put them there, those ribbons meant something important.

Alexei seemed shaken after the fall—and not just because of his arm. They all were. There was something unsettling about this place, as if the whole forest were holding its breath and watching them. Lina knew Alexei felt it too—however much he pretended he didn't.

Lina looked around. As far as she could tell, they were in a basin. There was no way back out—at least not the way they'd come. That meant they'd need to move extra quickly if they were going to reach the meeting point before dark.

"Hey, leader," she said to Vadim. "We'll just have to look for a way around this ledge and back up to the top. Maybe if we go far enough we can loop back on ourselves and—"

"Don't be an idiot," growled Alexei from over by the trees. He grimaced as he clutched his bandaged arm. "There's no way we're getting back up there."

Lina blinked back tears as it dawned on her what this meant. She vowed to make her voice stronger than she felt, however. "Come on. We don't have time for this. We've got to get a move on. Mamochka will be waiting for us."

Vadim turned to Lina with narrowed eyes, this time without the usual smirk. He was dead serious. "Alexei is right—there is no way back."

"No. Mamochka trusted you. We can't abandon her. She did her part for us, didn't she? That means we stick to what you agreed and we—"

"Did you really believe Katya would make it out after us?" said Vadim in his acid tone. "Let's face it, her chances were nonexistent, even with her luck. I didn't expect her to escape, and I doubt she did either—not really. Why do you think she promised us a reward from your grandmother? It was so we'd still take you to her, even if Katya wasn't there to make sure of it. The meeting point was just a half-hearted fantasy. Her first priority was always you, and she made that clear."

"No," Lina said again. If anyone could manage it, against the odds, Katya could. That's what Bogey had said. Lina turned to Bogdan. He frowned and looked away.

She turned her back on Vadim. On all of them. The tears were bubbling up now, forcing their way free.

She wouldn't accept it.

With a burst of energy that surprised even her, Lina took off marching back toward the slope. She'd get to the meeting place. She'd do it. She'd *show* them. And if her mother didn't come, she'd just march right back to the camp. She'd get her out. Somehow.

Lina's tears made a blur of the trees, the ribbons. She batted branches out of her way and clambered upward. The slope steepened sharply. The steeper it became, the more the ground crumbled under her feet. It wasn't long until her foot slipped. She couldn't cling on, and she slid all the way back down on her hands and knees, bashing into the odd hard rock on the way.

Lina came to a stop at the foot of the towering slope and looked up. She'd barely managed to get a quarter of the way up before she'd fallen. There really was no way back. It was hopeless.

A mocking laugh pealed out from somewhere behind her—Vadim's. Lina got to her feet stiffly and dusted herself off, but she didn't turn around yet. Her cheeks burned. She felt feverish from being upset, the way she would after a long cry as a child. Her hands shook. She wanted to kick something. Preferably Vadim. And yet she could see the truth now.

Lina wiped her eyes. She may not be able to see a way to save her mother right at this moment. But she didn't have to accept she'd lost her either. She'd go on to Moscow and find her grandmother. Her grandmother would help save Katya. All those stories Lina's mother had told her, about how powerful her grandmother was . . . She may even have the ear of the Great Leader. One word to him, along with information from Lina about which camp Katya was in, was all it would take.

Perhaps *that* was why Katya had made Lina promise to find her grandmother? So that Lina wouldn't do anything stupid—and so she really *would* stand a chance of helping her mother if she got stuck behind? That had to be it. Of course.

Lina took a deep breath to steady herself. If there was *any* chance to set her mother free, it lay in Moscow, with her grandmother.

Back with the others, Lina found handfuls of clean snow to wash her scratched hand—and the cut on Bogdan's head. Bogdan flinched, making a kind of inward hiss at the coldness. "You OK, Lina?" he asked gently, when she'd finished.

Lina couldn't reply. She wanted to, but her throat felt squeezed by grief. What an idiot she'd been to believe her mother could escape too. Even if she'd sneaked out of the guard tower, Commandant Zima would've been waiting. He'd told her as much. And with Lina gone, they'd surely suspect Katya had been in on the plan.

Heart racing with thoughts of her mother, Lina rested her hand against a nearby tree and felt a surge of heat travel down her arm and tingle through her fingers. She gave a little jump as the bark creaked and something scratched her hand. Lina pulled it back, fast. Where her palm had rested, a tiny jut of branch had appeared, with a few fresh, minuscule pine needles poking out.

Lina glanced at Bogdan to see if he'd noticed, but he was crouched down, pressing more snow to the cut on his head.

Lina turned back to the tree and the new bud. Strange. It had been the same feeling she'd had in the greenhouse whenever she touched the plants—but stronger. More concentrated. Had she imagined it? She held her breath and pressed her hand over the bark again. She focused on building the warmth, drawing it along her arm. When she pulled her hand back, there was no mistaking it—the branch was longer with yet more needles, bright green, fresh, and new.

How was it possible? What did it mean?

# 16

They carried on into the heart of the forest until dusk, with only a short stop to eat some of the food they'd salvaged from the slope: green beans and more of the black bread. Even so, Lina's stomach cramped painfully with hunger. She didn't mention it, although she didn't need to count up Alexei's remaining loaves of bread to realize they were going to run out of food soon. Surely *they* knew that too. Who would be the first to say so?

They collected large branches to make shelters and smaller ones for a fire. The smoke shouldn't be easy to see among the trees, they decided, and as far as Old Gleb was concerned, with ghost hounds around, a fire was the least of their problems. He was in charge again briefly— giving basic instructions, showing them what to do. They built the frames of their shelters out of the large branches, interlocking at the top, then threaded the frame through with twigs and used leaves for cover. As they did so, Lina couldn't help absently massaging her palm where she'd felt the tingle of heat—and seen the tree branch beneath it, newly grown.

Again, Lina and Bogdan built their shelter together. Lina glanced at him as they worked, and she wondered if she should tell him how she'd made a branch grow earlier. Her heart lurched at the thought of what he might say, and she decided not to. He'd think she'd lost it, wouldn't he? And he'd be right. Stuff like that was impossible.

Building took her mind off everything else, at least.

Old Gleb sent them out looking for kindling next: dry leaves and the like. While they scavenged, Lina approached him. He'd been keeping his distance since the fight with Alexei. Now, when he wasn't giving orders about the shelters and the fire, all he had to say were mumblings about angry spirits.

He didn't look at Lina as she sidled up, but said, "You saved us when you brought us down here, kid, but Vadim's done us in by camping in this forest. It'll find us—our Baba Yaga. Our evil spirit. It's only a matter of time. If we're caught by its ghost hounds, we're finished."

He stepped close, all of a sudden, and pushed his frowning face into hers. Lina jumped. It was the first time in hours he'd even looked at her. "Don't sleep tonight," he said. He tapped the side of his head, hard, with a bony finger. "Stay alert. There's things in the trees—spirits and wolves. This place is theirs, not ours. Listen hard—to *everything*. If you have to run for it, your best bet is to keep heading that way." Gleb pointed through the trees. The way looked dark and damp, with shadows overlapping shadows.

Lina nodded but didn't say a word. She worried that the fall into the forest had made mad Old Gleb even crazier. Her mother had told her to trust him, though, hadn't she? Despite everything, Lina realized with surprise that she did.

As night fell, everyone sat in a circle around the small fire. Nobody spoke about the day. Old Gleb in particular looked wracked with worries. Shadows cast by firelight danced across his brow and slipped down the slope of his cheeks.

"It's my birthday tomorrow," said Lina, breaking the silence. Then she laughed. Once she'd started, she found she couldn't stop laughing. It had more anger in it than she'd expected. Not even Old Gleb, usually so full of cantankerous spirit, laughed with her. Everyone just watched her until she'd finished.

"It's funny," she said, wiping her eyes. "If anyone had told me I'd be free on my birthday—out here, beyond the wire, stuck with all of *you* . . ." She trailed off.

Soon afterward, Lina and Bogdan made their way to

their shelter—this time, they were under a canopy of branches instead of a ceiling of snow. Once they'd settled down for the night, Lina tried her best to stay awake, to listen hard, as Old Gleb had warned her to. But each one of her bones felt heavy, with sadness as much as exhaustion, and the crackle of the fire and the sound of the others' low mumbling lulled her.

She couldn't be certain what had woken her up. The stone, perhaps, and its sudden flash of heat. Bogdan muttered something, but he was asleep—she could tell by his drawn-out, gravelly wheezing. She could've kicked herself for sleeping, after Gleb had warned her not to.

She listened. The others must be awake still, because she could hear them beyond the shelter—speaking in a hush. Despite their low voices, something about their tone told her they were arguing.

"I'll do it. I've got no problem with that." That was Alexei, blunt as ever. "I've still got one good arm."

It was Old Gleb who answered him. "Come on. Open up your heart for once, will you?"

"Idiot! I told you not to get friendly with her. You've only got yourself to blame."

"Who saved our skins from the hounds? That's right: *She* did. The kid. You can't do it. It's too brutish. There must be another way . . . And we've got plenty of vegetables to go on, for now. There's enough for all of us—"

"A handful of green beans. A few onions. We won't last on that and you know it, Gleb. Not after we lost so much food in the fall."

"Alexei, if nothing else touches your heart, at least think of the reward from her grandmother, would you? Vadim, what do you say? Make this brute see sense. Please."

"Reward," grumbled Alexei. "That's if there is one. Katya could never know that."

There was a pause. Then Vadim spoke in the voice he used when he'd impressed himself by being clever. "There wasn't enough food, even before this friend of hers turned up, and since the fall, there's even less. They may be sharing rations, but that's still more food than I'm prepared to lose out on. The reward for the girl means nothing if we starve first. We'll do it tonight—both of them. Gleb, you'll help me hold them still. Then, Alexei, you go in with the knife . . ."

"Vadim. No."

Lina covered her mouth with her hands to prevent herself from crying out. She thought she was going to be sick. What had she done to deserve this? They were going to kill her and Bogdan—for what? So they could eat their rations?

After a pause, Vadim spoke again. "Sacrifices have to be made here, Gleb." He laughed. "Unless you'd rather take their places, that is? You do eat a lot for a scrawny old man."

Old Gleb whimpered and said no more.

# 17

With her heart thundering in her ears, Lina gave Bogdan a rough shake and whispered, "Bogey. Wake. Up." His eyes snapped open, but she clamped her hand over his mouth before he could speak. Then she hissed, "They're going to kill us. We've got to go."

"Mmf!" Bogdan's eyes flashed wide in the dark.

"We've got to go right now, or we're goners."

Bogey shot upright and Lina pointed to the sack containing the few vegetables they'd managed to save from the trees earlier, now at their feet where she'd wedged it in. Together, they crawled over to tug at it. The material was caught on the spiky branches of the shelter and wouldn't budge. There was a horrible scraping, tearing sound every time they pulled.

"Shh," Lina said.

Outside, Vadim, Gleb, and Alexei fell silent. They *must* have heard. Lina and Bogdan stopped moving and waited, holding their breath in the dark. If Alexei and the others came to their shelter now, they'd be trapped.

It felt like a long time before the three men picked up their conversation again—this time in low murmurs that were impossible to make out.

Bogdan reached behind the sack to free it from the branches. He gave Lina a nod. With a final tug from both of them, the sack of vegetables came loose.

Lina edged to the exit and poked her head out.

The fire had reduced to embers. The last of the wood made loud whip-cracking sounds, sending up puffs of dark, acrid smoke.

The three men were silhouetted around the dying fire, their backs to Lina. A bright moon illuminated the forest in an eerie blue glow, so she could just make out Old Gleb, slumped like a sack of bones next to the huge figure of Alexei. The fur trim on Vadim's coat and on the *ushanka* on his head ruffled in the ice-cold breeze. She knew that the minute the embers faded and the heat died, they would come. Lina and Bogdan had mere moments before that happened. If that.

Lina crawled out of the shelter. The frozen earth at the entrance twinkled like a sky of stars but made little noise. Once out, she signaled for Bogdan to follow and then took a step forward. A branch cracked under her foot. They both froze. Lina tasted metal on her tongue—the taste of panic. She risked a glance at the three men.

They hadn't moved. The crackling embers had masked the sound.

Lina winced by way of apology while Bogdan passed her the vegetable sack, and then he clambered the rest of the way out. The snow around them was marked with dry branches and pine needles. Walking on it would be noisy.

All Lina knew was that, if they couldn't be quiet, they would have to be quick. She took Bogdan by the hand and tugged him in the direction Old Gleb had pointed out to her earlier.

They ran.

There was no mistaking their boots crunching on leaves and branches now. There was no mistaking the rage in Vadim's voice, either, when he screeched, "Stop them! They've got our food!"

Lina ran as fast as she could in the dark, dodging tree trunks. The cold air sliced through her lungs. A cluster of ribbons tied into the branches whipped across her face. Bogdan kept pace, slipping behind every so often, then racing ahead. Sometimes she dragged him; sometimes he dragged her.

Neither of them would be the first to let go of the other's hand.

"Run, kids!" Lina heard Old Gleb shout out to them.

"Run for your lives!" Vadim and Alexei would be angry with him when they got back to the campfire, that was for sure. He may have just sealed his own fate.

Behind them, the pounding of feet got closer. Vadim and Alexei were chasing them. It was Alexei who Lina feared most. They couldn't outrun a man of his size. Not in this. She could hear his shallow breathing as he caught up with them. She tried not to think of him edging ever closer with his long strides, his hunting knife . . .

The vegetable sack bashed against a tree and then her leg. It was too awkward to hold on to. Lina dropped it. Onions spilled out behind them with a dozen little thuds. If it was the food the others wanted, they could have it. But Alexei kept on coming. Gaining ground. *Why* did he always have to try to get the better of those he felt had injured his pride?

One long, ear-piercing howl rang out. Then from all around them came yelps and snarls. Lina gasped. Were there lights appearing from behind the trees? Yes, there were—from glowing lamps, but there was no one there to hold them, so they were floating like fireflies. Impossible . . .

Hot air blew against Lina's cheek and she smelled the rank breath of an animal. At the same time, something metal and sharp swished over her head and missed: Alexei's knife. Right behind her, Alexei cried out.

Lina and Bogdan kept running. Way back at their abandoned shelter, they could hear other yells and screams. It was Old Gleb—it had to be. Had he finally come face-to-face with his ghost hounds?

Lina glanced over her shoulder and got a fright. Vadim was right behind them now, though his face was a mask of fear: so white that the tattoos crawling up his neck looked completely black. He'd given up chasing. Now he was running *with* them.

Not for long.

He fell suddenly and was pulled backward into the shadows, as if something had dragged him away. A distinctly animal snarl came with it. Where Vadim had once been was nothing but a swirl of dirt and glittering frost.

Bogdan jerked Lina to a halt. Lina tried to pull him along again, but fear had made him strong, and confusion had made her weak. He held fast.

A loud growl rose out of the darkness in front of them. She could smell the breath of a meat-eating animal on her face again. It came in hot huffs, like the air from bellows. Maddeningly, she could see nothing but the outline of trees.

"Stay back, mutt," she called out. "Or I've got a boot here with your name on it." Lina had never hurt an animal, not even for food, and in normal circumstances, she wouldn't dream of kicking one. But these weren't normal circumstances.

Bogdan yelped. "It's got my arm!"

Lina barged in front of him. She felt coarse fur against

her hand, cold as frozen pine needles, and pushed with all her might.

"I said, back off!" To her surprise, the invisible furred body shifted against her hand, the hot breath evaporated into mist, and the next growl came from a few paces away. It had actually obeyed her. Why weren't any of them attacking?

"There's nothing there," said Bogdan. "I felt it on my arm—its teeth were so, so cold. But I can't see them. Any of them." His voice sounded strangled by fear.

It was true. There was nothing there but the yellow glow from the strange flickering lights dotted amongst the trees—and the trees themselves. Hundreds of them. For miles.

Or was there?

As they watched, what had at first looked like a tree started to change. To move. A tall figure rose as if from the darkness itself—or the air. It wasn't a hound or a wolf. It was a woman.

Lina could make out little more than her silhouette in the moonlight: the woman's long, straight hair and fitted clothes. She towered over them. She may even have been as tall as Alexei.

From either side of the woman came snarls, growls, and more hot breath. No matter how hard she strained her eyes, Lina still couldn't see the creatures.

The woman stepped closer, and her face emerged

from the deeper shadows, lit by the distant lamps, which appeared to have moved closer. She looked down her straight nose at Lina and Bogdan. There was no pity or warmth in that pale face. Her scowl reminded Lina of Commandant Zima's.

She said, "Tell me why I shouldn't have you wolf-bound, just like your comrades."

# 18

Whatever "wolf-bound" was, it chilled Lina's blood. It had to be something to do with the invisible animals she could still hear, snarling at them. The stone against her chest was hot again, as if it were on fire—though in the panic of the chase and her desperation to get away, she hadn't even noticed until now.

Lina tried to speak but stuttered into silence at the woman's appearance. She had to be around her mother's age, or younger, and she looked so healthy—so clean. Even more so than the guards at the camp. Her clothes were pristine and her cheeks didn't sink inward, like Old Gleb's and the others'. Her dark eyes glimmered and her hair looked long and heavy and soft. But there was something odd about her features. She could've been carved from ancient stone rather than made of living flesh.

Lina took a breath to try to speak again. She needed to choose her words carefully. That much she knew.

"With respect, they're not our comrades," she said. "They were going to kill us."

The woman's mouth curled in disgust. "What monsters would slay children? Humans are disgusting."

"If it hadn't been for you, they would have caught us. You and your . . ." Lina didn't know what to call the beasts that were there, but not there.

As if hearing her thoughts, the woman said, "In truth, there's something about you that my wolves don't like." She frowned at Lina curiously. "This has never happened before. Who are you?"

It struck Lina that not many of the people her wolves hunted probably had the chance to introduce themselves.

"I'm Lina," she said. "This is Bogdan." The sooner the woman knew their names, the more likely she was to see them as people—and treat them better. The same had been true at the camp. If the guards didn't know you, you could bet you were in danger. Same if they knew you but didn't like you. Unfortunately if they didn't like you, you were out of luck.

Lina hoped that she could make this person like them. Fast.

"And what's your name?" Lina asked as politely as she could.

Before answering, the woman dismissed the animals

with a wave of her hand. The snarling stopped and the rank smell faded into that of leaves and soil.

"Svetlana is the name given to me," she said after a pause. "Here they call me the Man Hunter."

A shiver skittered down Lina's spine at the words *Man Hunter*, and she glanced at Bogdan, who looked just as terrified.

Meanwhile, Svetlana watched them intently. "My wolves have never refused to bind a human before," she said. "You must come with me so that I can learn the reason for this." Svetlana held out her pale hand. Her fingers were slender and covered in silver and gold rings. She smiled at them. It didn't make her look friendly.

Svetlana shone with a cool radiance that took Lina's breath away. Yet she found herself thinking of her mother again. Svetlana was obviously powerful. Maybe if Lina did as she asked, she might agree to help free her mother from the camp. Still, Lina hesitated.

When neither of the children took her hand, Svetlana's smile became a scowl. She snapped her fingers. Lina glanced at Bogdan. They both placed their hands in one of hers. With her other arm, Svetlana drew her dark cape over them. The material seemed to grow—to spread around their shoulders, then down toward their ankles. Lina was sure it had only been waist length before.

One thing was certain: She'd never felt anything softer. This was nothing like the scratchy burlap sackcloth they slept in at the camp or the rough cotton of the standard-issue clothes she'd worn her whole life. The material was as soft and as cool as a breeze—so gentle against her skin it was hardly even there.

Pinpricks of light winked into life under the black cape, one by one. Lina gasped. She realized with a start that they were stars. Her heart skipped with excitement. Was Bogdan seeing this too?

The cape was gone. It was as if they were standing in the sky. They were surrounded by stars—all around. Even below. Her knees turned wobbly and she grabbed on to Bogdan for dear life, sinking her nails in like claws. "Aargh!" he complained. And then, "Ahh!" when he too took in the view, followed by a long, slow intake of breath as the wonder of it hit him.

What was she standing on, if not thin air? Yet whatever it was felt hard underfoot. And then Lina understood. It was an enormous frozen lake, so sheer and smooth that it reflected the sky like a mirror. And just ahead, at the center of the lake, was a pinnacle of ice as high as a mountain. Had it broken away from a glacier at some point?

Lina blinked and looked again. It wasn't ice. It was a grand, tapering tower—nothing at all like the squat, rectangular buildings in the labor camp or any of the houses she'd seen in pictures.

Did Svetlana actually *live* there? Out on this frozen lake?

Lina took a step. The surface underneath her groaned.

She could even hear the dark water lapping at the underside of the ice. As she watched, something else moved beneath it. She froze.

It was something big.

Just as she started to think she'd imagined it, Lina saw it again: the flank of some giant creature as it arched up through the water. The ice itself bulged under the pressure, creaking, before the thing sank away again. Into the depths. Out of sight. The image of what she'd glimpsed burned into Lina's mind. Huge body, silver scales, and a fish's tail.

Her sense of calm broke. She gripped Svetlana's arm like she wanted to crawl up it.

"You needn't worry, child," said Svetlana. "That was Pechal, who guards this place. Nor will this ice crack. Not with me here."

Still, all Lina could think about was falling through. The chill that would pierce her skull as she sank. She'd be knocked out cold and would sink, deeper and deeper, only to be caught in the mouth of that giant *thing*—with its glassy eyes and its needle-sharp teeth. It was all she could imagine until they reached the strange tower.

# 19

The door was smooth, silvered, and narrow. It looked more like a mirror than a door, with no hinges or handle—just carvings of trees, flowers, and fruit around the edge. Svetlana simply put her palm against it and pushed lightly. It opened. "Go in," she said.

Lina hesitated. She caught Bogdan's eye. Bogdan frowned and tilted his head toward the door to say they should go in. Lina frowned too and shook her head. But it wasn't like they had a choice. Finally, Lina shuffled through the door, followed by Bogdan. Svetlana swooped in behind them.

The hallway walls looked just like layers of ice, one frozen over another, and another, and tinged a translucent pale blue.

Lina was stunned. "Have you ever seen anything like

this?" she whispered to Bogdan. Unlike her, he'd grown up beyond the camp. Perhaps this place was normal . . .

Bogdan just shook his head and carried on staring at everything, his mouth hanging open. So did Lina. Awe swelled in her chest at the flecks of silver and gold that glinted from inside the walls whenever they caught the light from the oil lamps. These elaborately decorated lamps were clustered around the walls—seeming to hang all by themselves, all at odd heights and unequally spaced. Were these the same as the lamps she'd seen in the forest?

Lina hadn't noticed Svetlana light them. Had they already been lit when they came in? Even stranger than that was how the lamps swayed and moved—as if following them through the hallway. Were they *actually* following them?

They reached the bottom of a gold staircase, where there was a doorway into a new room. Svetlana shrugged off her dark cape and slung it across the ornate banister of the stairs.

Underneath she wore a high-throated bodice and trousers. Her clothes were smart, woolen, and well fitted, though the gray color reminded Lina of her own prison overalls.

Svetlana turned on Lina and Bogdan without warning, clipping the heels of her black boots together. Staring into that radiant face, Lina felt her skin prickle. For the first time since the forest, she realized the stone was white-hot against her chest again.

"There is no way to leave this place — not without my say-so," said Svetlana. "If you try, my wolves will alert me. They may refuse to bind you. For now. But that doesn't make you safe from me." She glared at them in turn. It was as if she were daring them to give it a go — right now. Her gaze lingered on Lina, who squirmed inside.

"However," said Svetlana. "Just to be certain . . ." She flicked her hand. The oil lamps from the hallway crowded around Lina. She drew her arms in, afraid she'd get burned by the hot metal. Beside her, the same thing happened to Bogdan.

"Go with them," ordered Svetlana.

There was nothing else to do. Lina let the lights usher her down some narrow, spiraling stone steps and into a room. Every time she turned her head, she thought she saw shadowy figures beside her, holding the lamps. But when she turned to look directly at them, they merged with the shadows of the hallway. They were always just at the edge of her vision.

The lamps retreated and the door banged shut behind them.

A shiver ran up Lina's spine. They were trapped.

# 20

"What *is* this place?" asked Lina, now that she and Bogdan were alone. She looked around the small, windowless space. Or cell, more like. And yet even the cell was incredible. These walls were the stone gray of permafrost, rough to the touch, and sparkling with what looked like silver veins. At the center of the room stood an ornate table with chairs on either side, and on top of that sat a rusted lamp. A tiny moth fluttered around it, making the light flicker. "I mean, *how* is this real?"

"How is any of it?" he said darkly, laying his hand against the silver-streaked stone walls. "Those invisible creatures in the forest? The way we got here? None of it's possible."

Lina rubbed her arms, despite the relative warmth here compared to outside. Like Bogdan said, none of it made sense. Those floating lamps just now — or anything about Svetlana. Even Lina's own stone necklace shouldn't have been able to do the things it did.

They searched the room for exits: hidden doors, loose panels, weak points in the walls. Over in the corner of the room, dark-blue curtains with silver-and-gold embroidery framed beds with soft duvets. Lina's eyes widened at the heavy, shimmering curtains, the beds. Did everyone live like this outside of the camp? Not in magic towers, obviously — but surrounded by such comfort? Svetlana's home was what Lina imagined the former czar's palace must have looked like.

The beds were all they found, however. No windows. Not even a hint of natural light filtering in from anywhere. The door was locked from the other side and there was no way to wrench it open.

There was nothing to do but to wait.

First Lina sat at the table. Then, when no one came, she crouched in the corner of the room. Bogdan was lying against the wall with the unfinished map draped across his chest, staring up at the ceiling. Unlike her, he barely moved. He seemed to be lost in thought.

Were they here to be interrogated? Lina had met people who'd been interrogated before. They weren't the same as the other prisoners.

"D'you think she's a sorceress?" said Bogdan suddenly, looking at Lina. "Or a witch?"

Lina shuddered. "Like Baba Yaga, you mean? I don't think so." Svetlana didn't look a thing like Baba Yaga was supposed to, and Lina definitely couldn't imagine her tower sprouting chicken legs. She shook her head. Then again, there were the invisible creatures that Svetlana commanded and the cape that had transported them here. "Maybe a sorceress, though," Lina added. Even as she spoke, she thought about Svetlana's lucent skin, her look of almost being carved.

Was Svetlana human at all?

Lina's stomach cramped with hunger. She didn't know whether it was the fact she'd barely eaten, the adrenaline from the chase, or the aftereffects of the cold, but she'd started shaking. "Either way," she said after a pause, "I hope she feeds us."

Bogdan nodded, resting a hand on his own stomach. Still he was lying against the wall.

The stone against Lina's chest warmed her until her shaking stopped. Then she pulled it off over her head and studied it again. She ran the odd-size beads through her fingers, counting them. Until she came across one that was different.

It was wooden like the rest—but bigger. She turned it around in her fingers. It had a second hole chiseled into it and, by its appearance, something stuffed inside. How had she not noticed it before? "Hey, Bogey," she said. "Look at this."

"Hmm?" Bogdan stretched around to look at her with doleful eyes.

Lina fished inside the bead and pulled something out with the nail of her little finger.

A tiny slip of paper.

It was yellow with age and tightly rolled. Bogdan was next to her in an instant. "What is it?" His voice by her ear, so unexpected, almost made her drop it. Lina gave him a glare, then unrolled the paper carefully and read the words written on it.

*"My darling Anri, I give you the gift of my heart."*

Lina almost dropped the whole thing. Again. This time in horror. Was it not a stone after all, but some sort of shriveled-up, mummified human heart? No—of course not. *Get a hold of yourself,* Lina thought. The note must mean something else.

"Whose writing is that?" asked Bogdan. "Your mama's?" He flinched after he said it. It was obvious that he wished he hadn't mentioned Lina's mother.

Lina brushed it off as best she could, because she didn't want to make her friend feel bad.

"Dunno," she said. "But Anri was my grandfather's name, so . . ." She looked at Bogdan, wide-eyed. "I'm guessing my grandmother wrote it?"

"Your grandmother?"

Footsteps clip-clopped outside: the sound of stiff leather boots against the flagstone corridor. "We can't tell her anything," said Bogdan in a hurry. "She definitely can't be trusted. If she asks us anything about anything, or *anything*, we've just got to lie. If she's a sorceress and she doesn't like what we say, she might turn us into something horrible."

"No way, Bogey. If she *is*, I don't think it's safe to —"

The footsteps stopped right outside the door. Lina rolled the note up again and tucked it back in its bead, then pulled the whole necklace over her head and stuffed it under her clothes.

Just in time. The door swished open as if of its own accord and in walked Svetlana. The door closed behind her, and she sat at the table. She beckoned to Lina and Bogdan to take a seat too.

The last thing Lina wanted to do was face Svetlana across that little table. She couldn't show her fear, though. That would be the worst thing either of them could do.

Lina and Bogdan sat down opposite her. The ragged bronze-tipped moth danced around them but quickly drew back to circle the lamp.

Svetlana clasped her hands on the table. Her silver and gold rings glinted on her fingers in the flickering lamplight. The rings were designed like flowers and vines. Leaves and tendrils. Feathers.

"Where are you from?" asked Svetlana. "What were you doing when I caught you?"

Lina and Bogdan glanced at each other. "We were —" Lina began.

"On an errand," said Bogdan. "An official one, for Commandant Zima of Prison Camp Nine. That's Lina's father. He's a very important commandant."

Lina stared at him, aghast. She hadn't wanted to lie—Svetlana didn't seem like the sort of person who'd respond well if she found them out. Lina wished they'd had more time to discuss it. And why, oh why, had Bogdan made it such a hurtful lie—of all things, about the commandant being her father? She hadn't even realized he'd heard the rumors. They'd never spoken about them. Yet he must have known how much they would upset her.

She'd never let him forget this.

Svetlana frowned. "What possible errand could you have been entrusted with?"

"Getting supplies," said Bogdan. "For the officers' winter banquet . . ." He looked at Lina as he spoke, wild-eyed and virtually pleading. It was as if he were signaling to her that he could no longer control his own mouth.

Bogdan had pitched their hopes on a gamble. An extreme one, at that. But what was it her mother always said? Life is a gamble. Lina couldn't tell the truth now without getting him into serious trouble. It was all or nothing.

Lina took a deep breath. "It's true," she said. "All of it. So you'd better be careful, because the commandant will be looking for us. He'll be angry if he thinks we've been badly treated. We're only here because our escorts decided to betray the comman . . . my father, and escape instead." She couldn't help thinking of Old Gleb, who'd done everything he could to help them.

"You're the daughter of the camp commandant and yet you're dressed in prison clothes?" Svetlana raised an eyebrow.

Lina shifted uncomfortably in her seat but gave no answer.

Svetlana opened her mouth as if to ask more, so Lina said quickly, "Please, what does 'wolf-bound' mean? You said in the forest that's what you'd done to the men. Are they alive?"

Svetlana waited. The only sound was the tapping of the moth's tiny wings against the lamp beside them. Then Svetlana said, "They are alive. In a sense. The wolves have infected them now. Clouding their minds. Their memories. Dulling their senses. They don't understand what's happening or even who they are."

She brushed a dark strand of hair out of her face and went on. "A long time ago, I brought my wolves into this world from another. First they came to protect me, but now their purpose is to help me find what I'm seeking. They are excellent at tracing a scent. If any humans should get in their way, that is unfortunate. Once humans are bitten, a slow change will begin. They become vacant. Confused. They stop craving nourishment from food, water, and rest—and yet are compelled to keep walking."

Beside Lina, Bogdan clutched his arm, as if remembering the wolf that had grabbed him—the one Lina wrestled off. Svetlana noticed too and narrowed her eyes. "Don't worry, child—my wolf didn't bite you hard enough to begin a binding." Her gaze flicked from Bogdan to Lina as she continued. "Eventually humans who are bitten will just fade into shadows, capable of nothing but following the most basic of orders. That's when I decide whether to let them roam or bring them here."

"That's cruel," said Lina before she could stop herself. "They're people and they're suffering."

A flush came into Svetlana's cheeks. "There's more suffering and deceit in this world caused by people than by my wolves. Besides, what can truly suffer without a mind capable of understanding such a thing? Humans take pleasure in hurting one another. Not my wolves or my shadows. I give the shadows a purpose—an honorable one, under my guidance—beyond causing misery and pain."

"And what's that?" asked Bogdan in a shrill voice.

"To aid the hunt," she said simply. "Whether it's alongside the wolves, reporting to me, or simply serving me here."

Lina remembered the lights she'd seen between the trees as they ran from Vadim and Alexei. So Svetlana's shadows had been in the forest too. Reporting on them. Is that how she'd found them there? Or had her wolves tracked their scent?

Something else was bothering Lina. "But what are you hunting *for*, exactly?" she asked. Svetlana's response surprised her. She frowned and looked distant, not saying a thing.

The moth landed on the table with a tiny thud, bringing Svetlana back to herself. Svetlana watched it awhile, coolly. "Little pest," she muttered under her breath. For a moment, Lina thought that Svetlana was going to squash it. She didn't. The moth flipped itself right side up and went back to its relentless fluttering against the lamp.

Svetlana leaned in suddenly, pushing her face toward them. "Why won't my wolves bind you, Lina?" she asked, still ignoring Lina's earlier question as if she hadn't spoken at all. *"Are* you entirely human?"

Lina looked to the side, trying not to think about the pulse of heat she'd felt travel through her so often in the greenhouse and again in the forest. Or the way the branch had grown beneath her touch. She couldn't help but see it all over again, in her mind's eye.

"The commandant will be expecting us back soon, and if we're not, he'll come looking for us, just like Lina said," chipped in Bogdan, filling the silence.

Svetlana sat silently, studying them both. Her glare made Lina worry. As if Svetlana could see everything she was thinking about. She shifted uncomfortably in her seat.

"When you next sleep, your words will leave you and become part of the other world," Svetlana said. "When

I find them, I will know if what you've told me is the truth. And understand this: It won't take me long to find out." Svetlana rose from her chair. "Don't for a moment doubt that I will get at the truth. Or that I'll find a way to put you to use. No one can find you here unless I want them to—not even your 'father.' My tower is entirely hidden, tethered to the world only by my and Pechal's life force." She raised her chin and looked down her straight nose at them. "Wolf-bound or not, you will give up your vile human ways and serve me, as these shadows do. I promise you."

Lina's blood chilled. If Svetlana really could do what she said she could—find their words while they dreamed and see their truth—then what chance did they have? They'd told a huge lie. A lie almost the size of Siberia.

And they could only fight sleep for so long.

# 21

Lina sank farther down in the chair. This was a disaster. All of it.

She risked a glance at Bogdan, then wished she hadn't. His expression was frozen somewhere between panic and guilt. "Bogey, why'd you lie to her?"

Bogdan folded his arms and huffed. "Oh, stop it, Lina. How was I to know what she's capable of?"

Lina drummed the table with her bony fingers. "All right, all right, you couldn't have known. But this *does* complicate everything." She stopped drumming the table, curled her fingers into a fist, and sighed.

"Yeah, I know." Bogdan spoke more quietly this time and shifted his chair closer to hers. "She's really scary and I panicked. Thought if we had more time, we'd work something out."

"Yeah. I guessed."

Lina listened to his wheezy chest for a while—the churning of breath in and out. Was it actually clearing a bit, after a couple of days free of the choking air in the mine? She broke the silence first. "Never mind, eh? We're here and we're alive, aren't we?"

Bogdan half smiled, but it was soon replaced with a frown. "What are we going to do, then?" He shifted closer again and lowered his voice to a whisper this time. "You think all that stuff about seeing our lies when we sleep is true?"

Lina ran a hand through her tufted hair. It could do with a trim, and there were tide lines of dirt caked onto her scalp. "Dunno," she said, picking at a bit of the encrusted mud. "I don't understand any of this—or what she is. Let's stay awake as long as we can, just in case. And try to work something out, quick."

"Reckon she'd hand us back over to Zima in a heart-beat if she could," said Bogdan. "Don't you? Or find some way to have us 'wolf-bound.'"

Lina nodded. "She's certainly dangerous."

For a while, they sat in silence.

"Bogdan?" Lina said. Bogdan raised his eyebrows at her use of his full name. "You know what you said about Commandant Zima being my father . . .?"

Bogdan winced. "Yes?"

"Why'd you say it?" Her voice came out louder than

she'd meant. "I know you were making it up, but . . . do you think the rumors are actually true?"

Shadows cast by the moth's wings danced across Bogdan's face. Already Lina dreaded what he might say next. Bogdan sighed. "Listen, my friend. I don't know. Your mama—and *him*? I can't see it myself. But *someone* must be your father. What about that doctor she works with—Vasily? Maybe he's your papa. Though you've got to say it's odd, how the commandant kept you around."

He was right. None of the other prisoners who'd had children at the camp had kept them. They were taken away to orphanages soon after they were born. Why had her mother been allowed to keep her? The commandant must have permitted it.

"Plus," Bogdan added, "you'll admit . . . you've got his hair." He must've seen the dismay on her face, because he squeezed her arm and said hurriedly, "Look. Who cares if Commandant Zima is your father, or if he isn't? You're nothing like him. Nothing. That's what counts, eh?"

"You're right. Who cares, even if he is." But it did matter. As soon as Lina had been old enough to understand the rumors, she hadn't been able to stop thinking about them. The older she got, the more she thought about it, and the more her dread grew. Bogdan's stories of his papa—kind, generous, fair—filled her with both wonder and heaviness at the same time. Surely that's what a father should be?

"Lina?"

"Yes?"

"Happy birthday."

Lina smiled. The pair sat still on their chairs, in silence. A familiar smell wafted into their cell. They both recognized it: cabbage soup.

Sure enough, when the door next opened, two bowls of the rank watery stuff and two hunks of black bread came in on a platter, surrounded by the oil lamps.

It all came in on its own.

Lina and Bogdan locked eyes in amazement. But then Lina noticed something else. If she stared straight at Bogdan, not at the lamps, she could see things moving at the edges of her vision. It had been the same with the lights that had brought them to this room. Again, by not focusing directly on them, she could make out something dark and fluttering in the corners of her eyes, like a bird's beating wing. Shadows? The shadows of Svetlana's "wolf-bound"? She could tell by Bogdan's face that he could see the same thing.

"Who d'you think they are, these shadows?" whispered Lina when she could catch her breath to speak. "Or were?"

Bogdan raised his eyebrows high into his hair and let them drop. "Around here? Herders and farmers. A mix of people from the smaller towns, maybe—even the odd big city. Probably all the prisoners who've ever escaped from the camp . . ."

This was what Old Gleb, Vadim, and even that thug Alexei would eventually become. It was what Svetlana wanted to turn them both into, as well. Lina shuddered at the thought.

Some oil lamps hovered by the door, guarding it. Growls gave away the presence of wolves too. The wolves may not be able to bind them, but that didn't mean they weren't dangerous. Bogdan had felt the jaws of one on his arm in the forest, hadn't he?

The shadow people set the tray down with a clatter, sending one of the hunks of bread skittering onto the floor. Keeping her gaze straight in front of her so she could still see the shadows, Lina swooped down to pick up the bread. She hesitated a moment. Instead of eating it, she held it out.

She had to know if what Svetlana said was true: that they really did no longer think, or feel, or want—like a person.

"Here," she said, holding the bread at arm's length. "Are you hungry? Take it." Bogdan squinted—trying hard to look without looking. Lina too kept her head very still. "You must be hungry," she said, addressing the room. "Don't you eat?"

The oil lamps drifted out of the room. All the shadow people left. All but one.

It was small—only up to Lina's shoulders in height—and it stood next to the bread. A whisper hung in the air. It felt as if it had grown there, like a piece of fruit, rather than having been spoken. *"Nevertell . . ."*

Then the small shadow person slipped away and the door shut tight.

Lina lowered her arm. She still held the bread in her hand.

"What did that mean?" asked Bogdan, frowning. "'Nevertell'? Never tell what?"

Lina had no idea, but she knew one thing now, at the very least: Svetlana's shadow servants weren't as mindless as Svetlana thought.

# 22

There had to be some way out. Surely.

They searched the room a second time, but just like before, they found nothing. It was no good. Lina and Bogdan were stuck.

They had vowed to stay awake until they had a plan. But the floor and the chairs were so uncomfortable they eventually decided that sitting on the beds would be better. And as the room was so chilly, they soon climbed under the blankets—just for a bit of extra warmth. Snuggled between the soft mattress and duvet, Lina knew deep down that staying awake was no longer going to happen. This was like lying on clouds compared to what she usually slept on. She couldn't help but utter a small sigh of delight.

Besides, there was no way out of the room—not until

someone opened the door again. Maybe they should just rest now, so they would be ready for when Svetlana returned?

Lina glanced at Bogdan. He was keeping his eyes half-open—just—but they rolled every now and then up underneath his heavy lids. Watching him, Lina felt the same happening to her. She listened to Bogdan's breathing, and it reminded her of her mother's soft breaths when she would press an ear against her chest. The sound had always lulled her. Made her feel safe.

She slept.

In her dreams, she was buried deep underground in the cold, but she could see a light above her and feel its warmth. She knew that, no matter what, she *had* to reach the light. She woke to find herself clawing and flailing at thin air, as if trying to dig her way out. Only to be faced with a room full of flickering oil lamps—and Svetlana at the foot of their beds.

Svetlana was pale. And furious.

"Liars!" she bellowed. "Did you think I wouldn't find out? *Me?*"

Lina felt groggy. She couldn't think. She opened her mouth to speak, but it felt like her tongue was still asleep.

"Think carefully before you utter another word, child. A second lie will cost you dearly." Svetlana's dark eyes flashed as if they contained lightning. And, if her eyes were lightning, her voice was thunder. "I know you weren't on a private errand. Humans—you're all the same. Liars. Betrayers. You only ever think of yourselves."

Lina knew Bogdan was awake too when he silently sank his nails into her arm. That, and his sudden intake of breath, betrayed his fear. He was right to be afraid. Lina had to be careful. One wrong word could mark the end of the road for both of them.

"The part about the other prisoners trying to kill us is true. But we weren't running an errand for Commandant Zima. We were trying to escape as well. I guess you saw all this? When we slept?" she said, testing her.

"It's not your place to question me," Svetlana snapped.

There was no point in lying anymore. "Mama and I were desperate to escape the camp," said Lina. "So Mama made a deal with those men you had wolf-bound in exchange for food, with the promise of a reward when we got to my grandmother's house in Moscow. I always kept my distance from them before, because they had bad reputations. Especially Vadim. Bogdan followed me because he was worried. He didn't want me getting into trouble. Because when I heard about the escape plan, I didn't care who the men were or about their reputations; all I wanted was to go with them. So I'd know what it was like to be free."

She paused to check Svetlana's face. Flickering light from the lamps danced on her skin, but her jaw was set firm. "You gave up the right to freedom when you became a criminal," said Svetlana.

"But I didn't commit any crime," said Lina. "Neither of us did."

"Both of you—explain."

Bogdan piped up first. "My parents are political prisoners. I don't think the secret police knew what to do with me, after they took them . . . I look older than I am, and I used to be strong, so they sent me to Lina's camp—to work in the mine."

Lina steadied herself. "I was born in the camp. It's where I've lived my whole life. I wasn't there for doing anything wrong either." Even if she had been, she mused, would she have deserved it? Would anyone? Knowing that place like Lina did, she didn't think so. "My mama was taken there when she was a teenager."

Something happened to Svetlana's face. Her stern white mask seemed to crumble, and a hollow look came into her eyes. But it wasn't pity. It was something else. Sadness? Fear?

A thought crossed Lina's mind. Maybe now was the time to ask if Svetlana could help her mother. It was worth trying—it could be her only chance. "Please," she said. "My mama is still in the camp. She's innocent too. Can you help me free her? Use your wolves?"

Svetlana scowled. "Why should I help you? Why should I even believe you this time?" she said, her voice quavering. "About any of it?"

Lina looked Svetlana dead in the eye. "Because it's the

truth and I think you're someone who specializes in the truth. And we're giving it to you now."

Svetlana's mouth and eyebrows twitched. This wasn't good.

"Enough," she growled. "Both of you." Her rage grew until it filled the room. "You are proven liars. Informants, no doubt. I wonder how many others you betrayed before your own imprisonment. And now you want me to *help* you! Enough of your tricks. As you cannot be bound, either you will agree to serve me in human form, or I will take you back to your prison camp where you will face certain execution for your escape. You have tonight to decide which it will be."

With that, she signaled to her shadow servants and marched out the door—a trail of glowing oil lamps, like fireflies, behind her.

# 23

The door closed with a clunk. The shadow people must have locked it from the outside. Lina felt sick.

"We're done for," said Bogdan. "We'll be killed."

"We have to escape," said Lina.

"They're probably standing guard. Listening in on us, right now." Bogdan was right. They probably were.

"There's got to be a way out." Lina scrambled out of the bed and hurried across the room. Surely they'd overlooked something. They searched the frozen walls with their fingertips, feeling along every crevice and crack. The moth fluttered next to the lamp.

It was useless. If not even a moth could escape from this room, how would they?

Bogdan rubbed his eyes and face. "There's the 'distract and attack' technique. We could always try that."

It was an old trick they'd seen other prisoners use the few times there'd been a minor riot. One person, or a small group, would create the distraction. Upturn a table or start a fire. Then, while the guards were dealing with the distraction, the other group would be waiting to attack.

They were fun to watch, these mini riots—for a while. Until things got ugly. In truth, however, Lina had never seen one that ended well for the prisoners involved. She'd always steered clear of them. In fact, Lina had never been in a fight before. She'd seen plenty, of course. She'd also seen her mother dish out a few black eyes and split lips—though only ever to protect their things, or herself and Lina. Her insides squirmed at the thought of wounding another human being—whoever it was. But what other choice did they have?

She looked around for things they could use. There was the lamp, of course. Or the chairs. Bogdan eyed them too. "When she next comes in," he said, "I'll grab a chair and hide behind the door while you stand there and distract her."

Lina screwed up her nose. "Distract her? How? With what?"

"Doesn't matter. Do a dance: Do the Barynya if you like. As long as she's looking at you and not me."

Lina considered it. She was many things, but a dancer wasn't one of them. And she'd feel exposed in the middle of the room with nothing for protection. "Right, then," she said finally. "I'll just grab a chair to wave at her too. OK?"

Bogdan raised the corner of his mouth in a lopsided

smile. "OK." Looked like theirs would be the "attack and attack" technique.

Lina took the necklace off again and studied the larger wooden bead. It gave her comfort to roll it around in her fingers. The moth flew headlong at the lamp and rebounded onto the table. It was hard to watch it try and fail, endlessly, to reach the light.

In one swift move, Lina scooped it up in her hand and set it next to the bead. "Here, little thing," she said. "Stick with us."

The tiny creature flitted onto her thumbnail and wiggled its antennae, which looked like minuscule ferns. It almost seemed to be thinking about her offer. Did it somehow understand her? Had this normal, plain little creature actually soaked up some magic, being stuck in this place? An idea occurred to her, and she tipped her thumb a little, to angle the moth toward the hole in the big bead. The moth with its shabby brown wings crawled inside, into the center of the paper scroll.

Lina smiled. If they were to try and fail, at least they would all do it together.

Neither Bogdan nor Lina slept properly after that. For Lina, thoughts of what Svetlana would do to her and Bogdan blurred into images of her mother—a flickering shadow just beyond her reach in the guard tower. And through it all ran Svetlana, braced against the cold, and with the snarling ghost wolves still giving chase. Always at their heels.

Lina woke with a burning feeling against her chest. The stone. Another warning.

Just at that moment, something clunked. It came from the door. What was it? The lock? Lina shook Bogdan awake. "What? What?" he said.

"The door," hissed Lina. "She's coming!"

Bogdan leaped across the room, grabbed a chair, and pressed himself against the wall, next to the door. All in one move. Lina had never seen him act so fast. Her head still felt foggy from sleep. She grabbed another chair, as they'd planned.

The door creaked open, but just a little—as if nudged by a breeze from the other side. They waited, but no one came. Lina thought she heard something from the hallway. A whisper, so faint it was barely there.

"Let's look," she said, frowning.

Bogdan nodded. They both put down their chairs and peered around the door.

The corridor was dimly lit and empty.

"Hello?" whispered Lina. Besides a dark movement in the corner of her eye that vanished when she turned her head, there was nothing—and no one. Only another whisper that came from nowhere and melted away like frosted breath. *"Nevertell."*

"Thank you," whispered Lina to the quiet, cool corridor. "Thank you so much."

It looked like they had a friend.

# 24

Lina led the way, first of all inching along the dark corridor, then up the spiraling steps of frozen stone, clinging to the gold banister. The way out ought to be just up these stairs and through the hallway. They were so close.

The house had a weighted silence to it—like a great body of water pressing down on them from above. They reached the ground floor. Lina had the feeling they were being followed, though she didn't know by who. Or what. The shadow person that had opened the door for them, she guessed. The one who'd whispered. *But what—or who—else could be lurking in this corridor,* she wondered.

Natural light filtered into the hallway from somewhere above. Lina had forgotten the translucent blue-green walls up here: the flecks of silver and gold frozen deep inside. Part of her wished she could hold them—or at least touch one.

Bogdan crept up the last step beside her and looked around. He tapped Lina's shoulder and pointed to the floor. Flakes of fresh snow peppered the rough stone. Something cold landed on Lina's cheek. She wiped it away and looked up. There were tiny flakes of snow falling from the ceiling. Actually . . . now when she looked, there was no ceiling.

Lina wasn't sure what was more bizarre—seeing the muddy-white sky far above them or seeing all the floors of the tower between them and it. The inside of the tower was split into two halves, joined only by the outer walls and the corridor they stood in. It was just as if an earthquake had opened a chasm through the center.

The gold staircase stretched up and up. In the daylight, Lina could see all the flourishes on it—flowers, trees, and birds—but also how scuffed and tarnished it was. Frayed blue curtains, like those in their cell, draped from an ornate rail on the floor above them. Lina guessed that was where Svetlana slept.

Hopefully she was still sleeping. If she did such a thing as sleep.

They made their way along the corridor toward the door they'd arrived through. There it was. No handle. No visible hinges. Just as if someone had blocked off the end of the hall with mirrored stone.

134

Svetlana had laid her palm against it to make it open, hadn't she? So that's what Lina would do. The stone on her necklace grew hot again. They had to move fast.

She stepped closer.

A growl came from the air in front of the door. A loud, low sound, like a rumble of thunder. She froze. A shadow wolf.

Lina's gut twisted. A snort of hot breath from the invisible animal tickled the fine hairs on her arms. "Stay back," she hissed, trying to make her voice forceful, like Svetlana's, without being too loud. She felt behind her for Bogdan and then pushed herself in front of him. The wolves had once before obeyed her and not attacked. Bogdan was another story.

A high-pitched whistle from behind them made Lina wince. It did something strange to her head. The sound traveled right through her skull.

Twisting around, Lina caught sight of movement on the stairs. It reminded her of how the rags they hung in the windows of the labor camp to keep out the cold would twirl and turn in a storm, as if alive. Could it be the small shadow person?

The whistle came again, in three short blasts this time. Then a huge force hit Lina in the stomach. Hard. Her legs gave way and she crumpled to the floor. Bogdan made a choked sound behind her—panicked, pained—but all she could do was gasp and clutch her own stomach, where an icy coldness spread out, chilling her bones.

The wolf had leaped at her.

As the pain of the cold subsided, Lina could pick herself up off the floor. Bogdan was lying beside her. He'd also been hurled to the ground when the ghost wolf had barged past them both, heading to whoever—or whatever— had called it off with that whistle.

Lina saw the subtle movement on the stairs at the same time as she heard the whisper. *"Nevertell . . ."*

That same phrase. Again. What did it mean?

The scratching, scampering of the wolf's paws on the stairs got farther and farther away. Lina groaned. The coldness in her stomach had turned to tingles, but her hip still felt numb. "Bogey—you OK?" She pulled him up by the arm.

"Think so," said Bogdan. He rubbed his leg and cautiously tested his weight on it, wincing.

Lina glanced up at the dark-blue curtains, which seemed to twitch. "Let's get out of here, quick." She pressed her palm against the door. Nothing happened. "Er?"

"Try again," said Bogdan. "Think about it opening, or something."

"What good's that going to do?"

"I don't know. Just try it!"

Lina tried again, focusing hard this time. "Open." The door swung back at her so fast she had to leap out of the way. A blast of cold air hit them from outside. It rushed down Lina's throat and into her lungs like a shock of icy water.

She struggled for breath. A clattering sound came from behind them—the wolf? Svetlana? There wasn't time to find out. Bogdan recovered first and grasped Lina's hand, limping out onto the frozen lake and dragging her beside him, across the ice—so perfect and clear they could see the snow clouds reflected in it from the sky above.

Only when they were too far across to even consider going back did Lina remember Svetlana's giant creature—Pechal, that monstrous fish guardian—and see the flash of its scales as it rose up beneath them.

# 25

The whole lake shook.

The body of the big fish slammed against the underside of the ice a second time, sending out a shock of hairline cracks. Lina and Bogdan tripped and fell.

"What's it doing?" shrieked Lina.

Bogdan gritted his teeth. "Doesn't want us to leave, that's for sure."

Another slam shook them as they tried to stand. The cracks deepened. If it kept on this way, it would soon break through.

Lina imagined the chasm that would open beneath them. How it would swallow them up. Plunge them into that icy water. Deliver them to those giant jaws. Her legs felt hollow. Her head swam. She had to push the thoughts away if she was going to save herself and Bodgan.

The next slam catapulted them forward. They clung to each other in the air before luck landed them on their feet. Then they were running. Running fast. What else could they do?

Something vast moved beneath them. Lina didn't want to look. But something inside her demanded it. She glanced down. A huge, round eye stared back, keeping pace with them below the ice: Pechal. The eye was gold-and-silver flecked—and pitch-black at its center, like a deep hole. The darkness of it widened a little, as if getting ready to swallow them.

The eye surged ahead. The ice beneath them bulged and creaked under the pressure of Pechal's gleaming body pressing upward. Lina and Bogdan started to slide. Without a second thought, they wrapped their arms around each other to save themselves from falling. Lina fixed her gaze on Bogdan. She had to, to stop herself from seeing Pechal's eye. The lake's depths. Bogdan only stared ahead, his jaw set, his sights on the nearing bank. "Skate," he said.

Skate? Of course. Not that they had any choice. They were already slipping down the ice as it curved against Pechal's scaled flank, ready to buckle. Bogdan bent his knees and angled his feet for better stability—and speed. Lina followed his example.

They turned their skid into a skating run. Lina focused on moving her legs, on breathing—and the strength of

Bogdan's grip on her. Beneath the ice, Pechal swam in bursts, speeding ahead before quickly falling back. If they kept up this pace, could they outrun him?

The bank wasn't far now. Another two minutes and they'd reach it. Pechal couldn't follow them onto land. But Lina's calves burned with the effort of driving forward, of keeping up with Bogdan. They trembled under her. If they buckled now, she would collapse.

Then came the mist.

It was wispy at first, but quickly it became white and heavy, like sunken clouds. The bank was swallowed by it completely. Still, it *had* to be there—even if it was hidden. Lina glimpsed Pechal again—not beneath them, as he had been, but a little farther off this time. His eye roved, as if searching. Had the mist confused him?

Lina gritted her teeth through the pain in her legs. Just a short sprint and they'd reach the bank. Safety. With a flash of tail, Pechal turned. Was he going back?

This time, Lina wasn't going to look around to find out. A weaker slam against the ice shook them, but not enough to knock them down. It had been some distance away—she knew that much. Pechal *had* retreated. Finally they'd lost him.

Lina couldn't keep going any longer. Her legs gave way. Bogdan's grip on her was wrenched away. She sprawled forward into the mist, into nothingness.

# 26

The mist had grown so thick that Lina couldn't see her own hands or feet, but beneath her was soft, heaped snow: solid ground. Relief surged through her. They had reached the edge of the lake. Groping around after her fall quickly led her back to Bogdan. They helped each other up and clung to each other as they stumbled through the fog. He was her lifeline now: the only way she could be sure that anything around her was still there. He, at least, was real.

"I don't like this." Bogdan sounded panicked. "This isn't right." He'd been so self-assured a moment ago. Now his fingers gripped too hard and his hand started to sweat. Lina didn't like it either, but for Bogdan—the boy of maps, of direction—this nothingness had to be torture. The emptiness must scare him as much as the thought of falling into the lake had scared Lina.

"It's just a mist bank, Bogey. It'll clear." That was rubbish and they both knew it. There was nothing normal about this sudden mist, totally surrounding them. But then, there had been nothing normal about Svetlana or her ghost wolves—or her impossible tower either.

"What if we're going in circles?" asked Bogdan, breathing fast. He squeezed and squeezed her arm.

"Doesn't feel like we're going in circles. Feels like we're going straight. Look, it's got to shift soon." Was she trying to convince him or herself? Both. Holding each other even more tightly, Lina and Bogdan hurried in the direction they hoped would be the right one.

Lina fought down her own panic. She dreaded the mist finally clearing to reveal they were back at the tower—that they had come around in a circle, just as Bogdan feared. She couldn't tell him that, though.

*What if the mist never cleared?*

Just as she thought it, Lina caught a glimpse of the snow-covered earth—and her own boot. "It's clearing. It is, Bogey. Look!"

Another patch opened up around them, and now she could see Bogdan's face again, damp with cold sweat. When she saw the relief in his grin, she knew it mirrored her own.

The mist cleared as suddenly as it had come. When they

looked back, they could see nothing but a white haze. No tower at all. It couldn't be. Lina scowled. "There's no chance that huge tower could be hidden. We'd at least see the top."

"Nothing was right about that place. None of it." Bogdan shuddered.

Did Svetlana control that mist, so no one would find her tower? What was it she'd said? That the tower was hidden, tethered to the world only by "my and Pechal's life force." Had they actually crossed a boundary—between worlds?

Around them danced tiny snowflakes. Beyond those, Lina could see for miles. Snow-cragged mountains and ice-filled valleys to the left and right, bluish and hazy on the horizon. Far ahead, vast forests covered everything. Their current path opened into a wide white plain. Lina gasped. Her pale breath faded instantly, as if it too felt humbled by the vastness of this place.

Lina couldn't help casting a glance over her shoulder again. Still no sign of the tower—not even the mist now. Only a wide, snaking river farther off, gleaming bright white where fresh snow covered its frozen waters.

Bogdan clamped a hand on her shoulder. "The Yenisei!"

"The what?" said Lina.

"That river, there. I bet it's the Yenisei. It flows from Tuva, where my papa's from. That's got to be it."

"How can you be sure?"

"Well, I can't be totally sure, can I? But if I'm right,

that means . . ." Bogdan fumbled around in the back of his boot, searching for his maps. "Yes! That's it. Look. Look at the way it curves on the map, and then at the curve of the river." He shoved one of the maps under Lina's nose and pointed so hard she thought he might poke a hole through it.

"Bogey, there are hundreds of rivers on that map. And they all curve."

He ignored her. "We're somewhere along here, that means. Between the Central Siberian Plateau and the West Siberian Plain. So we're getting closer, Lina. Svetlana might actually have done us a favor, transporting us under that cape."

Lina tried to get involved in his calculations, but he was busy murmuring and measuring, then scribbling things down on another sheet with the stub of his pencil. Lina left him to it. She stared at the bluish mountains in the distance and tried to ignore the crushing feeling in her chest. It was that same feeling she'd been used to at the camp. She didn't know why, but she felt certain they were being watched. A feeling that, despite this great wilderness, they weren't alone.

She could just ignore it. It had been with her since they escaped from Svetlana's tower. It was probably nothing more than adrenaline. But then, the same thing had happened on the night of the escape, when Bogdan followed them. If she'd ignored her feeling then . . .

A high-pitched screech rang out: the unmistakable cry of a falcon. Call it paranoia, but before the stone against her chest had even started to get hot, Lina was on the move.

So was Bogdan. "Get down!" he hissed, just before he barreled into her. They ducked under the cover of a large snow-heaped rock and peered out to watch the sky.

A giant falcon soared overhead. Bigger than any natural falcon. And it was definitely looking around. Hunting. For what? For them, thought Lina. She felt it in her bones: It was hunting for them. It had to be something to do with Svetlana. Another one of her strange servants? Lina remembered the falcon she'd seen circling them just after they left the mine—back when they were with Old Gleb and the others. If she remembered rightly, it had also appeared just before the ghost wolves had chased them into the forest.

The falcon scanned the ground, its feathers whistling and rustling under the strain of keeping that giant body aloft. Both the rock they were under and the snow cover worked a magic of their own, however. The falcon passed by, then soared far into the distance until all Lina could see of it was a dark smudge against the clouds.

"Lina." Bogdan tugged at the sleeve of her jacket—formerly his.

"What?" She took her eyes off the falcon and looked where he was pointing. Something stirred beyond a small rise of land, sending up a plume of mist and snow. Heavy footsteps—and lots of them. They sounded too large and too regular to be human. Something with lots of feet, then.

It rose over the ridge and crunched toward them—a white fur-covered beast with a pot belly, four stubby legs, and a long gray face with the blackest eyes. Its hair framed its face, just like a human's might, but tracked all the way down a long, thick neck. It wasn't human, that much was clear. A knot of fear formed in Lina's gut. Would a beast like that hurt them?

She now noticed with surprise that it had a human rider. A person covered head to toe in animal pelts.

The rider pulled their face covering to the side. A girl peered out of the fur, which twirled around her face in the bitter breeze. She had to be older than Lina by a few years, with high cheekbones and dark eyes that sparkled when she grinned. She said something in another language before switching to Russian.

"If I were you two," she said, pointing at the sky, "I wouldn't let that thing catch me."

# 27

Snow quickly filled in around Lina's and Bogdan's feet as they spoke with the girl—named Tuyaara—but Lina hardly noticed it. She'd never seen a creature like the one Tuyaara sat on before. "What is it?" she asked, mesmerized, but felt her ears get hot when the other two stared at her in surprise.

"A horse!" said Bogdan, once he could do more with his mouth than gape. Perhaps it hadn't crossed his mind that Lina would never have seen one, growing up in the camp.

"Not just a horse. It's a Yakutian horse," Tuyaara told them proudly as she dismounted.

So this was what a horse looked like. Lina only knew of them from stories. She gazed into its brilliant dark eyes, itching to run her hand over its soft-looking fur. But she held back. It looked powerful. Especially its legs, which it might use to kick.

Tuyaara patted its side and eyed Lina curiously, as if wondering what kind of strange person had never seen a horse before. "Its fur's extra thick, see, so it can survive the cold. No need to be afraid of it. It belongs to my parents, so it's part-tame. My family are herders and farmers, here in Sakha."

The horse shook its head from side to side and showed the whites of its eyes, making Lina jump back. Tuyaara made a puzzled sound. "She seems wary of you two, though. What are you doing all the way out—?"

Bogdan cut her off. "Did you say Sakha?" he said, aghast. "As in, the Yakut ASSR? That river over there—that's not the Yenisei?"

Tuyaara laughed. "What? You're way off course if you think that's the Yenisei. It's miles over that way. Listen, you're obviously lost." She looked over Lina's thin jacket, her gray prison overalls. "You'd better come home with me so I can help you find your way."

Tuyaara seemed trustworthy enough. And what was the alternative?

Lina and Bogdan followed a little ways behind Tuyaara, because any time they got close to the horse, it stopped and wouldn't move or shook its head and tried to rear up. "Something's really spooked her," said Tuyaara with a shrug and a look at Lina and Bogdan. "Maybe it was the bird. My father would take one look at that thing and say it came straight out of the Lower Worlds. He'd want to get you checked over by a shaman immediately in case you needed spiritual protection. Probably an Orthodox priest too, to be extra safe." Tuyaara chuckled. "He does like to keep traditions alive however he can, in these *challenging* times."

"Are there shamans near here?" Lina asked. Perhaps the shamans might be able to explain what had happened to them. They might even know who Svetlana was.

"That depends who's asking," said Tuyaara. "I wouldn't want to get anyone in trouble with the authorities for any sort of banned religious practice . . ."

That went for the Orthodox priests as well as the shamans, no doubt. Almost every religion had suffered under Stalin's laws, his horrific purges. Lina knew a lot of former priests in the camp—and those were the lucky ones, because they were alive.

Tuyaara walked instead of riding—that way, she said, she could talk more easily.

"What's your story?" Tuyaara asked over her shoulder. She looked them up and down again. "You're wearing prison clothes, I see."

"It's a long story," said Lina, glancing sideways at Bogdan, who was still staring at the snow, frowning.

"You can speak freely with me," said Tuyaara. "We've had our share of *difficulty* with dear Comrade Stalin out here. Besides, I know a boy who's also in a forced labor camp. They took him away for criticizing our dear comrade's methods. He's the son of family friends. I've known him since I was four." She pulled her furs across her face and turned away from them for a moment.

"It's nice to talk to people who aren't just the same old villagers or my brothers, actually," Tuyaara went on, a little more quietly this time. "It's a small farming collective we're part of: us and just a few other families. It's been weeks since I've gone to a town or seen any friends there. I met prisoners like you when a bunch got brought here to build roads and things. I haven't met any escapees before, though." She turned to look at them again, eyebrow raised. "I mean, I'm guessing that's what you are?"

Lina hoped they could trust Tuyaara. Her words had hinted that she was willing to protect others, even if they might be on the wrong side of the law—just as they were. It probably meant they'd be safe with her. But then, nothing had been the way it seemed since she started this journey. Lina chewed her lip. The stone against her chest wasn't giving out any warnings. "You're right," she said, glancing at Bogdan again for reassurance but getting none. "We broke out of Prison Camp Nine just a few days ago."

Tuyaara stopped walking and stared at Lina. "Prison Camp Nine? I'm sure that's where my friend is. Do you know Keskil?"

"Keskil?" Lina asked. Did she mean Keskil who shared his quarters with Bogdan?

Even Bogdan now looked up. "We know a Keskil."

"Tall," said Tuyaara, staring from one of them to the other. "Sixteen. Always trying to solve other people's problems. Pretty handsome . . ."

"Yes!" Lina laughed. She couldn't believe it. "Yes, I think we might know *your* Keskil."

They chatted for a while about their mutual friend before Lina's thoughts came back to Svetlana and their escape. "Do you really think that big falcon is what scared your horse?" she asked. "Because we think the bird might have something to do with a woman who captured us. It seemed like she could do things . . ." She hesitated, then said: "Things that should be impossible."

"Right," said Tuyaara with a grin. She didn't sound convinced, but she didn't seem to totally disbelieve them either. "You should tell my brothers all about that. They love a good story. You know, some people around here do say this place is troubled by a bad spirit."

"A bad spirit? Really?" Lina remembered what Old Gleb had told her. Poor, mad Old Gleb. Always teased because of his "fairy tales." Where was he now? Where were the others? Alexei and Vadim. Had they all turned into those shadow people already, or were they still lost and wandering, in what must seem like a nightmare?

"That's right. They call it the Man Hunter," said

Tuyaara. "They reckon the spirit comes here to hunt, and it captures anyone it comes across. So the story goes, anyway. I thought it was just a fairy tale."

Lina scanned the horizon where that giant falcon had been. The Man Hunter. That's what Svetlana had called herself on the night she captured them. But what *was* she?

The stone warmed Lina as they trudged, and the warmth moved around her body to the tips of her fingers and toes — until her cheeks felt hot and pink.

Tuyaara brought them to a log cabin, with a single funnel for a chimney rising from the center. It was her family's *balagan*, she explained — where they lived in order to farm with the rest of the collective in winter.

Inside, it was warm, with rugs on the floor and a fire crackling at the center. Tuyaara stripped off her furs, smoothed out her silky black hair, and introduced her family — her youngest brother, still a baby, her mother, and her father.

"They're from Prison Camp Nine," Tuyaara told her parents, straight out. "They know Keskil."

Tuyaara's father reached out to clasp Bogdan's shoulders. "Keskil? Is it true?" He was clearly eager to know whatever they could tell him, although Lina noticed Tuyaara's mother withdraw a little, a stern frown on her face, despite the happy chubby baby wriggling on her hip.

While Bogdan and Tuyaara's father talked, Lina couldn't stop staring all around her. Everything was wooden: the walls, the seats, the table. Bright tasseled tapestries hung from hooks and a large radio covered in knobs and dials, like the ones the guards at the camp had, sat in the corner. The delicious smell of cooking tinged the warm air—something milky but savory. Ornaments and keepsakes were clustered on shelves—and in full view. These people didn't need to hide their belongings, Lina realized, because what belonged to one belonged to all of them. But it was more than that: They trusted one another. They were a family. Lina immediately thought of her imaginary Moscow apartment. Her heart ached with a wonderful hurt.

Tuyaara frowned. "Are you crying?"

Lina wiped at her face. "It's just the change in temperature making my eyes water." But she couldn't help an involuntary sob into her sleeve.

After Tuyaara's father and Bogdan had spoken awhile, Tuyaara's mother beckoned Tuyaara away, and the three family members retreated to the stove, where they murmured to one another in low voices. Perhaps they were trying to work out what to make of these two escapees. Perhaps they were even worried about being punished by the authorities for helping them. Who wouldn't be? A stab of guilt ran through Lina's heart at the thought of bringing this family trouble. She exchanged a look with Bogdan, who'd been examining the radio. Perhaps they shouldn't have come here.

"I know you couldn't leave them out there, sweetheart," she overheard Tuyaara's mother say, "but we have a problem now because of your rashness. They're fugitives, after all. The other villagers we can trust, but are you *sure* no one else followed you?"

"Oh, Namiya, my love! Can we worry over practicalities later?" came her father's frustrated voice.

Lina occupied herself by playing with her necklace, while Bogdan took his maps out. They were both trying not to listen anymore.

Tuyaara's other two brothers had been out rounding up the horses for the evening when they'd first arrived, but soon they came home and Tuyaara introduced them too. The eldest, Michil, wore a fur *ushanka* balanced high on his head, which made him look very tall, and a wide grin just like Tuyaara's. The other, Dolan, had flushed cheeks and seemed serious and shy.

Michil and Dolan wanted to know every detail of their encounter with Svetlana and listened with solemn frowns while Lina and Bogdan explained what had happened. Lina kept expecting them to laugh—but mockery never came.

"She's taken Yakuts and many others as well," said Michil. "Her and her spirit wolves. Shamans and Orthodox priests have both tried to deal with her, in their own ways—even to help her—but she's a stubborn one. She

154

won't budge. But the longer she stays here, the more bitter she gets. That's what they think. It's bad news when a powerful spirit gets like that."

"It is for anyone who gets in the way," added Tuyaara.

"How long has she been here, then?" asked Lina.

"Only a short time in this part of Sakha," said Tuyaara. "But years, supposedly, in one region or another. The stories have been around since I can remember. I know that much."

Michil nodded. "I was three when I first heard the tale of the Man Hunter and the spirit wolves that roam the plains, turning humans into ghosts. They came when she did—so they must be drawn into this world by her."

"Michil, you know those tales were just Mama trying to get you to go to bed without making a fuss." Tuyaara punched his arm and grinned.

Michil wrapped his arm around her shoulders, winked at Lina and Bogdan, and said, "Our sister likes to think she's above all this talk. She thinks she'll move to Yakutsk one day and study to be a teacher. But it won't last—she'll get homesick in two minutes flat and wish she could trade the cars and classrooms for her old horse."

"Says you!" Tuyaara wrestled Michil off while Dolan smirked and shook his head.

Lina glanced away. It felt hard to breathe all of a sudden. Could this have been her life too, growing up, if it hadn't been for the camp?

Lina glanced at Bogdan, who strained to lift the corner of his mouth. He was still smarting, she could tell, after discovering he'd been wrong about the river and where they were. Despite the warmth and the welcome, a kind of creeping despair had come over Lina as well. Every second she did nothing felt like failing her mother. Being held captive in Svetlana's tower had wasted yet more time. They still had thousands of miles to travel.

Moscow and her dreams had never seemed further away.

If Tuyaara's parents had been discussing their worries about harboring two escaped prisoners earlier, they didn't mention it when they called everyone to the table. Dinner was a frozen salted fish dish called *stroganina*, a horse-milk drink called *kumis,* and a deliciously warm and fatty millet porridge. After years of cabbage soup, Lina's tongue tingled with all the new flavors.

Tuyaara's father rose from his seat every so often to stoke the fire, tending it with great care. Finally he sat down with them, straight-backed at the table. "Any friend of Keskil's is a friend of ours," he said firmly. He put his hand to his heart. "It will be wonderful to be able to bring our friends news of their son. They will be overjoyed to hear that he's still alive." Tears sparkled in his dark eyes, and he blinked them away. "You can stay with us for the winter, if you need to," he announced.

At this, Tuyaara's mother, Namiya, pursed her red lips

and turned her attention to the baby, the same troubled frown on her face again. Lina shifted in her seat with another guilty twinge.

But Tuyaara's father went on as if he hadn't noticed his wife's displeasure. "If the Man Hunter is after you, as you say, you'll need to stay hidden until it moves on or forgets. It's far too dangerous, otherwise."

Lina stood next to Bogdan, outside by the cattle shed. Night had come quickly and stars pricked the sky like snow that had been frozen in time. They had borrowed Michil's and Dolan's coats and hats to keep warm. It was quiet out here. Only the occasional snort of a horse echoed from the gloom, and the odd rumble came from inside the cattle shed, along with a strong whiff of hay, as the cows shifted their feet.

Above the outlines of the other distant village cabins, light flashed and rippled across the dark sky in shades of green, with the occasional pulse of purple or yellow. "The Northern Lights," said Bogdan, gazing out at them. He looked different with Michil's *ushanka* balanced on top of his head, the way Michil had worn it earlier.

Lina stared at the lights too. So much more was possible than she'd ever realized. Her stone necklace—which both warmed her and warned of danger. Lost spirits, terrorizing and abducting humans. The existence of furry, pot-bellied horses. And now these rippling lights splayed across the night sky, flashing and changing as if trying to tell them something.

How was it that, in the face of all this, reaching Moscow could seem so impossible? They had thousands of miles to travel—and Svetlana hunting them on top of that.

"We were never going to get to the city on foot," said Bogdan. "Perhaps this is for the best, after all. Staying here, I mean."

Lina hugged herself. Spring was months away. Part of her wanted to go back to the camp right now to check on her mother. But only her grandmother had the power, the influence, to free her. All she needed was Lina's knowledge of which camp her mother was in—names, places, specific details—and she could make it happen with just a single word in the right ear. Lina *knew* it.

She'd promised her mother she'd carry on. That was what she must do.

The longer they stayed here, the further away her dreams of meeting her grandmother and rescuing her mother would slip. Anyway, could they really stay hidden for the whole winter with Svetlana searching the skies and plains for them? Something told Lina she'd never stop—not until she found them. She'd seemed fixed on finding out why her wolves wouldn't bind Lina. And then they'd defied her by escaping. She'd be angry.

No. As kind as it was of Tuyaara's father to offer them shelter, food, and company, they'd be endangering everyone if they stayed. Tuyaara's mother knew it—Lina could see that she was worried about her family. Their baby.

Lina steeled herself. Now she just had to work out how they were going to get to Moscow.

"Bogey," she said. "What d'you think Vadim planned to do when he got to that farmhouse? Would they have stayed there or moved on eventually?"

"Doubt they would've stayed for long. Not the sort to keep to himself, was he? He would've gotten bored before long without anyone to bully. Think about it—he even got bored at the camp, and there were plenty of people there he could bother."

"So a city, then?"

"Probably back to Stalingrad, where his gang operates."

Lina thought about it. She was definitely missing something. She had to be. "He couldn't have been planning to do it all on foot. It's impossible. He must've had another way. Another plan." And he must have told her mother something. He'd promised to take Lina to Moscow. Katya wouldn't have let Lina go without knowing how Vadim planned to get her there.

Bogdan shrugged. "Got no idea what Vadim's plan was, but Tuyaara's family might lend us a sled. Maybe some of their dogs, to pull us. We could go from town to town picking up supplies until we finally get to Moscow. But it'll still take months."

Lina let her mind drift. She felt it going out to meet the Northern Lights.

Everything snapped into focus in a rush.

"Bogey!"

He flinched away from her. She'd shouted in his ear by accident. "Aargh! What?"

Lina couldn't believe she hadn't thought of it before.

She could barely keep still. She felt like she was going to explode. "Think back, Bogey. How did you get to the camp, when you first arrived?"

"We walked a ways, towing carts . . ." Bogdan said. He was silent for some time. Then he set his jaw. "Train," he said. "Before that, I came by train."

# 28

Lina and Bogdan ran back into the *balagan* together. "Excuse me," said Bogdan. "Where's the nearest town with a station along the Trans-Siberian railway?"

Tuyaara's father stared into the corner of the room as he considered the question. The harder he stared, the more he frowned, and the harder he appeared to be thinking. "Far," he said at last. "Too far by horse or by dogsled. And it's too much of a risk with that thing searching for you."

"There are the practicalities to consider too. Money. Tickets," Namiya chipped in, but she didn't sound as against the idea. She squinted as though also thinking hard.

Tuyaara leaped to her feet. "I can take them to the train station at Bratsk," she said. "We can stop with Uncle and his family on the way and borrow their car. It's old and won't go far, but it'll at least get to Bratsk. *Then* the journey won't take long. I can lead Lina and Bogdan to Uncle's. I know the way—I can do it."

Moscow. The train would really take them to Moscow.

"Wait a minute," said her father. "It may be dangerous, Tuyaara. Let's not rush into this."

"We need to rush," said Tuyaara. "Never mind your Man Hunter, guards could come looking for them any day now. And Lina needs to reach her grandmother as soon as possible."

"She's right, you know," said her mother. "We've already discussed the possibility that search parties may come looking. And no one is quicker or more capable of this than Tuyaara."

Lina felt guilty for causing a division in the family, however small. She would've been happy to leave—just her and Bogdan, on their own.

But Tuyaara's eyes gleamed. "Is that a yes? Papa, they're friends of Keskil's, remember. They need our help. So can I take them?"

Her father looked at his wife, frowned, and tutted. "Yes," he said, at last. "I suppose you can."

That night, Lina snuggled down in a bed of blankets and furs. The floor was hard underneath her, but she didn't mind it. Buried in all that warm bedding, she finally thought she knew how mice must feel, snug in their little nests.

At daybreak, they would take horses and head out to find Tuyaara's uncle. From there, they would drive onward to the train station at Bratsk.

Lina knew it wouldn't be easy to leave. For the first time, she'd glimpsed a real family home, and her heart ached at the thought of leaving it behind to face more snow and ice, cold and danger. But, like Tuyaara, she could also hardly wait. She would be on her way again, moving closer to finding her grandmother.

This had been the most eventful birthday of her life. At certain points, she hadn't thought she would survive it. And yet, here she was.

When Lina slept, she dreamed of Tuyaara's home and of all the talk, the laughter, and the feeling between her whole family: so tender it was painful. But beneath the noise of her dreams, she kept hearing another voice. A whisper close to her ear, which woke her several times into the still darkness of the room.

*"Nevertell."*

# 29

Come first light, not one horse would go near them. Even those most docile and used to riders reared and bucked when Tuyaara and her brothers tried to guide them over. "Maybe they sense something around you," said Michil at last. "According to Yakut folklore, they're very perceptive of spirits. They see them."

Tuyaara frowned and tapped her toe. She wasn't interested in her brother's musings, and she wanted to get moving, Lina could tell.

"Maybe you should just forget about this journey and stay," Tuyaara's father said. "It would be for the best."

"Thank you," said Lina. Every kindness Tuyaara's family showed them made her flush with gratitude. But she shared a knowing look with Tuyaara's mother and understood that he was being helpful—but not practical. And they were fugitives. Carrying on their journey still felt like the right decision.

"Thing is, I think I know what it is," Lina went on. She'd had her suspicions all morning since she woke from that terrible disturbed sleep, her head aching, her face puffy and rubbery. She fixed her gaze on Bogdan. "I think we've brought our friend with us. The one who helped us escape."

Bogdan looked puzzled at first. Then understanding flashed in his eyes.

"Who is it?" asked Tuyaara. "Why can't we see them?"

"It's one of the shadows, from Svetlana's tower," said Lina. "I didn't realize before, but then all night I kept seeing and hearing things. I'm sure of it now. She must've been with us since we escaped into that mist. I bet that's why your horse wouldn't go near us too."

"She?" said Bogdan.

Lina shrugged. "Pretty sure she's a girl. Don't know why."

Tuyaara raised her eyebrow. "Interesting. Is it—'she'—friendly?"

Lina nodded. "She did help us. So I think so."

The sun blazed an orange rainbow across the sky as they argued about what to do. The light dragged their blue shadows over the snow, as if urging them to get moving. After a lot of discussion—including Michil insisting they stay another night to carry on the debate and Tuyaara shrieking with impatience—they decided Lina and Bogdan should take the dogsled while Tuyaara rode her horse.

"Make sure you bring those dogs back, Tuyaara," said her mother, wagging her finger. "We need them. And you're not to get on the train."

"Don't worry, Mama. I can handle the dogs and I'll come straight back."

Tuyaara's family lent them felt boots and furs, food for their journey, gifts for Tuyaara's uncle and his family—and even more food parcels for the train. Each kindness weighed heavier on Lina than the last, because she could barely offer anything in return. "I promise we'll send the boots and furs back somehow," she said, clutching Tuyaara's mother's hand in her own, "as soon as we get to Moscow and find my grandmother."

Namiya patted Lina's shoulder. She must've known that returning the clothes would be all but impossible but, unlike Lina, had accepted it. "Thank you, Lina. But bringing news of Keskil that we can pass on to his family is enough. To them—and to my Tuyaara—knowing he's alive is worth more than furs and food."

Lina nodded, said goodbye to Tuyaara's father and brothers, and climbed aboard the sled with Bogdan.

"We'll know if the spirit has gone with you by the horses' reactions," said Michil, "and you ought to be able to tell by Tuyaara's horse." He was clearly wary of the spirit. Lina felt fine about it, though. It had helped them escape from Svetlana's tower, after all. And she was fairly certain it was going to come with them. If she tilted her head a certain way, she could see the small shadow, perched just behind Bogdan on the sled.

By the time they set off, the morning sun had turned white, and a bitter wind whipped up the snow. Lina knew by the weather and the fall in temperature that a bad storm was on the way. They all did.

After a great start and a break for lunch, they rode on long into the afternoon. Dark clouds began squeezing the sky from above. They pressed down and down until only a sliver of ice-blue sky remained. It swamped the friends in an eerie green light and made the mist of glittering diamond dust that hung all around them a murky, marshy color.

From high above came a falcon's shriek. Lina jumped and called the dogs to a halt. Tuyaara stopped her horse too and sat as still as she could. "Hard for it to see us in this," she said. But she still didn't take her eyes off the sky.

The dark shadow of the giant falcon passed through the clouds above them, circled twice, and glided off ahead. Had it spotted them, after all? Lina guessed they'd know for sure if they heard Svetlana's wolves. She dreaded hearing their howls and flinched at every sound from then on.

"If you're lucky, this 'Svetlana' won't follow you all the way to Moscow," said Tuyaara. "Surely she wouldn't track you that far."

"Let's hope we lose her somewhere between here and there," said Bogdan, "so she stops bothering all of us."

They talked about other things after that, to distract themselves, chatting over the racket of the horse and the dogs and over the snow spray kicked up by the sled. Bogdan shared stories of his past and of his hope of finding his parents, while Tuyaara talked about wanting to study to be a teacher in a city like Yakutsk. She talked about how there was such an imbalance in the world between people, and how, by becoming a teacher, she wanted to make it better. Or at least try. She was excited to hear all about Bogdan's upbringing in Leningrad.

Lina stayed quiet. She thought about her grandfather's gardens. With her knowledge and abilities with plants, she hoped she could get a job there one day without much trouble. Her knowledge—and her abilities . . . But what were those abilities, exactly? Just a way with plants, the same as her grandfather had had? Or something else? Her experience in the pine forest suggested there was more to it than a normal talent. Could she do it again, make something grow like that? And, if so, could she do it from a seed? From thin air? She longed to try, but now wasn't the time.

Funny, she thought, how she'd only ever wanted to be a gardener like her grandfather. And now here she was, thinking about magic.

Her stone necklace kept her warm, though her new furs did an excellent job of that too. But despite that, she felt uneasy. A pressure gathered at her temples with the coming storm, and she wondered if *any* distance would be enough to escape from Svetlana. If the stories were true, and she'd spent all those years hunting . . . Lina didn't need to be an expert to know she wasn't the sort who just gave up and let things go.

Lina checked again to make sure their shadow friend was still with them. Yes, there she was: the merest flicker of movement at the edge of Lina's vision. To see her had become a comfort. Lina knew nothing about her—who she'd once been or what she even knew of her own past. But she trusted her. That was important.

She trusted them all: Bogdan, Tuyaara's family, and Tuyaara too. Especially Bogdan, though. He'd been her first true friend. She was so glad that he was here with her. All this talk of Leningrad and the future made her fearful of what might come. What would happen when they reached Moscow and Lina finally found her grandmother? How long would Bogdan stay with her before going on to find his own family?

Now it was really cold. Lina's face felt numb. Ice droplets formed in her eyelashes and in the fur that encircled her face. The same was happening to Tuyaara and Bogdan. Even the horse's lashes were completely encrusted with the sparkling frost.

Tuyaara and Bogdan were still chatting. Lina noticed

another sound in the background, though. A kind of swishing, tinkling sound. "Wait," she said. "What's that?"

Bogdan stopped the dogs this time, and Tuyaara brought her horse around to stand next to them. They listened in silence.

Nothing.

"You sure you heard something?" said Bogdan. "I can't. Oh, wait! Hang on . . ." They looked at each other, wide-eyed. As he was speaking, Lina had caught the noise again: that same swishing, tinkling sound.

"There it is again." Lina heard it a third time as she spoke—and gasped. "It happens when we talk. Without a doubt."

"Aah," said Tuyaara. Awe and fear mixed in her eyes. "The whisper of the stars."

"The what?"

"It means it's cold enough for our breath to freeze," she said. "Look." She cupped her gloved hands in front of her as she spoke and then showed them what she'd collected: tiny, sparkling grains of ice.

"You caught your own words?" Lina gazed at the glittering grains. "Imagine actually being able to *keep* what you say. Better make it something important . . ."

Bogdan stretched out his arms and cupped his hands dramatically. "One day, I WILL find my parents again," he said. He showed them the words, sparkling in his mittens, and grinned.

Tuyaara laughed. "My turn," she said. She pouted and put on a funny voice. "I will move to the city and teach."

"What about you, Lina?" said Bogdan. "Aren't you going to try?"

Lina cupped her hands a little ways in front of her mouth as the others had done and paused. It felt very serious, all of a sudden. She closed her eyes and an image of her mother sprang into her mind, vivid and overpowering. "I will find my grandmother and get help to rescue Mamochka," she said. The words froze in the air and tinkled into her palms.

She gazed at the collection of twinkling little crystals. The words had shuddered through her like a wave just now, and though she couldn't explain how, it felt like they'd carried the image of her mother with them, out into the world. Was it her imagination, or for one split second did she see her mother's face flash across each surface of the ice grains, just as Lina had pictured it in her mind just now? No—that wasn't possible. It had to have been her own reflection, if anything. She carefully tucked the ice grains into her pocket.

"As fun as that was," said Tuyaara, "if we can hear the whisper of the stars, it means it's already too cold. We've *got* to reach my uncle's before this storm hits."

*Or it won't just be our words that get frozen solid* was what Tuyaara was thinking, but she didn't have to say it. Lina understood.

They raced on. The clouds darkened and so did the gloom around them. Frozen wind drove ice dust at their faces. They covered all but their eyes and kept going. Then came the snow.

"I can see their house," said Tuyaara, her voice muffled under layers of fur. "We have to get the dogs inside. Now."

Lina could see it now too—another log cabin, like Tuyaara's, on the horizon. As they charged closer, the silhouette of a man—Tuyaara's uncle, perhaps—waved at them, urging them on. Lina knew by how frantically and forcefully he flapped his arms that they were in trouble if they stayed out a moment longer.

By the time they reached the *balagan*, thick snow, driven on the wind, stuck to them horizontally, head to toe, and kept on coming at them like a solid wall. Everything looked dark gray to Lina, except for the white snow slashing across her eyes.

By then, Lina could no longer tell the ground from the sky.

# 30

Tuyaara's uncle ushered them onto the raised porch at the front of the house, while his children rushed out and took the horse and dogs to shelter around the back. At the door, Lina glanced one last time at the snow behind her.

In the midst of the storm, a dark-haired girl reached out toward Lina from the plains before the wind-driven snow obscured her. Lina let out a cry of shock. The girl couldn't have been more than four years old. She wore no coat or furs. Her face had been bunched up into a cry and she held her arms out in front of her, begging to be held.

"There's somebody out there—I just saw her! A tiny girl," she shouted, gripping Bogdan's arm.

Bogdan looked between Tuyaara and her uncle, fast.

"Is someone missing from inside? From another home, maybe?"

"There are other families nearby. Children, possibly," said Tuyaara sternly, hovering between them and the warm hearth of her uncle's home. "Show me where."

Lina pointed to where she'd seen the girl.

Tuyaara frowned. "I can't see anything, Lina. I'm not my brother, but I have a bad feeling in my gut about this. Don't trust your eyes."

Lina's stone pulsed with heat. She couldn't be sure what it meant. Something was definitely wrong. It could be a trick of Svetlana's. What should she do?

Then Lina remembered all the times she'd cried for her mother with her arms held up to her like that. How small, selfless acts—of fellow prisoners, of Tuyaara's family—had no doubt saved her life. The child's sob carried on the wind. It wrenched at her. What if it wasn't a trick?

She couldn't leave her to freeze in the storm.

Lina strained her eyes to see the girl again and thought she caught a glimpse of dark hair whipped by the wind. "She's just over there," said Lina, looking at Bogdan. "I'm sure of it. If I run quickly, I can grab her and bring her inside."

Tuyaara shook her head. "Lina. Bogdan. My friends. Don't do it."

Her uncle said, "No, please stay. There's nothing out there but your own deaths."

Just as doubt crossed Lina's mind, the child's cry came again, clear as anything, carried by the wind. "I've got to," she said. "I'm sorry."

"Lina! Bogdan!" called Tuyaara.

But Lina wasn't listening anymore—and Bogdan was right beside her as she dashed into the swirl of the storm. If she could just grab the little girl and carry her indoors, she could save her. But where was she now? The girl had been just there. She was sure of it.

All Lina could hear was the howl of the wind. All she could see was a blur of white and gray. Her own breath, blown back at her, turned to ice when it touched her skin, pulling tight and pinching as it froze.

Bogdan grabbed her arm. He shouted something, but she couldn't hear over the noise of the storm. He had frost flowers blooming across his cheeks. It felt as though they were being buried alive.

Lina glanced behind them. Snow and haze and darkness obscured the house. No doubt Tuyaara was pacing inside, by the hearth, raging because she knew she couldn't help them, her uncle and aunt trying hard to comfort her but failing. Lina shouldn't have run out here like this. She ought to have listened. It was a hard truth—and made worse because she couldn't tell which way was which anymore. She couldn't go back to the house even if she wanted to.

※

Lina fought against the wind and flailed her arms to keep from being buried by snow. Forward, backward, up, down—direction lost its meaning. The safety of the *balagan* was gone.

Fingers slipped around Lina's upper arm and gripped tight. For a second, Lina couldn't breathe—a scream rose in her throat and froze there. Coldness seeped from the fingers through Lina's furs. First she looked at the hand—bony, covered in papery pink skin. Then at the owner's face—that of an elderly woman.

A second wave of shock jolted through her. The woman looked just like her imaginings of Baba Yaga—one of Russia's oldest fairy-tale villains. Fear left a tingle in her arms and legs. The coldness of the old woman's touch reached Lina's bones.

They'd come for a young girl. They'd found an elderly woman. This was Svetlana's work. It had to be.

But even as Lina thought it, the idea seemed to evaporate on the wind.

"Please," said the woman, her voice cracking, "help me. My home is just over there, but I can't make it alone."

Her words were clear despite the wind's roar, as if carried through Lina's body along with the coldness. Lina saw that the woman held Bogdan's arm too.

They shared a look. Bogdan seemed as doubtful, as confused, as Lina was.

"Wait. Have you seen a young girl out here?" Lina asked.

"No, no young girl, child. Only me here. Only me for miles."

Lina knew that wasn't quite true—Tuyaara's family was nearby—but she let it go. It didn't seem to matter anymore.

"Come, my home is this way," the woman said. "Help me walk and I'll give you shelter until you can find your friend."

Lina moved as if in a dream—unable to stop herself. It was a struggle just to think, to focus her mind—those cold fingers clouded everything—and then, a new certainty settled over Lina. The woman was so light and so frail. The bare skin on her wrists, folded tightly around her bones, had started sparkling and cracking in the cold. They *had* to help her to safety.

But there was something that Lina was trying to remember. A name. Svetlana? She could barely remember who that was . . .

The large, dark shape of a circular hut loomed out of the haze, snow plastered up one side and stuck like mud. They'd be there in moments if they could just keep going straight and resist the force of the wind. Lina struggled to breathe, but she quickened her pace anyway. Stopping now meant dying on the doorstep.

Linked together, all three of them burst through the door as one.

# 31

The elderly woman was the first to rise from the floor where they had collapsed.

She shook out her white hair and straightened her back. She looked much taller than she had before, hunched against the wind. "Your kind act will be rewarded," she said in a much stronger voice. "I promise you."

She barged the heavy door shut with her shoulder and pulled curtains across it. The winds still wailed and howled, but the heavy tapestries draped over every wall dampened the sound. Lina's head swam. She felt numb inside, but her nerves jangled—like the feeling returning to a deadened limb. Panic fluttered in her chest. Who was this old lady? She'd felt only concern for her moments ago, but now a creeping sense of distrust slithered over her skin.

Lina scanned her surroundings for clues. She couldn't

tell what the hut was made from, but it had a stone hearth with a fire already burning inside. Every time the wind rose, a cloud of black soot billowed down from the chimney. The rugs echoed the patterns of the tapestries hanging on the walls: fruit and flowers, suns and moons, animals and birds. They had a Georgian look to them, Lina thought, remembering the stories her mother had told her of the family's home in Moscow.

Lina's head felt oddly empty, though. She could remember the stories of her grandparents. She could remember her mother, of course, and the escape from the camp—but little after that. It felt like something important was missing.

While Lina took in the room and tried to gather her thoughts, Bogdan spoke up warily. "I'm Bogdan, and this is Lina. So . . . what do we call you, Babushka?"

"Babushka. Ha! Babushka will do." The woman sneered at them the way Vadim used to as she moved back toward them. "Here. Take off those cold furs, or you'll be soaked through."

Lina's insides lurched. That sneer gave her the urge to crawl to the farthest end of the room. This "Babushka" resembled the Baba Yaga of her mother's most terrifying bedtime stories so much—even down to the one sharp tooth occasionally peeking out from behind her thin lips—that it took all her control not to run out into the wilds again.

Where would she go, anyway? For as long as that storm raged, they were trapped here. Besides, Baba Yaga wasn't *real*. And it was dangerous to say otherwise. Fairy tales like those were not allowed.

Still, this old woman made Lina uncomfortable. To hide her nervous shakes, Lina busied herself unbuttoning her coat and hood. The chill in her blood started to thaw. At the same time, her memories came back to her in flashes. Vivid, alarming memories. A falcon circling. Wolves howling—and a tall woman with a cloak. The images were hazy, unconnected, but fear pushed its way into Lina's heart. The stone necklace radiated heat. Whether it was still fighting the dire chill of the storm or trying to warn her, she couldn't tell.

She had to take off her things so they could dry out, but she didn't want to lose sight of where they were—just in case she needed them again in a hurry. Nor did she want to show how afraid she was.

"Have you lived here for long, Babushka?" asked Lina, trying to sound breezy. "It's lucky we found you out there." She glanced at Bogdan. He stared back, open-mouthed. As Lina looked at him, it all came to her in a rush: the journey from Tuyaara's house, the little girl in the snow, the old woman, and . . . Svetlana! She gave a gasp. But was this Svetlana? Or *another* like her? How many beings were there with these kinds of abilities?

The babushka slung their clothes over her arm and

began laying them around the hearth. "Yes, yes," she said. "Lucky. Who knows what would have become of me in that blizzard if you two *rebyatishki* hadn't helped me."

They sat by the fire, covering their mouths and noses every time a cloud of black smoke billowed around them. The feeling was just about returning to Lina's face, feet, and hands, which stung like they'd been slapped with sticks. Inside, her anxieties writhed and wouldn't be still—made worse somehow by the unnatural calm that had repressed them until now. At her side, Bogdan wrung his hands.

The babushka bustled into another room and came back wrapped in a bundle of dark-blue silver-trimmed shawls. "No need to look so afraid, little ones. I just want to help you, as you helped me. I'm heating water so that you can wash, and I've laid out some new clothes for you on the beds. They belonged to my children," she added when they looked at her, puzzled and afraid. "A boy and a girl, who are now fully grown."

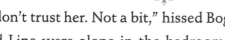

"I don't trust her. Not a bit," hissed Bogdan the minute he and Lina were alone in the bedroom. There were more tapestries in here, as well as beds covered in blankets and, just as the woman had promised, a change of clothes. She'd even filled tin buckets with steaming hot water, one for each of them, so they could clean up. It took all Lina's strength not to dive straight in.

"Doesn't it feel like we've met her before?" Bogdan went on.

Lina rubbed the back of her neck. "Could be," she whispered. "Do you think Svetlana can change her human form?" Given everything else she could do, Lina could believe it.

Bogdan chewed his cheek and nodded.

"We can't know for sure who or what she is," Lina whispered even lower. "But I don't trust her either, so let's stay on our guard. Try not to let her touch you, Bogey, because that's how she tricked us into coming here. We'll just keep close to our coats. If we have to, we'll grab them and run."

Bogdan agreed. "Might as well get changed into the clean clothes, though," he said. "No harm in that, eh?"

Lina found her outfit neatly folded on one of the beds next to her coat, which had had a chance to dry. Bogdan picked up his clothes from the other. There was a moment of fluster and blushing until they realized they could pull a curtain across the room between them for privacy.

Once behind the curtain, Lina stripped off—laying the stone carefully on the bed within sight—stood in the bucket, and splashed herself with the hot water. She rubbed it into her face and hair. Grime ran down her legs in rivulets. Then she dried herself and put on the new clothes: a green tunic with a silver-and-gold leaf motif embroidered around the hem and warm wool trousers

182

underneath. She traced the embroidery with her finger and thought of what had happened the last time she touched a real plant.

As she reached for the stone, the moth crawled out of its bead and fluttered around the room, as if inspecting these new surroundings. Lina had forgotten it was even there. The way it dived and danced in the air, it looked like a piece of ash, riding the hot currents from the fire they'd sat around with Old Gleb and the others. She watched, hypnotized by its twirling and twisting, and by the strength of her own memory.

To her surprise, the moth soon returned to her. It settled itself down inside the same bead. Lina frowned, then shrugged. "Fine, little moth friend. Make yourself at home."

She found a small, beaten-up old mirror on the wall by the bed, lit a candle to see herself better in the dimness, and ran her fingers through her tufty sand-colored hair. It had been a long time since she'd seen herself in a mirror. Her hair had really grown. But it still stuck up in patches when she pulled and twisted it, even while damp. Her bottom lip looked fuller somehow—her face longer, her jawline more angular. As for the tunic, she'd never worn anything so soft, so fitted, and so . . . girly.

Something moved at the edge of her vision. Like rags floating underwater. Lina knew instantly what it was. "You!" she said, and then lowered her voice. "So you came with us? Good for you. I'm glad you're here, friend. And don't worry, because I won't say anything to Babushka, I promise. I don't trust her—whoever she is."

The candle, burning in its brass dish, flickered as if caught in a breeze.

*"Nevertell . . ."*

A little cough came from behind the curtain. Lina guessed that meant Bogdan was ready. When she pulled it back, he was dressed too—in an embroidered knee-length jacket in deep red, with long sleeves and trousers underneath. He looked amazing.

"You look . . ."

"Amazing!" said Bogdan. "You look amazing."

"You too, Bogey."

"Better than standard-issue overalls, isn't it?" said Bogdan, stretching out his arms. He giggled, and Lina remembered how their laughter had always been dark and tinged with bitterness. She struggled to think of a time when Bogdan had actually sounded so happy.

"Hey, Bogey," said Lina, "she's still with us, you know. The shadow girl. She—"

*"Nevertell."* The candle, over by the mirror, flickered again. This time the flame dipped—once, twice, three times. It looked deliberate.

Lina and Bogdan stared at each other. "Are you doing that?" whispered Bogdan to the room.

*"Nevertell,"* came the voice, and the candle flame

dipped three more times. They realized with excitement what this meant: that they could find out more about their shadow friend, using the candle. Lina had suspected before that Svetlana was wrong when she said the shadows were mindless or beyond suffering—and now it was confirmed. Even if their memories were locked away at first, they clearly returned to them over time, as their shadow friend's had.

Bogdan was already on the case. "Flicker once for yes and twice for no," he said, and asked a flurry of questions.

"Are you a girl?" One flicker. That meant *yes.*

"Are you young?" *Yes.*

"Are you the same age as us?" *No.*

"Younger?" *Yes.*

Bogdan narrowed her age down to eight. Lina glanced at the door, through which came the occasional muffled clank of a pan, or a thud and crackle as Babushka stoked the fire. She was busying herself on the other side. But for how long?

"Where are you from?" Lina asked the shadow. She hadn't quite gotten the hang of the yes-or-no questioning. "I mean . . . Are you from Siberia, originally?" *No.*

"The countryside somewhere?" *No.*

"A big city?" *Yes.*

"Moscow?" *Yes.*

"Did Svetlana take you away from your family?" The light flickered once. *Yes.*

"How did you come to be trapped by Svetlana?" said Lina. She slapped her own forehead. "I mean—"

"Lina, my friend, you're doing it totally wrong," said Bogdan. "Watch me." He began again, "Are you—?"

"Are my little *rebyatishki* dressed?" It was Babushka's voice on the other side of the door.

Lina looked at Bogdan, startled. "Coming," she called.

Babushka was warming more water on the hearth when they came out—this time for them to drink. "Hot water is as good as medicine, out here," she said.

Lina sniffed it suspiciously, then breathed more deeply. The steam filled her lungs. Fresh, warm, delicious water. She drank.

"I can take you to where you're going," said Babushka suddenly. "*If* you'll just tell me where. And why."

Lina froze and peered over the rim of her cup.

Babushka smiled, showing her sharp tooth. "I promised to help you, didn't I? Don't I remind you of someone who could?"

In the stories, Baba Yaga did sometimes help people. Other times, she tried to hurt them. Often, she tried to eat them. One thing was certain, though: Baba Yaga could never be trusted. Lina looked the old woman up and down. If this was Svetlana, what was she up to?

"How could you help us?" asked Bogdan slowly.

"My house will take us there."

"Your house?"

"Just tell me where you're going, go to sleep in your beds, and in the morning—we'll be there."

Lina and Bogdan looked at each other. "Moscow," said Lina finally. "That's where we're going."

Babushka laughed. "Moscow! Then you really are going to need my help." Both of them were silent. "What is it, *rebyatishki*? Do you still not believe me?" She took a potted plant from a shelf. It looked leggy and unwell. Lina could immediately tell that it needed sunlight.

Babushka touched the plant. Its tendrils sprawled out like a person stretching after a deep sleep. Leaves unraveled, bright green and waxy. The stalk plumped out and darkened, turning flaky and woody. It became a miniature potted tree. But Babushka hadn't finished. Several furry green fruits bulged from its branches, flushing yellow and pink as they grew, and became fat with juice.

Lina gaped. She remembered the branch that had sprouted under her touch in the forest. Was *she* magical like these people too—like Svetlana and Babushka? Were there others?

# 32

The stone burned against Lina's chest in warning. Babushka plucked two of the blushing, globe-like fruits and offered Lina and Bogdan one each.

"What is it?" asked Lina. She could barely keep the dread out of her voice. The stone's reaction had shaken her. And yet her heart thudded with excitement. The sweet smell had made her mouth water involuntarily. Could *she* grow something like this?

"Try one," said Babushka, watching her again through narrowed eyes. "Fruit like this grows in my homeland but not here. Except with a little encouragement."

Lina still hadn't taken the fruit that the old lady held out. As if to tempt her, Babushka made its stem bulge a little, and a tiny, waxy leaf popped out. A cold smile stretched across Babushka's lips.

Lina took the fruit from her carefully. Her stomach felt knotted.

"Can you make anything grow?" asked Bogdan, studying the fruit in his hands. He seemed more interested than afraid. Lina felt a twinge of hope. Perhaps he'd believe her, after all, if she told him what she'd done—what she could, perhaps, do again?

"Yes," said Babushka. "In the right conditions."

"You could feed whole villages like that, couldn't you?"

"Or a labor camp," muttered Lina.

"That is my warm magic," said Babushka, "and warm magic needs warmth. I come from more temperate climes, far from here, and I haven't been back in many years. So my warm magic has suffered. And besides, it takes a certain *positivity* of spirit to grow more than a few peaches, which I am not so inclined to anymore."

Bogdan took a bite of the fruit. It made a sucking noise against his teeth, and a blossom-like smell wafted around Lina's nose. As Bogdan chewed, his eyes got wider. "Lina!" he said after he'd swallowed his mouthful. "You've got to try it!"

"Go on, child," said Babushka, smiling. "Your friend is enjoying his."

Lina looked at Bogdan, who nodded, his eyes still huge and flickering with excitement. The peach didn't seem to be poisoned—which was good for Bogdan's sake.

"What are you waiting for?" snapped Babushka impatiently. "Try it."

Lina hadn't expected her sudden flare of temper. She flinched from the lash of Babushka's words and bit down, deep into the fruit. "Ow!" She'd bitten through soft flesh and into something hard. Her teeth ached. She ran her tongue over them. It was fine. None of them seemed loose.

"Be careful of the pit," said Babushka. She still sounded irritable. "Have you never eaten a peach before?"

Lina sank her nails into the puncture marks her teeth had left in the skin of the peach. Pink juice welled up around her fingers and trickled down her wrist. She peeled a chunk of the velvety fruit flesh away. Beneath it there was a stone.

A stone just like the one hanging around her neck.

Without a word, Lina handed the fruit with its exposed stone to Bogdan, who stifled a cry with his hand.

"If you're impressed by peaches, I can show you some *real* magic while you eat the rest," said Babushka, who must have misunderstood Lina's and Bogdan's reactions. "Powerful magic." She bustled to the edge of the room and grappled with something behind one of the tapestries, chattering as she went.

The juice from the peach dried onto Lina's skin in sticky trails as she waited. She was still reeling from what she'd just seen. The magic stone she wore around her neck wasn't a stone at all but a peach pit. Her heart pounded. She could barely believe it.

# 33

Her mind still whirring, Lina thought of that note, tucked inside one of the beads on her necklace: *"My darling Anri, I give you the gift of my heart."* What did it all mean?

"Help me with this, please," said Babushka from across the room. Now that she'd wrestled a tapestry to one side, she tugged at an old, round frame propped against a battered chair. It came up to Lina's chest when she got close.

"It's heavy," said Lina, eyeing Babushka. "Do you usually do this all on your own?"

Together, all three of them rolled the frame into the center of the room and lowered it down flat onto the floor.

The raised edge was beaten silver. The inside of it was black. Babushka took a glass jug filled with water from the shelf above the hearth. "Some melted snow that

I had left over," she said as she poured the water into the frame. It created a shallow, swirling pool. Light bounced and wobbled all over its surface, reflecting the cobwebs dangling from the ceiling's rafters.

"It's a water mirror," she said. "Kneel down around it with me, and I'll show you how it works." She crouched next to it and laid her hands on her knees. Opposite her, Lina and Bogdan did the same. Out of the corner of her eye, Lina saw the telltale flutter that meant their shadow friend was with them.

Babushka narrowed her eyes. Her smile was gone now. "Cold magic comes from coldness—of spirit and of place. What better place than this for it? And living so long in isolation, I have cultivated my coldness of spirit. The reward? It lets me peer into other worlds. Summon spirits. Even see a person's real self in their words." She paused as though noticing something for the first time, before continuing, "And it allows me to spot *secret snakes*."

Before Lina knew what was happening, Babushka leaped to her feet in a whirl of blue shawls and tussled with the air.

Not the air, Lina realized. Their shadow friend.

Babushka shrieked, "Insolent servant!"

Now Lina knew for certain who they were dealing with: *Svetlana.*

She leaped to her feet. So did Bogdan.

The babushka—Svetlana—was shouting, "Do you

think you can abandon your duties? Sneak around here without me *knowing*? Your punishment is to wander the nothing world." She pushed her hands toward the water mirror. To push the shadow in.

"Stop!" shouted Lina.

Bogdan dashed behind Svetlana, trying to pull the old lady backward, away from the mirror. From the other side, Lina tried to pull the invisible girl from Svetlana's grasp. It felt like her arms flailed in slow motion against a great weight of water, as if she were moving through a nightmare. Svetlana only laughed—a callous, bitter sound. Above that came a piercing squeal, like an animal in pain or fright.

Lina realized it had to be the shadow girl, screaming.

"Stop it. Stop," shouted Lina again. "She's our friend!"

Lina couldn't hold on. Her fingers slipped through the shadow girl. Bogdan, thrown back by Svetlana's struggling, launched in a second time to try to hold her still. "Do as Lina says," he yelled. "Let go of her!"

Noise bounced around the room. Filled Lina's head. But all their voices paled against the sudden roar of the wind down the chimney. A billow of black smoke covered everything. It clung around her face and caught in her throat, lingering too long to be normal. It drifted and swayed in front of her, like a reflection in dark water that had been disturbed.

A hand clasped Lina's, and she screamed.

*"Nevertell,"* came the whisper.

Time slowed down. The hand held tight. Svetlana and Bogdan were nowhere to be seen. Hidden in the smoke? Or gone? Was Lina even in the hut anymore? It felt like dreaming and fainting, mingled together.

The billowing, inky black hung around her.

With it came other things. The echo of an unfamiliar voice. Small scratching sounds. A smell of wood shavings and lead. The cloud shifted and she saw an outline: a girl with pigtails. She was sitting at a desk, writing. On the cover of a second notebook next to her was written a name: NATALYA.

Lina looked at this child and knew exactly what she was witnessing: a memory. "This is you, isn't it? From before. So your name's Natalya . . . Were you at school?"

"*Nevertell.*"

The child at the desk dropped her pencil and froze. Lina froze too. Her stomach lurched. The memory-Natalya was looking right at her. Or was she? Was she actually looking *behind* her, at something that would've been there? Out of a window, perhaps?

The vision of the girl at the desk collapsed in on itself. Split. Became two new shapes. Natalya again. This time crouching rigid on the ground, a hand raised to protect her face. In front of her was the faintest outline of a wolf in silhouette, a ghost wolf, poised with its hackles up. A voice rang out, and it was Natalya's, clear and pleading: "Please. I won't tell what I saw. I'll never tell!"

The wolf leaped.

The smoke cleared. Natalya's memory—if that's what it had been—vanished along with it.

Lina staggered backward. It took her a moment to remember where she was. In front of her, Svetlana still grappled with the shadow girl. It was as if nothing had happened. Had she been the only one to witness the memory?

Bogdan was clinging to Svetlana's arms, as he had been before the smoke cloud. He'd definitely regained some of his old strength since being away from the mine—and even stopped coughing as much. Lina leaped forward again too, determined more than desperate this time. Perhaps Svetlana knew they were about to overpower her, because she let go. She whisked her hands behind her back like a naughty child and laughed.

Anger flashed in Lina's heart. Svetlana had tried to hurt their friend. Now she was mocking them. She clenched her fists. "What's so funny?"

The fluttering at the edge of Lina's vision told her that the shadow girl had hurried to the corner of the room, where she looked much smaller. All bundled up. She had to be crouching, clutching her knees.

Lina turned back to the old lady. "Well?" she demanded. "What's so funny? That's our friend you just tried to, to . . ." Lina realized she had no idea what Svetlana had tried to do. Banish her to the "nothing world" of the water mirror? Kill her? A thought flashed into Lina's mind, connecting what she'd just seen with what Svetlana had done. "Is it because she saw something she wasn't supposed to, once? Out of the window of her classroom?"

Lina bit her lip when she saw Svetlana's look. She'd given away too much.

Svetlana raised a wizened finger. "She showed you something. Didn't she? Somehow you and she made a connection. Ha! I've caught you. I *knew* you had powers."

Lina stood, panting. "I don't know what you mean," she replied after she'd caught her breath. "Come on, Bogey. Let's leave." She knew as she said it that, even if Svetlana let them, they couldn't really just leave. It would be dark out there, and the storm still raged. She was starting to think they'd be better off taking their chances in the storm, however. To the old woman, she said, "We know who you are. You're Svetlana! You're dangerous."

Svetlana smiled sweetly. "I haven't said I'm anyone, my darling. But look at me. I'm an old woman, yes. I'm a sorceress as well. You've seen I have powers. I can help you to understand *your* power. Don't you want to know what you're capable of? I do. I want to see what you can do with the water mirror when you try. You want to know too, don't you? Be honest."

Lina hesitated. The truth was she was both desperate and terrified to know what she might be able to do, in equal measure.

"Come, look into the mirror," Svetlana said. "Let me

show you what I mean." She sat at the edge of the frame, tucking in her skirts.

Bogdan looked from Lina to Svetlana and back, astonished. Lina felt queasy. He had to be wondering what powers Svetlana was talking about.

Slowly, Bogdan and Lina lowered themselves too.

Svetlana sat back and smiled. She looked smug. "Think about the men you traveled with, Lina. Concentrate on them while you stare into the water—and make them appear."

Lina and Bogdan looked at each other.

"Go on," said Bogdan.

"Why would I want to see them again? They tried to kill us," Lina argued. But something stirred inside her even as she spoke. It was the feeling she got when she touched plants and made them grow—yet it was more like the forming of a cold shudder than a rush of warmth. She really *did* want to know if she could look into this "mirror" and make the men appear.

Lina tried to picture their faces. The memory of Old Gleb poking his head into the snow shelter that she and Bogdan had shared came to her. She thought of his face, broad and freckled, his gray-streaked mess of hair—and his eyes, with the odd dark fleck in the white. More than anything, she remembered his singsong voice. The way he'd spoken to them both, so cheerfully. As if they were his own children.

The reflections in the mirror twisted and took on new shapes. The cobwebbed ceiling was no longer visible.

"A face!" cried Bogdan. "I can see a face!"

The water swelled and rose until it looked like an upside-down drip. "It's turning into the shape of a person," said Lina in awe.

Not just any person. It was Old Gleb. Only not quite as Lina had remembered him. His cheeks were more sunken than ever, his skin ashen. Colorless. And his eyes. His eyes were dull: seeing but not seeing. She thought she could read pain and confusion in them—and in the way his teeth were set together. As far as Lina could tell, he walked in endless mist.

"You've done it!" gasped Bogdan. He jiggled in excitement before he composed himself enough to sit still—but his look of awe remained.

Svetlana narrowed her eyes at Lina. "And quickly too," she said. "So you have power with the mirror as well. But how much of it? And why?" She drew back, the way you might from something that could bite.

Behind the image of Old Gleb, two more bulges rose out of the mirror. Alexei and Vadim. Both were hunched and sallow-skinned. The sight of them made Lina feel ill. She remembered what Svetlana had told them about the men being wolf-bound. They were becoming shadows like Natalya. "How long will it take before they disappear?" she asked.

"A while yet. At the moment, they are still changing—into something not quite human, not quite animal. And they are displaced while they change. They crave warmth but won't find it here. This is a place where spirits live. What an honor for them, as former criminals. Now they will finally be able to serve a purpose."

"The person who did this was callous and cruel." Lina's face felt hot with anger. "Just another tyrant the world doesn't need. Like Commandant Zima."

"Perhaps. Or you might say they've been given another chance, beyond the limits of their otherwise base little lives," said the old woman curtly. "The opportunity to be productive. To finally contribute to something greater than themselves. That *is* an honor."

Lina's anger frothed into silent, spitting rage. How could Svetlana think it was OK? Whatever they'd done, no one deserved this torture. If her mother had been here, she would've argued her piece relentlessly, but . . .

The faces swirled away, replaced by a shifting darkness. The water in the frame bulged and writhed like an animal. No shape formed, but a sound, muffled at first, came out of it: a desperate sound.

"Is that someone crying?" Bogdan gasped, wide-eyed. "Who is it?"

"Lina," sobbed the voice. "Please be safe, Lina." A blast of wind roared down the chimney again and engulfed them in black soot. It blew the fire out altogether.

Lina knew exactly who the voice belonged to. It was her mother. She lurched back from the mirror, her heart pounding.

# 34

Bogdan looked between Lina and the water mirror and back again. "What just happened?"

"She let other thoughts interrupt her concentration," said Svetlana. "It happens, when you lack experience. Nevertheless, Lina, your self-control was impressive. I've never seen such talent from an untrained human child. Even my own."

Lina's heart fluttered like a panicked bird's. "That was my mamochka. She's suffering in that nothing world, and she's . . ." Hot tears welled in her eyes. After everything they'd been through, it was too late. Her mother was dead.

"Not necessarily in the nothing world *yet*," said Svetlana. She drew her white wiry eyebrows together, as if working out a puzzle. "Though that is the most likely answer."

"So there's a chance Lina's mama isn't . . . That she's still alive?" asked Bogdan.

"Perhaps. But death will be close—and all but certain."

Lina couldn't focus on what they were saying. She could barely even breathe. Her mother was gone.

"Lina," said Bogdan, gripping her shoulders tight. "Did you hear that? Your mama might still be OK."

"For now," said Svetlana.

"Can you save her?" demanded Bogdan. "Lina's mama? With your powers, I mean." He kept one hand gently resting against Lina's shoulder as he spoke, and the warmth of him was as healing as any magic stone.

"That depends," said the old woman, waving dismissively.

"On what?"

"On whether or not I care to."

Lina's anger exploded. She jumped up. So did Bogdan. He stood next to her in silent but clear support.

"Who do you think you are, treating people like that?" Lina's voice wobbled. She was on the verge of shouting.

"Lina," said Bogdan, a warning in his tone. This was dangerous.

"No, Bogey. She can help my mama and she won't." Lina looked up. Her face felt hot and puffy. Her eyes burned. "Fine. Take us to Moscow, then, like you said you would, so we can find my grandmother, who *will* help! Or does *that* depend on 'whether or not you care to' as well? I bet it was just a trick to make us trust you."

The old woman stood in one swift motion, straightening out her back to stand tall. She unbundled her hair and shook it over her shoulders. As she did so, it grew and darkened until it was long and black. The face they now looked into was no longer Babushka's, but Svetlana's.

"Why should I help you *humans*, when humans have never done anything for me?" she raged. "You will stay here and serve me. You won't escape this place."

In two strides, Svetlana stood in front of them, a hand on each of their shoulders. Coldness trickled through Lina's blood, and she shivered.

"Calm yourself," Svetlana said, close to Lina's face. "We can't have someone with your powers getting over-excited. Go to your room and sleep. I'll decide what to do with you back at my tower."

"I'm sick of these people who think they can rule over us like czars. Commandant Zima. Svetlana. Even Stalin!" Lina wiped her tears on her sleeve. Her rage felt impenetrable.

She and Bogdan were alone now in the bedroom.

"Not even Vadim and Alexei deserved what she did to them," she said.

Her fury wasn't dulling at the moment. It hadn't even dimmed. If anything, it had been growing since Svetlana had locked them in here.

"They say they have our interests at heart," Lina went

on, "and yet, what have any of them ever done in our interests? Taking away your parents, Bogey. Sentencing you to hard labor. Sending my family to a camp because my grandfather criticized the wrong person and had some unusual beliefs about real-life fairy-tale magic. I've spent my life in a prison—and for what?"

Bogdan said nothing while Lina blinked back more tears. He must have been waiting until the silence settled. When he spoke, his voice was soft.

"What you did back there with the mirror . . . it was amazing. Did you know you could do that? Magic?"

"Not *that*, exactly." Her voice was quiet and wavered a little, but she carried on. "But I think I can make plants grow, sometimes, when I touch them."

Bogdan hugged her. "That's incredible" was all he said. The hug said more.

"And I did see a memory of our shadow friend—she's called Natalya. I saw her at school. She witnessed something . . . something that she shouldn't, and Svetlana had her wolf-bound. And . . ."

Now that the truth could flow freely between them, Lina was relieved—but her heart still ached over what the mirror had revealed. "Do you really think she could be dead? Mamochka?"

Bogdan wrapped his long arms more tightly around her shoulders. "Svetlana said there's a chance she's still alive, didn't she?"

Lina rested her head against his, the way she had at the camp when she'd turned to leave through his window. It felt like another lifetime now.

*"Nevertell,"* came a whisper by Lina's ear. She noticed a pressure against her arm—neither warm nor cold—and knew their shadow friend, Natalya, was comforting her too.

They stayed that way for a while until Lina had composed herself. She needed to believe she could still save her mother. But time was running out. That meant she had to reach Moscow and find her grandmother. Right away.

Finally, she turned to face Bogdan. He nodded at her. "Right, my friend. What are we going to do about this situation we're in?"

"We'll escape," she said. "As soon as possible."

*"Nevertell,"* said the shadow girl, as if in agreement.

"Let's wear our coats and boots to bed and keep our hoods with us," Lina said. "We'll pretend to sleep but instead be listening," she went on. "If we can sneak out tonight and find Tuyaara again, we will."

Whatever might happen, they'd be ready.

# 35

Two candles burned by the beds where they huddled—one small, the other bright and new. Lina had left them both going so they could see. The old one was down to its dregs now. Just a pool of wax in a patterned brass dish that also cupped a violet flame growing dim.

Bogdan breathed deeply.

"Bogey?" Lina whispered. He didn't answer. He must've actually dozed off, instead of pretending like they were supposed to be doing. They'd decided to wait until they were sure Svetlana was asleep and then try to pick the lock so they could sneak out of the house. Lina turned her head toward the candles.

"Natalya?" She kept her voice low, so Svetlana wouldn't hear through the wall.

One candle flame dipped in answer.

"That was you I saw earlier in the soot, wasn't it? Memories, from your past." The candle flame dipped once more—a definite *yes.*

"How many others has Svetlana done this to? No! I mean . . ." *Questions with yes or no answers,* Lina told herself, screwing up her eyes at her own mistake. "Has it been over fifty?" *Yes.*

"Over one hundred?" *Yes.*

Svetlana had made more than one hundred men, women, and children into shadow-like servants. Lina was quiet for a while before she asked, "Is Svetlana human, Natalya?" *No,* came the answer.

Bogdan snored a little. Lina nudged him in the ribs through all their layers of coats and blankets. His legs twitched as if jolted with electricity. He said nothing, though the snoring stopped. He was awake.

The door to their room opened. Through a half-open eye, Lina saw Svetlana come in and pause for a moment. Lina closed her eyes, slackening her jaw to mimic a sleeping person. She didn't dare peek as Svetlana's footsteps came closer. It struck Lina that Svetlana must really fear her if she wanted them to be asleep before she took them back to the tower.

Lina tried to keep her breathing calm. Not easy, with Bogdan squeezing her hand as hard as he was. Her fingers started to go numb. Lina risked opening one eye.

Svetlana stood tall, a few paces away. She wore her waist-length cape.

The cape.

*She's going to use it to transport us,* thought Lina. *We can't let her. It's now or never.*

Svetlana turned toward them. Lina quickly shut her eyes again. She heard Svetlana's footsteps get louder as she approached the beds. The inside of Lina's eyelids grew darker as her shadow fell over them. She could even smell Svetlana's skin and hair: a cold, metallic scent, mixed with the faint sweetness of blossoms.

A rustle of material. And silence.

"Now!" shouted Lina. They kicked up a flurry of blankets. With horror, Lina saw that Svetlana's dark cloak had already grown. It draped all around them. Inside it she could see stars—even the glint of moonlight on some large, near-invisible shape that shimmered and then broke away from the night sky, moving closer. A looming pinnacle of ice.

The tower.

Lina grabbed at what was closest: a candle. She hurled it. The weak flame turned to a slender stream of smoke as it sailed toward Svetlana. The wax, however, stayed molten. Svetlana shrieked. The stars sparkled inside the cape by Lina's face, as did the tower, just as the material whipped back. Svetlana pulled sharply away, clawing at the hot wax hardening on her skin.

Bogdan tried to cover Svetlana with a blanket, but she fought back. In the struggle, the blanket glided over Lina's head. With it came darkness. Lina kicked and clawed it off—just in time to see Svetlana recover from her shock and surge forward.

Bogdan leaped off the bed. Lina followed, but her leg got caught in the blankets. She half leaped, half fell. Her palms smacked hard against the floor. The stone around her neck swung out from inside her tunic and dangled, spinning on its beaded string. No time to worry about that now, though. She scrambled to get to her feet.

Before she could make it, Svetlana's long, pale hand darted under her chin and grasped the stone, yanking Lina toward her. Svetlana was pallid and trembling. Lina stared into her dark eyes, which were hot with rage.

Svetlana tugged again on the stone necklace. "How did you get this?" she hissed.

"It's mine," said Lina, clawing at the necklace drawn tight around her neck. "Get off—you're choking me!"

"You're a liar," said Svetlana. "A liar and a thief. Where did you get this? Who did you take it from?"

Lina gritted her teeth. It was getting harder and harder for her to breathe, let alone speak. "My mother gave it to me," she managed to get out.

Svetlana let go suddenly. Lina fell back onto the bed. Svetlana had gone pink. In fact, she seemed to be having trouble breathing.

"You'll come back to the tower and explain," she said at last. "Now." With a flick of her wrists, the cloak encircled Lina and Bogdan again—the coolness of the night sky inside it pressing in around them, settling over Lina like a veil.

Something clicked. Then and there, Lina knew exactly what to do.

As a corner of the cloak fluttered past her face, she grabbed it. Tugged.

The material made an electrical buzz as it tore—like a lightning strike. Lina wrenched it as hard as she could. The corner ripped away in her hands. *Grow,* she urged the scrap of cloak. *Grow now and take us away from here.*

The black material rippled and slipped around her fingers. It felt like trying to hold running water. Lina twirled around and her eyes met Bogdan's. They grasped each other's arms—tight.

Just in time. Lina's piece of Svetlana's cloak—seconds ago, nothing but a tiny scrap—gathered them up entirely inside itself.

# 36

Lina remembered the first time they'd traveled under Svetlana's cape. The dark. The calmness. The stars. That slow, gentle realization that they'd arrived somewhere new.

This was nothing like that.

It felt a lot like falling into darkness. Fast. Except Lina didn't know from where or toward what. If it had been one of those falling dreams, she'd have already woken up, her heart pounding as she reached out for the nearest thing to cling to. Now, her stomach lurched—and lurched again. Pressure built in the back of her head. Between her shoulder blades. All she could hear was a rushing noise, like gushing water.

She screamed.

"Not falling," she managed to say to herself. "I want flying, not falling . . ."

The pressure on her body shifted. The rushing noise became the whistling of wind, blowing back her hair. To her left, Bogdan still held on tight to her hand, and she to his. He looked at her with a frightened grimace. But there was something else with them.

Some*one* else.

A young girl with mousy hair tied back in pigtails and cream-colored skin clung on to Lina's other arm. Now that their momentum had shifted, Lina could feel the pressure of her grasp. She didn't look at Lina—not once—but gazed down with lagoon-colored eyes. Lina recognized her immediately: Natalya, their shadow friend.

Lina looked down now too. Below them, a snowy waste opened up, only just visible in the dark—full of mountains, chasms, and crags. In among it sat Svetlana's tower on the lake, clear enough for Lina to see the giant fish moving and circling in the depths beneath it.

Soon the tower was far behind them, swallowed up in gloom.

There were forests ahead. Forests stretching for miles, with a pale mist rising between the dark trees. On the horizon, three bands of color—burnt orange, fading to white, and then a deep royal blue. The moon rested, heavy and bloated, in between where the blue turned to black. Little veins like silver filigree sprawled across its surface. A night or two ago it would have been full. Now it had a slice off one edge. It had started to wane.

Lina noticed something else: a little cluster of lights, with something long and mechanical moving along a straight black line through the snow away from them. Some kind of giant, snaking, motorized monster.

"A train," called Bogdan. The wind stole most of his voice away—but Lina lip-read the rest. "Head to that town, Lina, if you can."

She'd been aware from the start that this bizarre journey through the sky hinged on her, and Bogdan clearly knew it too. Where they ended up would depend on her focus. On how well she could concentrate.

The thing was, now that they were out here, she just wanted to keep traveling farther.

They soared toward the cluster of lights on the horizon. They overtook the train, riding its dark rails. Wisps of clouds zipped past them, sometimes obscuring the ground below. Lina gripped Bogdan's hand tighter. They were speeding up.

"Slow down!" shouted Bogdan. "We're going to . . ." It was too late. They had already passed the town. Now they were rushing faster and faster.

Lina didn't want to make it to the nearest town. She wanted to go on—and on. If only she could get them all the way to Moscow. Her mother's life depended on it.

"Keep to the train lines, at least," came Bogdan's voice, so distant and quiet against the rush of wind.

Lina closed her eyes and pictured the apartment she'd

always dreamed of. The kitchen. Her neighbors. Food. Laughter. But something wasn't the same. She snatched at the images but couldn't keep them. They turned transparent—and cracked like ice. Blew away from her like snow dust.

Other thoughts replaced them. Men in uniforms, searching buildings: officials from the Party, perhaps. Secret police. Frightened people watching from windows and through cracks in their doors. Their fear infected Lina too. She glimpsed a woman clutching a doorframe, heard her wail as the uniformed men marched someone away. Behind the woman, gripping tight to her clothes, was Natalya.

Of course. These were Natalya's memories again. Her memories of Moscow, this time. The truth hit Lina like a physical blow. Natalya's memories were real. Hers? Only dreams. How could she take them all somewhere she'd never even seen?

Somewhere she didn't truly know.

She fought against her own thoughts. *16 Gorky Street, Apartment 4,* she said to herself. *16 Gorky Street, Apartment 4 . . .*

The words were paper-thin and blew away from her lips.

They flew even faster. As soon as she glimpsed something, they'd passed it in an instant. Lina's mind reeled. She could hardly breathe, let alone think. Her head started to throb with pain. What little control she'd had crumbled to nothing. Just like her visions of Moscow.

Thick clouds covered their view of the ground completely. Lina lost all sense of direction again. Were they flying forward? Falling again? Were they even moving at all? Panic writhed inside Lina's chest. They were dipping into the other worlds. She could hear strange creatures—cawing, calling, barking—but couldn't see them.

She could feel the hunger of the nothing world now, too, distinct from the others: like something alive. They weren't just passing into it. It was rising up—to claim them.

She looked in despair at Natalya, who was still hanging on to her arm.

Lina found herself staring directly into the girl's broad face, her glittering marine-colored eyes. Natalya placed a hand against Lina's cheek. It was as cold as death. The shock of it jolted Lina out of her panic.

"Novosibirsk," said Natalya.

Novosibirsk.

Lina had heard of it. It was a city in West Siberia. One of the prisoners had been from there. She closed her eyes. Novosibirsk. That's where we're going. Novosibirsk. *Novosibirsk.* Images of a vast city flashed in front of her. What looked like a blue palace. People everywhere. Natalya's memories again—except this time they were helping. This time, Lina had no impressions of her own to battle against Natalya's.

When she opened her eyes, the clouds had turned to a thin mist and then curled away behind them, Lina's pale breath riding out to meet the clear sky. They were lower to the ground now, and a sprawl of lights— yellow, orange, pale green—glowed against the brightening sunrise. Lina gasped. The lights could have been a field of spring flowers. That was the feeling they gave her.

Lina and the others sank into the city lights, down past high-rise buildings and houses, tram rails and street lamps, until their feet touched down on a road peppered with fresh snow.

In front of them stood a building the size of a palace, painted turquoise and white. It was the one she'd seen in her vision. Vast pillars stood on either side of an enormous central window, arched at the top, with a pale orange glow coming from inside. Across the top, written in Russian, large letters that stuck up like placards spelled the name of the town.

## NOVOSIBIRSK

When Lina turned to thank her shadow friend, she could no longer see her there.

# 37

"Whoa. I mean, let me just . . ." Bogdan sat down in the middle of the road and rocked a little, with his eyes bulging and his jaw slack. Lina thought he might be sick. She felt weird too. Raging hot and cold—all at once. Maybe she needed to worry about being sick herself.

She tucked the scrap of cape into her pocket, sank onto the pavement, and sprawled out, stomach down. With her head resting against her arms, she breathed deeply. She breathed in the coldness of the snow-dusted road.

"Lina," said Bogdan. "That was amazing. Terrifying but amazing. I've never seen the world like that before. Your magical abilities are *unbelievable*. Just imagine, you might be as powerful as Svetlana one day! It's no wonder she keeps on after us."

Lina lifted her head to look at him. He seemed to be staring at something far away, his eyes flickering with the kind of fire they got whenever he talked about ships or airplanes or his father's work. "When we were flying, the world looked just like a map, Lina. But not just any map. The best I've ever seen. And it was *real*. Imagine how quickly we'll get to Moscow if you can do that!"

Lina took a huge breath and let it out slowly, her mouth in a little "ooh" shape. "I can't do that again, Bogey," she said. "It's too dangerous. I lost control. I knew I should take us down to that first town, just like you said, but I *really* wanted to keep going—all the way to Moscow. It seems like it was too much, though. Because I couldn't see Moscow clearly, I couldn't take us there. And, Bogey, the other worlds were close—but especially that 'nothing' world. It's hard to explain, but I'm *sure* it tried to catch us. I'm sure, if we'd ended up there, the nothing world wouldn't have let us leave. We'd have been lost—forever."

Bogdan shuddered. Maybe, like Lina, he was remembering the terror he'd felt when they were lost in the mist that surrounded Svetlana's tower.

"We've got Natalya to thank for our lives," Lina said.

Bogdan climbed to his feet and stretched his arms to the sky. "Thank you, Natalya! Wherever you are!"

*"Nevertell,"* came the familiar whisper next to them.

Lina smiled. She didn't know if it was the half-light of

sunrise, or because she'd seen Natalya in her true form during their journey, but she could see her outline a lot better now. She was sure of it.

"If it helps, *I* think you can do it." Bogdan's eyes twinkled. "Get us to Moscow with the cape, I mean. You sure you don't want to try? Compared to getting the train, it *would* be much faster."

"I wish I could," said Lina. Every time she thought of the way the mists of the nothing world had surged after them—chased them—she felt sick.

The journey had also done something to her. The ground didn't feel solid anymore, but as if it kept on melting and reforming beneath her. It was happening to her body too. It felt like small creatures kept wriggling under her skin. She could barely think straight with that going on or focus on one thing for more than a few seconds.

Bogdan frowned. "What if we take it in small jumps, a bit at a time?"

If Lina thought about the scrap of cape hard enough, she could feel the coolness of it seeping through her pocket. Spreading. She shook her head quickly. "I nearly got us killed. If it hadn't been for Natalya, the nothing world would've closed in on us, and we'd never have gotten out."

Bogdan's shoulders sagged. She hated to see him so disappointed.

But she knew she could never control the cloak. In her

heart, she wanted two things, neither of which she could let go of: Moscow and her mother. But both were too far away. Not to mention in opposite directions. She couldn't guide them to either. The nothing world would claim them first.

Lina heaved herself up slowly, but the ground shifted under her again, seeming to open up like a chasm. She stumbled into Bogdan.

"Lina, you OK? Lina, I'm sorry. I didn't realize . . ." He looked so concerned when he frowned that it made Lina laugh—but that started off another violent wobble.

She gripped his collar to pull herself up. "Train?" she managed.

Bogdan nodded. "Train."

Bogdan ran off ahead. He must've been feeling better. He paced up and down with his back to her, studying the giant turquoise palace, and Lina imagined she could see his brain fizzing and popping with excitement as he surveyed the building.

She loved seeing him so full of energy. And he clearly felt at home in this kind of place. Now that she'd recovered somewhat from the journey, Lina couldn't stop looking around her in fascination. It was all so vast: the enormous buildings, the stretching roads, the wide, deserted sidewalks. Everything. She could barely believe the world was big enough to contain it.

Lina took a few steps to test her balance—slowly, so she didn't sway and fall with dizziness—and took the scrap of cape out of her pocket to study it.

She hadn't even been aware of holding it while they were up in the sky. What if she'd let it go? Would they have been lost among the other worlds, with no way back? Would they have dropped to the ground like stones? Best not to think about all that now. She stuffed the scrap back into her pocket.

Her fingertips grazed something cold and gritty in there. She remembered the whisper of the stars. The vow she'd made when they were riding with Tuyaara—that she would find her grandmother so she could save her mother. How was it possible that it hadn't melted while they stayed in Babushka's cabin?

"Know what this is?" Bogdan said when she arrived beside him, opening his palms out toward the turquoise palace. He sounded smug.

"No. Never seen anything like it before, have I? They don't build labor camps like this, Bogey."

Bogdan winced. "Sorry," he said. "But I *do* know. It's the *train station*."

A train station. Who knew getting the train was such a grand thing to do that it required a palace? Did they all look like this? Lina zinged with excitement at the thought of going inside—then had to rest her hands on her knees to steady herself again.

"Thing is," said Bogdan, "it won't be open to the public yet. It's too early. And we'll need a ticket—or we'll get caught."

Lina chewed her lip. "Svetlana could turn up at any moment. We'll have to be careful she doesn't find us first. Better lay low for a bit while we work out what to do."

"Agreed," said Bogdan.

# 38

They found a doorway to shelter in while Lina rested, and from where they could also keep an eye on the station. First came people in uniforms with keys to let themselves in through side doors. Then the commuters arrived.

A steady stream of people headed into the station—some walking, a few running. Often they carried cases and wore smart, long coats and hats. Lina had seen this many people before, but not so well-dressed, and never without armed guards as chaperones. She gazed at them all in their gorgeous clean clothes, with their proud, straight backs, milling around in what looked like chaos—as if they'd never once been ordered to do anything by a man with a gun.

They were mostly adults—or sometimes an adult and

a small child. So far, Lina couldn't see any way of sneaking in. She bit her lip and paced in the confines of their doorway.

An hour went by. And another. Despair played in Bogdan's eyes and stuck in Lina's throat. How would they get on board a train?

A train must have arrived because a crowd of people came flooding out of the station and kept on coming. Out came a school group. And then another. And another.

"I remember," Bogdan said, "when we visited Novosibirsk once—Mama and Papa and me—there were loads of schoolkids on the train heading here too. Mama told me every school goes to visit at some point. The Monument to the Heroes of the Revolution is built here. It's where some of the people who died overthrowing the czars are buried. Plus, there's a massive statue of Lenin somewhere around here, as well."

Lina grabbed Bogdan by the arm. "I've got it, Bogey," she said. "We'll tag along with a school group. Maybe that way . . ."

"We can sneak on board the train," finished Bogdan. "To Moscow. Come on, Lina. If we listen in, we might be able to find out where some of them have come from."

Bogdan sidled up to a group of schoolchildren wearing black and white, while Lina stalked a group in navy-blue button-down coats and jackets. Their clothes, the way they had their hair—they reminded Lina of how Natalya had looked.

*She was just a schoolgirl*, thought Lina, *a child, when Svetlana took her*. Lina had been wondering if there was a way to reverse what had been done to her—the same thing that was happening to Gleb and the others. But once the transition was complete and their bodies were gone? Well. She guessed there was no coming back from that.

The chatter of the group overwhelmed Lina. They all seemed to be talking at once: about what food they were going to have for lunch, gossip from the train, rumors of the hard justice of one particular teacher. She didn't hear any of them mention Moscow, though.

Bogdan shrugged and pointed at his group. *From Novosibirsk,* he mouthed.

Lina turned back to her group and bumped into something round and squishy. It turned out to be one of the group leaders.

"Pardon me," said Lina, looking down to hide her face and feeling the heat rise in her cheeks. But before she scuttled away, she caught sight of the papers in his hands. Group train tickets—and printed on them clearly was: MOSCOW.

Lina darted off in search of Bogdan. Bogdan grinned when she told him. "Now we follow—from a distance. It's the best spy way. Espionage. We stay out of sight until the very last minute."

"One teacher's already seen me," said Lina, shrinking

into her furs. "If he spots me hanging around again, he might tell someone. Maybe the secret police."

"Don't worry, Lina," said Bogdan. He winked at her and raised one corner of his mouth in his usual lopsided smile. "Just follow my lead."

"You? What do you know about espionage?"

"Kept those maps a secret all the time I was at the camp, didn't I?"

Lina had to give him that one.

They followed the group around the town until dusk. Lina started to panic that perhaps the school had booked lodgings for the night, and they weren't getting the train back today at all. Svetlana could catch up with them any second. She'd found them at Tuyaara's uncle's cabin, and she'd find them again. Lina was impatient. The sooner they got on that train, the better.

She grew tired, and her stomach cramped with hunger. They hadn't eaten or drunk anything all day, and her head ached and her skin still crawled from the experience with the cape. Then again, she was starting to feel better. Would it really hurt to use the cape once more—even just to get onto the train?

No. She couldn't trust herself. Just getting them onto the train could so easily become "just" taking them all the way to Moscow—which is what she truly wanted, deep down. That, and to save her mother. What if she took them back to the camp by mistake and landed them both in worse trouble? Getting shot wouldn't help anybody.

Bogdan grabbed her arm. "We're heading back to the square—look, we've been down this road before. Won't be long now, Lina."

Lina was so tired she could've rested her head on his shoulder and slept standing up. But she slapped her own cheeks and vowed to wake up.

"This is it," said Bogdan as the school group neared the station doors. They walked arm in arm. Nothing would separate them. "Now!" he cried. They darted through the crowds and tagged onto the end of the group.

It seemed to take forever to pass the men in hats at the doors of the station. Lina walked right under the nose of one. He watched her. She felt it. She and Bogdan looked so different from the other children, after all. Their clothes. Their hair. Everything. The station guard was probably still watching as they neared the platform. She could feel his gaze on the back of her neck.

Only when she dared to glance behind her did she see that he was busy, speaking with one of his colleagues. No one seemed to have noticed them. Not yet.

The line of children snaked along in pairs. Lina stared at the train in front of them—a huge green metal beast with a gold star stuck on its nose. She could hardly take it all in—she'd never seen anything like it.

"Now to get on board," said Bogdan.

A girl just in front turned and looked Bogdan up and

down—and then Lina. She finally turned back and whispered something to her partner.

The teachers stood by the train door, showing a guard in a smart uniform their group ticket. Lina felt sick with nerves. The girl in front had noticed them. She might tell someone. One of the group leaders might spot them. The guard by the train door might grab them.

So many things could go wrong.

The guard watched the children getting on board for a while before turning her attention to some of the other passengers. The teachers started chatting among themselves. The girl in front of them looked at Lina again—but this time she gave a half smile.

Relief flooded Lina. The girl wasn't going to tell. They were going to make it. They crossed the large gap between the platform and the train into a new world of warmth and bustling bodies, with suitcases and the smell of stale air and mint.

They'd done it. They were on the train to Moscow.

# 39

Lina and Bogdan split from the group of school-children as soon as they heard attendance being called. They edged away from the school's carriage and into the cramped walkway, working their way down the train until they found an empty compartment. It was snug, with a large window and two seats on either side that converted into four beds, top and bottom.

"What do you think?" Bogdan whispered. "Try to get some sleep in here?"

"We'll have to take turns sleeping," said Lina, "in case they come around checking tickets." If they got caught, they'd be handed over to the authorities at the next station.

Or worse.

*"Nevertell."*

They both turned around at the same time. For a second, Lina saw the silhouette of a young girl flickering against the walkway windows. She understood and smiled. "It's OK," she said. "I think our friend is going to keep watch."

Nevertheless, they stayed awake into the night, trying to find out more about their shadow friend. It turned out she really couldn't say anything more than "Nevertell." But when Bogdan found out she could make their compartment's light flicker, just as she had the candlelight in Babushka's house, he thought up some more questions for her.

Did she have brothers or sisters? *No.*

Had she always lived in Moscow? *Yes.*

Any pets? *No.*

Every time they found out something new about their friend, they felt closer to her. But there was something Lina wanted to know more than anything. She couldn't stop thinking about the memory Natalya had shown her in Babushka's hut. What had Natalya seen out of the window that day?

Lina and Bogdan talked in low mumbles about how they could find out. It would take a lot of yes-and-no questions to even start to get a clear picture. Perhaps if Lina could "connect" with Natalya's memories again, she could *see* more?

"Natalya, what do you think?" Lina asked. "Can you show me another memory somehow? If we both try together?" A pause—then a wavering *yes*. Perhaps Natalya wasn't sure if she could.

Even so, they'd give it a try. Lina held out a hand, and Bogdan held her other one. Maybe with all three of them focusing they would stand more of a chance. It couldn't hurt, anyway. Almost immediately, Lina's outstretched hand felt strange. A little numb—as if pushing against something. She wiggled her fingers. They felt slow and heavy. Natalya was trying to touch her.

Lina slowly let out her breath and relaxed her shoulders. She felt a little dizzy, as though she were drifting. The tingling feeling built in her chest and traveled down her arm.

The carriage lights went out. Small fingers grasped her hand. Natalya!

Bogdan gasped. "Look, Lina." The carriage window had previously shown nothing but nighttime darkness. Now daylight shone, and a city square, grass, and a fountain were reflected in the glass. The weather looked balmy. People strolled in the sun. Some were lying on the grass. At the center of it all, next to the fountain, a woman with long dark hair paced back and forth. Lina recognized Svetlana immediately. Despite the warmth of the sun, this Svetlana hugged herself as though she were freezing.

Svetlana—or the memory of her—stopped pacing next to a budding rose. With her shoulders hunched and her bedraggled hair hanging down, she looked like someone ready to scream. But instead, she reached out a hand as fast as a viper and gripped the rosebush as if she wanted to strangle it.

The roses on the bush all blossomed in seconds—great red petals peeling back as lips might over teeth, revealing more and more petals inside. The plant stretched out its branches. New leaves popped open like little green eyes. Bloodred petals began to fall around its base. They darkened and shriveled. The way they curled into themselves, so quickly, made them look like small creatures in pain. Now just the centers of the flowers remained, rotten-looking, and the plant bowed into the ground. The leaves folded and fell away until the whole thing crumbled back into earth.

Lina lost her grip on Natalya's hand. The carriage lights flickered—and came back on. The carriage window showed nothing but darkness—as it should. Lina's breath shuddered out of her. Making plants grow was one thing. But this? The third time watching Natalya's memories felt just as shocking as the first.

It took Lina and Bogdan a while to digest what they'd witnessed.

"Is that what you saw from your classroom window that day?" asked Lina eventually, once she could form words again.

The carriage lights flickered. *Yes.*

"Is that why she had you wolf-bound?" said Bogdan. "Because you saw her do magic?" His own voice trembled at the edges, and no wonder after what they'd just seen.

*"Nevertell."*

"How many people did she have wolf-bound before you?" asked Lina in a small voice. The lights stayed on. At first, Lina thought it was because of the way she'd asked her question, but then they dipped slowly—and stayed dipped for a long time.

Did that mean . . .? "Were you the first?" The lights dipped again. *Yes.*

She and Bogdan exchanged a look.

"Svetlana must truly hate people," said Bogdan, "to hurt a kid like you. Does she, Natalya?" *Yes.* But then the light flickered a few more times. It seemed like there was more to it than a simple yes or no.

Lina shuddered. She had powers like Svetlana—and who knew how many others out there? Did some of this hatred live inside her too?

"I'm sorry this happened to you, Natalya," Lina said softly. "You didn't deserve this. No one did. We'll either find a way to stop Svetlana for good, or . . ." But she couldn't finish her sentence. She didn't know what the "or" might be. She didn't want to think about it, either.

While they were starting to get ready for bed, Bogdan discovered a stash of individually wrapped cookies in his bunk—perhaps left behind by a previous occupant. They were dry and tough, though Bogdan and Lina ate them gladly. It wasn't much of a meal, but it would at least stave off the hunger—for now.

After they'd eaten, Bogdan fell asleep immediately. Lina was lying in one of the bunks and rolled the smooth wooden beads of her necklace between her fingers, her head clouded with dark thoughts. The beads felt warm to the touch—if only in the way that wood normally does.

The little moth came out to crawl over her hand. It tickled and made her laugh, stopping to twirl its fern-like antennae at her when she did—as if distracting her from her troubles had always been its intention. She smiled and helped it back into its bead. Perhaps it liked the warmth in there? Or maybe it was busy chewing its way through that note—the one written to her grandfather. Either way, it was a companion now. She'd be sad to lose it.

Lina finally shut her eyes and, when she dreamed, she dreamed of Moscow. She was happy in her little apartment block, sharing a meal in the communal kitchen and laughing with her neighbors. Bogdan was there—Tuyaara too. And now, so was Natalya. Except she looked just as she had when they'd traveled under the cloak: a normal little girl with deep, thoughtful eyes and a warm smile. Her laughter filled the room.

Lina dreamed of her grandfather's gardens next. Persimmons and palms grew there—and peach trees. Their leaves were deep green and firm to the touch, their trunks flaky and gnarled. Lina breathed in their perfume and brushed all the plants with her hands. They pushed back against her fingertips, growing, budding, flowering. Snow dripped off the unfurling leaves, and suede-skinned berries bulged out from white petals, peeling back and fading. Tendrils reached up high above her to make grand arches overhead, which blossomed and sagged, heavy with fruit.

The power surging through her arms and out from her fingers became stronger and stronger—until she felt like she couldn't stop it even if she tried. The green growth around her thickened. Tightened. Her heart beat faster. Plants crowded her. Closed in. She couldn't make it stop. The garden loomed over her, monstrously tall, on all sides.

Someone was with her in the gardens, keeping out of sight. A woman. Lina knew, in the way that you know such things in dreams, that this person was her grandmother. She tried to chase her but turned every corner too late. Thorns snagged Lina's clothes. Gaps between trees squeezed shut right in front of her. She caught just a wisp of hair or the flash of a hand.

Lina never once saw her face.

# 40

When they woke up, Natalya had gathered them food. The porridge was still warm. Most exciting of all, however, was that they had an egg each. She must have sneaked the food from other passengers or (Lina hoped) the catering carriage. Neither Lina nor Bogdan were about to complain, either way—they were so hungry after eating only cookies the night before.

"Thank you, Natalya," said Lina.

Just as they finished up, Natalya called them anxiously. *"Nevertell!"*

Voices traveled down the carriage. Bogdan darted to the walkway and peered out. "They're checking tickets," he said. They dusted down their seats and scooped up their eggshells. Lina hoped it would look like no one had been there.

They spent the rest of the day dodging train officials. They passed several in the walkways but did a good job of smiling and looking calm as they went by. Inside, Lina's guts knotted. Sweat prickled at the back of her neck. Bogdan, however, couldn't have looked calmer or more at home. He really was good at this.

Lots of people got on at the next station. The train filled up. Their old compartment became occupied by four people. As the second evening drew on, they'd been walking, hiding in the toilets, or lingering between carriages all day.

"We've got to find somewhere safe to rest," said Lina. "The longer we have to keep moving about like this, the more likely it is that someone will catch us."

They made their way to the back of the train. Bogdan was convinced that they'd been coupled up to some freight carriages at an earlier stop. "Wouldn't be prisoners. Not going in this direction," he said.

When they reached the back of the train, it was just as Bogdan had suspected. Wooden carriages clattered along behind them, snaking around the track as it curved, then whipping out straight again like a tail.

"Should they be doing that?" asked Lina. "Do we really want to go out there?" Then she got angry with herself. *Stupid.* She'd been through too many things, seen too many horrors in her life, to let a train frighten her.

Even if it was the first train she'd ever ridden.

There was a door separating the rest of the train from the freight compartments, and Lina pressed her face against the glass of its tiny window. The freight carriages were little more than trucks, but if they could climb up the little metal ladder on the side and get in under the tarpaulin, they ought to be safe—and hopefully able to stay hidden, all the way to Moscow.

"Natalya, are you with us?" asked Lina. Natalya dimmed the lights in the carriage. "Good." Lina slapped her hand on Bogdan's shoulder. "We can do this, Bogey."

"Who you trying to convince, Lina?" He winked and grinned, but Lina could tell he was fighting his own nerves too.

They put on everything warm they had, including their gloves. Together they undid the stiff latch. The door flung itself open. An icy gale blasted them, stealing Lina's breath.

Lina went first.

She tried to ignore the clanking of the couplings, the sickly jolting of the freight carriage, as she climbed up the ladder and then under the tarpaulin. She made way for Bogdan.

The stacks of slate chippings underneath weren't exactly comfortable. But at least they could duck completely under the tarpaulin and stay warm. For now, they decided to keep their heads poking out to watch the mountains retreat and the rivers snake away like their breath. Perhaps this was the last time they'd see anything like it before they reached the city.

"We'll be in Moscow by morning, I reckon," said Bogdan. "What will you do first?"

"Find my grandmother," said Lina without hesitation. "Tell her everything about the camp so we can save Mamochka together. I know her old address." *16 Gorky Street, Apartment 4.* "But if she's not there, I . . . I don't honestly know. I'm not sure where I'd start."

Bogdan nodded silently. "I'll stay for as long as it takes you to find her. Got to make sure you're OK, don't I?" he said. Then he looked away quickly. "That's if you want me to, obviously."

"Of course I do!" Lina glanced down, blushing—she'd shouted. The next time she spoke, it came out softer—and sadder. "What will *you* do after? You know, you could always . . ."

She stopped.

"Lina? What is it?"

Lina stared at Bogdan, shocked. "The stone," she said. "Peach pit, I mean. It's getting hotter."

Howls echoed all around—wolf howls—from the hills and the valleys. Yet there were no wolves to be seen anywhere. Lina sat bolt upright and scanned their surroundings. It couldn't be. Not now that they were so close to Moscow. Svetlana couldn't have found them. Her breath came quicker so that mist obscured her vision. She waved her arms to try to clear it. Yet she already knew: The howls came from nothing.

*"Nevertell."* Natalya's frightened voice gasped beside them.

Before they could say another word to each other, even to whisper "ghost wolves," a high-pitched animal shriek from above cut through the roaring of the wind past their ears.

Lina glanced up. Just as the giant bird descended on them. And as the body crumpled in on itself like burning paper, it became a dark-haired woman with wings, gliding on the air. Svetlana. But not as they'd seen her before. This time, she looked unhinged by anger.

Svetlana gripped the edge of the tarpaulin and clung hard, pressing her face toward theirs. "Liars, thieves, and vandals!" she screeched, and her voice had the same tone as the falcon she'd been moments before. "Is there any creature that's worse than you? Is there a human alive who doesn't spoil *everything?*"

The peach stone burned over Lina's heart. It sent stabs of pain through her chest. Svetlana clawed for her and missed. "Neither of you deserve the second life I can give you," she hissed. "You deserve to die instead."

She tore back the tarpaulin, sending the sturdy metal hooks that once held it in place flying over the sides as if they were nothing. The tarpaulin flapped and twisted like something alive. Svetlana made another swipe for them. Lina scrambled backward and hit the far end of the carriage. They were trapped.

Bogdan kicked out to try to drive Svetlana back while Lina grabbed Svetlana's fingers to twist them—anything to push her off-balance. But Svetlana was strong. One of her flailing hands clamped down on Lina's arm and yanked it. Lina felt herself dragged by a force she couldn't fight. Svetlana would throw her from the carriage. To the ground. To die.

Lina yelled for help. Bogdan tugged at Svetlana's arm, but it was useless. She had to throw something.

Anything.

She grabbed a handful of the slate with her free hand and threw it at Svetlana's face. It bounced off and tumbled away, not even leaving a scratch. In desperation, Lina fumbled in her pocket. She scooped up the whisper of the stars—those hard grains of ice, like frozen millet.

"You can't stop us!" yelled Lina. She threw the whisper of the stars right into Svetlana's eyes.

This time, Svetlana reacted instantly. She closed her eyes and cried out. Her voice sounded pained. Urgent. She let go of Lina's arm to claw her own face.

"Quick!" Lina shouted, tugging Bogdan's sleeve. Her whole arm was throbbing with cold. They clambered to the edge of the carriage, but looking down turned her stomach. So did the wind whipping past and the clattering of the wheels against the tracks. Jumping would mean broken bones. At best. And that's if they didn't get dragged under the wheels.

She had to act fast. Svetlana would recover in seconds.

Lina reached for the scrap of cape in her pocket. She couldn't take them to Moscow—but surely she could land them safely on the bank of a river that she could see with her own eyes.

*Grow,* she willed it. *Grow now.* She kept her eyes fixed on where she wanted them to land and barely waited for the cape to become half her size before diving headfirst into it with Bogdan.

Pitch darkness. Tumbling. Any sense of up and down gone. Just Bogdan, his hand in hers, and Natalya clinging to her waist. All around came terrible echoes—impossible to tell human from animal. Lina knew it was the nothing world, snapping at their heels. Trying to claim them. *Picture the riverbank,* she told herself.

Then she felt searing cold.

Snow went into her mouth, her ears—even up her nose. She thrashed, clawed it off her face, and gasped for air. Beside her, Bogdan did the same. They were waist-deep in the snow of the riverbank—but at least it wasn't the nothing world. They'd made it.

Lina wiped her eyes in time to see the train carry Svetlana away—just a flurry of hair and feathers on top of the slate carriage, growing ever more distant beneath a darkness broken only by stars.

# 41

Lina watched their hopes of reaching Moscow disappear with the train.

Bogdan struggled to his feet and bashed his clothes all over to get rid of the clinging snow. "It's gone down my neck!" he said through gasps and yelps.

Lina couldn't yet speak. Her jaw felt locked shut and all her joints were rigid. Partly from the bitter cold. Partly the aftereffects of such a narrow escape. She still watched the train, so tiny now she could cover it with her thumb, and felt something tug painfully at her heart.

Bogdan finished patting himself down and grabbed her by the arms. "Come on, my friend." He heaved her to her feet. Moving made the melted snow that had found its way down her neck feel sharp as knives against her skin. "You here, Natalya?" asked Bogdan.

*"Nevertell."*

"Good."

With ice daggers sliding down her back, Lina shook involuntarily while Bogdan helped her pat off the rest of the snow. The peach pit warmed her, but so far the cold was winning.

"I'm sorry, Bogey," said Lina through chattering teeth. "We were so close, and now . . ." Now the train had gone without them. And despite their best efforts to get all the snow out of their clothes, plenty of it had melted against their skin. Soon they'd be frozen. The peach pit could only do so much. Any chance of finding her grandmother had dissolved, just like the whisper of the stars in Svetlana's eyes.

"Aargh!" Bogdan backed into her. Then she heard what he must have: the growl right next to him. Another down by her elbow. A snarl just behind them. Ghost wolves.

They were surrounded.

Ahead of them on the empty train tracks, something moved. A dark mass rose. Lina already knew what it was, even before it stretched to the height of a very tall person. Even before the black material unfurled like a flower, revealing a pale woman.

Svetlana.

Their leap from the train—Lina's risk with the cape—had been for nothing. She'd found them again in moments.

Svetlana paced toward them, stumbling occasionally

and shedding feathers as she came. She kept wiping her hand across her eyes where Lina had cast the whisper of the stars into them, as if they stung, or she couldn't see properly. Lina trembled. Svetlana was going to kill them.

When Svetlana reached them, Lina could see that her irises were black and round, the whites of her eyes bloodshot. She stared straight at Lina. Her chest heaved. "It looked like truth, but is it somehow a trick?" she said after long seconds.

"Trick? What trick?" Lina's mouth had gone dry.

"The ice words you threw at me. It was cold magic—and powerful. It looked like truth, but I need to hear this from your own mouth. Tell me. What is your mother's name?"

"Don't tell her anything, Lina," said Bogdan, pressing his shoulder into hers and glaring at Svetlana. "We'll die before we give up the names of our families, you monster. Even if . . ."

*Even if they're already dead.*

Lina's throat tightened. Svetlana pointed toward Lina's chest, where the peach pit sat beneath her furs. A gash ran along the center of Svetlana's palm, and dark blood trickled down her wrist—perhaps a cut from the slate. "Then I will tell you this," she said. "Inside that necklace of yours is a note. It reads: MY DARLING ANRI, I GIVE YOU THE GIFT OF MY HEART."

Lina and Bogdan gaped at each other. "How do you know that?" asked Lina. "Unless—"

"That necklace was a gift—from me to my beloved. Now," said Svetlana through gritted teeth, "stop wasting time. Tell me your mother's name."

"Katya," said Lina, gasping. Her mind reeled—her thoughts couldn't settle on anything concrete.

Svetlana's eyes shimmered with brightness, and she took a step back. "Then your magic found its true target, and your ice spell has opened my eyes. You didn't steal that necklace, as I thought. Now it's clear why my wolves won't bind you and why a human like you has such powers. You, Lina," she said, "are my granddaughter."

Lina shook her head. She couldn't believe it. It couldn't be true. "No. My grandmother is in Moscow. She's . . ." Lina remembered the startling clarity with which she'd pictured her mother's face at the very same time she'd spoken those words into the ice: *I will find my grandmother and get help to rescue Mamochka.* "But it wasn't cold magic," said Lina, looking at Bogdan. "The whisper of the stars was just a silly game we played." Uncertainty was already surging through her, however.

Svetlana raised her chin. "You instilled it with magic," she said. "You fused an image of your mother into the words, and although she may be older, I know my daughter's face. You may not have realized, though, because you have so little mastery over your abilities. I've been trying to fathom the extent of your power. It shouldn't be possible. Not for a *human.* Now I understand why."

Bogdan held Lina's hand in both of his and muttered close to her ear. "Keep your wits, Lina. It could all still be a lie. She might have—I dunno—read our minds or something." But even he didn't sound that convinced.

On the other side of her, she heard: *"Nevertell . . ."*

The peach pit was doing something very strange: sending out strong, regular, sharp pulses of heat, in a way it never had before.

"Why didn't you come, then?" Lina snapped. "If it's true, and you're my grandmother. With your power, you could've rescued us. You could even have saved their lives! Grandfather, and—" She broke off at the sight of Svetlana. Her forehead had furrowed and she stared into an apparent void just ahead of her. She barely seemed to breathe.

The earth creaked, and fine cracks appeared on the snow's surface, radiating out from Svetlana. Much deeper cracks split the earth wide open. Lina and Bogdan wobbled on their feet as a chasm opened between them and Svetlana.

"What's happening?" Bogdan squeezed Lina's hand.

Chunks of snow tumbled down into the opening at their feet, scraping against the sides just like frantic, clawing fingers. Lina held her breath. The ice of the frozen river at their backs splintered and groaned.

As suddenly as it had begun, the ground grew still. Svetlana clenched her fists and scowled at her knuckles, which were bluish white. Her voice came out as a whisper. "So it's true. After all this, he is already gone." She looked up into Lina's eyes. "And Valentin? Him too?"

Lina shifted under Svetlana's gaze and didn't answer. She didn't know how to tell her that her son was dead.

"I see," came Svetlana's soft voice.

"Svetlana?" Lina tried to look into her eyes but found them black and fixed ahead of her again. "Svetlana." She reached carefully across the chasm for Svetlana's hand, to try to bring her around. She hesitated, then put her hand over Svetlana's and felt an involuntary pulse of warmth flow out from her palms.

Svetlana snatched her hand away. Lina jumped and pulled her own hand back, as if stung. Svetlana glared at her. "You accuse me of doing nothing, and yet I have been searching! All these years, I've searched. But there are things you do not know, and we have no time to discuss them." Svetlana stepped neatly across the deep split in the earth and marched past them to the frozen river's edge.

"Come here." She beckoned them over. Lina and Bogdan glanced at each other and then followed carefully down the slope, testing the ground to make sure it was safe.

"Do you remember what you heard in the water mirror at my hut?" As she spoke, Svetlana touched the ice of the river. It melted, enough to create a shallow, circular pool.

Lina choked back tears, remembering. "Mamochka."

Svetlana squinted down at the pool she'd made. "What the water mirror reveals is spirits. Those of people, animals—even words. But"—she looked up at Lina—"it doesn't always bring us the spirits of the dead. As I told you, sometimes, as with your fellow escapees, it will also show those who are alive but close to death."

As Svetlana stirred the water, the surface began to wobble and writhe. Reflections bounced off in bright flashes. "Help me, Lina," said Svetlana. "We must check on Katya. Think about your mother. I cannot summon her image myself; she is hidden from me by magic. But you can. You have clearly inherited some of my magic—both warm and cold."

Lina could hardly believe what she'd heard. Svetlana was her *grandmother*. It didn't seem possible. Lina had so many questions about her mother, her grandfather, and about her abilities, not to mention Natalya and the other shadows—and why Svetlana had created them. But she couldn't think about that now. It wasn't the right time. She took a deep breath and pictured her mother instantly. The water writhed and wobbled even more violently. She squinted at it, forcing herself to look. What would she see? Even if her mother was alive, she was still close to death. The thought squeezed at Lina's throat so she could hardly breathe.

The movement stopped. In a second, the water's surface became completely flat, and this time the figure of a seated woman rose out of it, as before. She looked like she was leaning against something—a wall, perhaps.

As Lina watched, an even darker shape rose out of the murky surface of the water but didn't fully form. It sank back down like a wave. They heard shuffling and more coughing. Then: "Will you *shut up* in there, Katya? Your constant hacking is driving me mad." It was a man's voice, sounding exasperated. Lina recognized it as one of the guards': Danill.

"Why don't you try being in here, Danill?" retorted Lina's mother, once she'd finished coughing. "It's the air. It's too damp. How long is Zima going to keep me in here?"

The guard sounded gentler when he next spoke. Lina thought Danill had always had a soft spot for her mother. "You know what Zima's like, Katya. He's angry about losing Lina. And about his greenhouse . . . He's stringing it out, waiting for the officers to arrive. The ones he planned that ridiculous annual banquet for. He wants to make an example of you." Danill sounded very sorry for her.

The little figure in front of them coughed again, then leaned over and spat. "And when will that be?" she said angrily.

"Oh, Katya, don't grill me! Soon. Actually . . . I expect it will be the day after tomorrow, at first light. You know"—Danill lowered his voice before he carried on—"all you have to do is speak with him. Say sorry. You're the only person he'd ever show mercy to."

"Never," came Katya's instant reply.

Lina's fear for her mother overwhelmed her, and the figure fell back into its vessel. The water rippled and went still. Lina and Bogdan were speechless. There was only one place her mother could be, and that was in the *karker*. It was a dank underground cell where prisoners were put for punishment. The rank, stifling air was already making her mother weaker—Lina could tell by her voice and her terrible cough. Zima had been true to his word, all right. And what would happen when the officers arrived? What would Commandant Zima do?

# 42

Lina fought back tears.

"Can you do it?" she asked, fixing her eyes on Svetlana. "Can you get us back there in time to save her?" Lina didn't trust Svetlana yet. But if they were going to stand a chance of saving her mother, she'd have to try. Besides, Svetlana's clenched jaw and fixed eyes betrayed her very great concern. Lina knew they wanted the same thing: to save Katya.

Svetlana's bedraggled hair fell across her face as she seemed to contemplate the enormous task ahead. She narrowed her eyes. "I have never traveled such a great distance in one day, nor with anyone but myself to consider. But I will do anything for my daughter."

"Good." Lina could feel her own heart, thudding hard, sending fire through her body. She nodded and turned to

Bogdan. "And, while we're at it, let's shut down the camp, once and for all. What do you reckon, Bogey?"

A beam spread across Bogdan's face. He had fear in his eyes, though. Lina recognized it as the same fear that was inside her too. But fear wouldn't stop them. Not now.

"What's our plan?" asked Bogdan. "If we're saving everyone and not only your mama, Lina, we need one. It's not like we can just sneak in there. Or can we?" he said, glancing at Svetlana.

Svetlana shook her head. "I cannot use the cape to set foot inside the camp. For reasons Lina will, in part, understand."

Svetlana looked at Lina as she said this, and Lina remembered how she'd nearly lost them in the nothing world, all because she couldn't clearly picture Moscow.

Of course. Svetlana had never been to the camp. So she couldn't picture it.

The ghost of a smile played across Svetlana's lips. "But Lina can."

"Can I?"

"As soon as we're close enough, Lina, you can steal silently inside, beneath the cape. If it was just your mother who needed rescuing, you could spirit her away under the cloak with no one knowing."

The thought of using the cape sent a shudder through Lina. Could she do it? Even close up?

"However," Svetlana went on, "if you do truly wish

to liberate the entire prison, then we will need another approach." She lifted her head and stared at them both, hard. "Bogdan and the shadow child and I will find the men you escaped with and lead them back to the camp, along with twenty or more of my wolves," she said. "We will bring chaos with us, and with our chaos, the prisoners will have their chance to overpower the guards. I do not believe that these people deserve freedom—but I will do it for you, child, after what I've put you through. *If* this is truly what you want."

Lina and Bogdan nodded in silent agreement. "No one deserves to live that way," said Lina to Svetlana. "No one. Perhaps when you see the camp for yourself, Svetlana, you'll understand." Then she went on, "So you'll all cause a scene and help the other prisoners escape while I sneak in and free Mamochka." Lina looked at Bogdan. "The old 'distract and attack' technique."

Bogdan nodded and grinned his one-sided grin. "Sounds good to me."

*"Nevertell,"* said Natalya in agreement.

In one swift move, Svetlana was next to them, holding out her hand. It reminded Lina of the night they'd met: their first journey beneath Svetlana's cape to her frozen tower. Svetlana's palm, she noticed, which had been badly cut earlier, now looked almost healed. As Lina watched, the last sliver of a scratch knitted itself back together—the dried blood drifting away like dust.

Lina and Bogdan each slipped a hand into one of Svetlana's. With the other hand, she flicked the cape, tattered at the corner where Lina had torn a piece off, and swirled it around them as it grew. Instead of blackness, they entered a rich royal blue, just like the color of the horizon on the night Lina had taken them on a bumpy ride to Novosibirsk. And, just like on that night, Natalya with her pigtails and her big, serious eyes was also holding on to her, tightly.

Lina breathed in the blue and felt hopeful and sad all at once. She was weightless. Lifted. The blue beneath their feet began to lighten until it was utterly white. A white globe pierced through the remaining blue and grew. Lina realized it was the sun rising.

Her weight settled. The white at her feet grew shadows and crags. Even through her boots, she felt the familiar sting of the cold.

They were standing on a mountaintop, overlooking a range of snowy peaks. Above them, and despite the cold, the sun blazed.

"We are in what humans call the Ural Mountains," said Svetlana. "I tracked you through here as you traveled on the train. Except you were far lower down then."

"You're not joking," said Bogdan, wobbling to keep his balance.

Lina laughed. There was a mix of fear and awe in his eyes as he took in the mountains—all laid out below them like a map. Up here, Lina felt exhilarated too, but for different reasons. With her head tilted toward the sun, she drank it in through her skin. It filled her up with energy—with what felt like magic.

A question came to her. "Svetlana, if I'm your granddaughter, does that mean I've inherited *all* your powers?"

"No," said Svetlana. "You are part human, after all—though how much so, and the extent of your abilities, remains to be seen. You've already shown great talent, however. I feel you may surprise even yourself. My children never showed any sign of being anything but human—though Katya has always had an affinity with luck. An arcane skill in itself."

Lina knitted her brows. "I used to think she was, but it doesn't seem like she's been that lucky to me now. Not overall, anyway."

"It's not as simple as that—and I remind you, she is part human." Svetlana looked sideways at Lina with a faint smile. "She does like to gamble. You may have noticed that. Even as a child, she liked dice games."

Every time Svetlana said something like this, Lina's heart skipped. She could barely believe it still—but everything pointed to the same fact: Svetlana really *was* her grandmother.

"What about my uncle?" Lina asked. "What was he like?"

"Valentin? He was gentle and kind. As it should be."

Lina said no more. She sensed Svetlana didn't want to speak about the dead yet—but to stay focused on saving the living instead.

"Lina's good with plants," chipped in Bogdan. "*Great* with plants, actually. Go on. Tell her what you told me when we were in her hut." He gave Lina a forceful nudge.

Svetlana raised an eyebrow. Lina felt herself blush. "I . . . There have been a couple of times when I felt like I could make plants grow. Like you did, with the peaches." Her cheeks burned, but she went on, "I don't understand it and I don't know how to work it exactly, but I *do* want to learn. Can you teach me?" She blurted out the last part and wished she hadn't when she saw Svetlana's look of surprise. A pink flush even came over Svetlana's pale face. Although Svetlana didn't look entirely *un*happy to be asked.

"Yes," she said finally. "I can teach you."

Lina looked away to hide her smile.

"We'll fly, for now," said Svetlana. "It will be slower but less exhausting. Slightly. This way we can see where we're going, and we can use the cape again when we get closer. You'll need to cling to my back."

Bogdan stifled a cry as Svetlana became a giant falcon. Staring into those eyes was like looking into the depths of the silver-flecked lake. Lina felt she could be looking at Svetlana's truest self. Or at least the truest form she'd yet seen.

They clung to her back, around the base of her broad wings, and Svetlana took off into the air. The mountains shrank away, and they could see for hundreds and hundreds of snowy miles. Bogdan screamed. So did Lina—and even Natalya cried out. Whether their screams came from fear or out of pure joy, not even Lina could tell. Far below them, howls echoed out from across the mountaintops and valleys: the invisible spirit wolves' voices joining a chorus with theirs.

# 43

After hours of traveling, Svetlana's falcon chest heaved, and wrinkled silver-gray eyelids pulled back and forth across her eyes. Lina knew she must be exhausted.

Svetlana could fly incredibly fast. How long she could keep it up for, though, Lina didn't know. In truth, at that moment, Lina could only worry about the well-being of her mother. She knew she would push Svetlana on, no matter what—and that Svetlana would be doing the same to her.

Yet as time stretched on, all Lina could see were more mountains, more forests, more snow. It hit her just how far they had to travel. Even with Svetlana's magic, there was every chance they might fail.

Lina kept thinking about her mother, down in that

disgusting cell. Her mother, awaiting the arrival of those officers. To make it worse, the memory of Katya from that first water mirror kept coming back to her. The way she'd called out for Lina.

Her fingers went to the scrap of cape, still stuffed in the bottom of her coat pocket. It felt as fluid as water but much, much colder. What if she used it now? Could she make it back to the camp from here?

"Lina." Bogdan touched her shoulder, making her jump. "If even Svetlana won't use it from here . . ." Lina knew he was right. She pulled her hand out of her pocket and clutched Svetlana's feathered back. Losing herself to the nothing world wouldn't help save her mother—or free the other prisoners in the camp.

As the sun moved through the sky, they came to a place filled with towering flat-topped rocks. But Svetlana didn't stop. They flew on, the relentless wind wrenching at Lina's fur hood, freezing the water escaping from her eyes into rivulets of ice across her face. They went on until Lina felt so weak with hunger she could barely grip the giant bird's feathers.

They plunged into a mist bank. Everything became eerily silent and still. The air Lina breathed felt heavy. Smothering. When the mist cleared, Svetlana's tower stood there, right at the center of its mirrored lake, gleaming against the rays of a powerful sun. They hadn't seen the tower in the daylight before.

Bogdan and Lina shared a frightened glance. Why had Svetlana brought them back here? Had she tricked them?

Svetlana carried them over the top of the tower. Peering around her powerful back, they could see right down into the gaping split through its center. Svetlana pressed her wings flat against her body and dived down into it.

In her terror, Lina found new strength to cling on—hard. They plummeted past every exposed floor. Lina glimpsed the snaking gold staircase, which seemed to wind like a gleaming ribbon alongside them, the translucent walls and corridors flecked with precious metal, the dark-blue curtains with their golden frayed edges, which billowed as they rocketed by.

She felt like she was clinging to a knife as it sliced through the layers of a giant cake.

Svetlana opened her wings. Lina's stomach lurched. They glided down into the very heart of the tower—a courtyard—and landed softly. It was large, enclosed on all sides by walls, with a small, round pond at the center. The whole thing was an indoor garden—and pristinely kept. Despite the open roof, it felt sheltered. Warm. It had vines, plants, and bushes of every kind. Trees too. Peach trees.

Before Lina could blink, Svetlana was a person again. "We must eat," she said. "We need all our strength, physical and otherwise, for what is to come."

Lina could relax. Svetlana had brought them here to feed them, not trap them.

260

Svetlana went on, "Lina, this is a chance for you to learn. We need nourishment. Will you grow our peaches for us?" She gestured toward the peach tree with an open palm.

"Um." Lina gritted her teeth at Bogdan. He gave her an excited grin and nodded his encouragement. *"Nevertell,"* came Natalya's voice, undoubtedly offering her support as well. Lina smiled weakly. "Suppose it doesn't hurt to try, eh?"

She placed her hands among the leaves. They felt warm and smooth against her fingertips.

"Cold and warm magic are bound together," Svetlana said softly, close to her ear. "One is not necessarily bad and the other is not necessarily good—that depends on who uses them and what for. Cold magic gives insight and crosses boundaries. Warm magic is growth and creates boundaries. Remember that."

Lina nodded. She closed her eyes and willed the electric heat to build in her chest, as it had done before. Willed it to travel down her arms and into her hands, to push out into the leaves. *Grow,* she urged. *Grow.*

Nothing happened.

Lina opened her eyes again. "I—I don't understand." Had she imagined her power before? In the greenhouse? In the forest?

"Never mind, Lina," said Bogdan quickly, ruffling her hair. "You'll do it next time."

"Indeed," said Svetlana with a small sigh. "It can take time, and the right conditions, to master such a skill."

Even so, disappointment swelled in Lina's chest.

"Next time, focus on what you wish to achieve and why—not the feeling of power itself," Svetlana said, as if sensing her sadness. "If we succeed and survive," she added, "I can teach you more. If you would like?"

Lina nodded, although she couldn't yet muster any words.

In seconds, Svetlana had grown fruit and plucked it from the trees for them. She did it with such swiftness and ease that it made Lina feel worse, and where she took the fruit, more grew in its place. "These peaches will restore us more than any other food," Svetlana said. As soon as she'd passed some to Lina and Bogdan, she bit into a fruit herself. Judging by the urgency with which she ate, she must've been ravenous.

Lina looked around in awe again. "You keep a garden here?" she said. "I had no idea. Is it . . . ?" She hesitated, worried about probing too far. "Is it to remember my grandfather?"

Svetlana brushed a leaf with her fingertips. "That, and our home. We met in the Caucasus Mountains, many years ago. Humans had often traveled that way. I would just hide and watch them pass. I knew better than to get involved with them—cruel and bullying, with their wars and their love only of violence and killing. But your grandfather seemed . . . different. He had a certain energy to him. Almost a touch of a natural spirit like my own kind. When we spoke, I realized it came from his passion for making things grow."

Svetlana took another peach and carried on. "His dream was to go to Moscow. He wanted to use his talent for growing for the good of the people and to be part of a new way of doing things that, he said, would be fairer for all. Yet he stayed with me for many years. We had two children, as you know. Valentin and Katya.

"I didn't want to leave my home in the mountains," Svetlana went on. "It's where I draw my strength. My power. But I knew if I wanted our family to be together, I would need to. He loved our home there too, but Moscow still called to him. So I agreed to move, as long as I could journey back to the mountains whenever I needed to, to feel at peace. It was a true torment, being split between my family and my home."

When they had all eaten their fill, they left the courtyard for the frozen lake, to give Svetlana more space to take off. Before she transformed, she stood apart from them and stopped still, as if listening. Then she knelt down and placed her hand against the ice.

The ice moved. Thin cracks appeared. Even from where she stood, Lina could hear the deep groaning sound it made. She found herself reaching for the bead in which her moth friend lived, for comfort. Beneath the ice, she caught a glimpse of Pechal's silver scales pressed against Svetlana's hand. The fish had come to see Svetlana—though there would always be the ice between them.

In that moment, Svetlana was the loneliest figure Lina had ever seen.

As they left the lake with its tower, the three of them clinging to Svetlana's falcon back once again, Lina gazed behind her. The courtyard had felt like a place of true calm. Of peace. In her bones, she yearned to create something as beautiful—as magical—as that.

# 44

hey hadn't flown far before Bogdan pointed and cried out. "Down there," he shouted. "Look at that, Lina. Look!"

"What? What is it?"

"I recognize that river. Follow it that way a little and over to the right. What do you see?"

Lina gasped. "Tuyaara's farm village. Bogey—well spotted!"

Bogdan beamed.

Lina could see the rooftops of the several lonely *balagans* now, with smoke rising from the chimneys and the horses moving on the ground. They looked like they were the size of millet grains. Among them was a smaller shape that had to be a person.

"Svetlana, can you please take us down over there?" said Bogdan.

Lina glanced at him. She wanted to see Tuyaara again as much as he did—she missed their friend—but time was so short. What about her mother?

Bogdan reached across and gripped her arm. "We won't be long, don't worry. But Tuyaara should know we're alive. And she's got a right to be there. For Keskil. Anyway, we'll need all the help we can get, I reckon."

Bogdan was probably right. As usual. Lina still had no idea how they were going to manage all this, or if the plan would work at all.

All she could think about was getting to her mother.

As they landed, the horses bucked and scattered. Tuyaara saw the bird coming and hurriedly swung her leg over her horse to escape, but Lina called out to her. "Tuyaara, wait!"

"Lina? Bogdan?"

They scrambled off Svetlana's back and ran to their friend. Tuyaara climbed down from the horse. She gathered them both up in her arms, which were thick in all her furs and barely able to bend. "What are you doing with that thing?" She scowled at the bird. "Is it safe? Has it hurt you?"

"It's fine," said Bogdan.

Tuyaara frowned. "I don't know what's going on. But"—she raised her voice—"you are a pair of absolute half-wits. What were you thinking, running off like that into the storm? I thought you must be goners. Do you know how it felt to go out the next day, to look for your bodies?" She studied their faces hard until her anger softened. "When we didn't find you, I did wonder. I hoped, anyway. Ah, it's so good to see you alive and well."

They hugged again—until Tuyaara pulled away.

"Come on," said Bogdan. "We'll tell you everything on the way."

"On the way? To where?"

"We're going to rescue my mother," Lina said. "And liberate the camp, if we can. We thought you might like to help—maybe to bring Keskil home to his family. It'll be dangerous, of course . . ."

Tuyaara's mouth became a thin line of resolve. "How many can the bird carry?" she said.

Lina and Bogdan looked at each other and shrugged. "She's pretty strong," said Lina. "But then, she's carried us a long way already . . ."

"I can carry as many as can fit on my back," came Svetlana's voice.

They all turned to see her, standing where the falcon had been. Tuyaara leaped backward, her arms spread in front of Lina and Bogdan protectively. But when they showed no sign of surprise or fear, she relaxed a little and nodded. "I'll get my brothers, then," she said. "They won't want to miss this."

It was a lot cozier with six of them clinging to Svetlana's back. It had taken a lot to convince Michil, in particular, to go anywhere near Svetlana's falcon form and not to tell their parents. They'd had to threaten to leave without him in the end.

Now Lina and Bogdan told Tuyaara and her brothers everything. Already they were steeling themselves for a fight—Lina could tell. And she recognized herself in the way Tuyaara looked to the horizon. It was her own burning need to save her mother—but different somehow. Keskil must have meant a great deal to her.

Soon the dusk rolled in. They came down near the edge of a forest, and Svetlana became a person in among the shadows. If Tuyaara and her brothers were shocked this time, they hid it well.

"We will keep on, through the night," said Svetlana between shallow breaths. "There'll be no sleep for me, if we're to make it now. You should all rest, however, if you can."

True to her word, Svetlana transformed again into a falcon and took to the air. The others closed their eyes. Even if they couldn't sleep for fear of falling, they could at least *try* to rest, as Svetlana had encouraged them to.

All but Lina. She had too much on her mind.

What state would her mother be in when—if—she got to her? And what about Commandant Zima? She hated to think of him: the man who might be her father. How would she react if she saw him? How would he react to her?

Through it all, her failure to grow the peaches in Svetlana's courtyard weighed heavily. What was the true nature of her powers, if not to grow things? It didn't make sense. That was the thing she loved doing the most.

She looked to Bogdan, as she usually did when something worried her. Somehow, now that she really studied it, his face looked older than she remembered. Even in the semi-dark, his complexion glowed in a way she'd never seen before. Perhaps it was his returning health. It was true that his terrible churning cough had all but disappeared.

Buried in Svetlana's feathers, her thoughts blurred with dreams until she couldn't tell the difference anymore.

# 45

As dawn broke on the horizon, there was still no glimpse of the camp. Svetlana brought them down in the middle of nowhere. Lina scrambled off Svetlana's back and ran around just in time to see two pale arms reach up out of the feathers to brush the falcon face away—as if it were a costume. Svetlana's own face rose up from beneath the beak. All at once, she was a person again. Lina ignored her surprise at Svetlana's transformation. "What's happening? Why've we stopped?" she said.

Bogdan came to stand close to Lina, and she could just see Natalya's shadow on her other side. Svetlana clutched her stomach and caught her breath. It was clear she couldn't yet speak. In the silence, Lina paced. She felt like shaking Svetlana and demanding to know where they were.

She had to breathe. Control her own frustration.

"We are close enough," gasped Svetlana, "to the camp—for you to use your piece of the cape. Do not worry. I enchanted the peach you ate yesterday. It will protect you from the other world for long enough to allow you to make your journey."

Lina was stunned. "Here? But how do you know we're near the camp?"

Svetlana put her hands on her hips and straightened out her back. "We are close to the men you escaped with. They have been wandering in this wood since that night. The wolf-binding has been taking place and they are becoming shadows. It is time for the rest of us to find them. We will bring them to the camp with my wolves and other shadows and stir a mutiny, as we agreed."

Lina and Bogdan looked at each other and nodded.

Tuyaara shared a glance with her brother Michil and then looked at the floor. "I wish I had my horse," she grumbled. "It sounds stupid, I know, but somehow it doesn't feel right, doing this without one."

"I can arrange a horse," said Svetlana. She closed her eyes.

Tuyaara frowned. "What's she doing?"

Lina and Bogdan shrugged.

"There are spirits other than wolves—and other realms in which to find them," said Svetlana without opening her eyes. Her voice sounded hushed and sharp all at once.

Her breath shuddered out of her as if she'd been running for a very long time. Then Lina heard a new sound. The pounding of hooves.

It came from the forest. Lina turned just in time to see a horse leap from the trees. It galloped toward them.

The horse's body looked as if it was made of ice. It had mist dancing inside it—like dappled tree shade that had been captured. Its face and mane were feathered with frost. Tuyaara let out a small cry, which she stifled with her own fist. Lina could see tears welling in her eyes. Watching her, Lina felt the hot sting of her own tears.

Her thoughts soon turned back to their task, though. There wasn't time to be awestruck.

"So this is where I go and get Mamochka," said Lina. She turned to Bogdan. "Ready to 'distract and attack'?" Looking into his eyes, a lump rose in her throat that she couldn't swallow. This was the first time she'd be apart from Bogdan in what felt like a lifetime. "Bogey . . ."

"Lina." Bogdan crossed the space between them in an instant and hugged her so tight she struggled to breathe. "You are my friend, Lina. My best friend. Be safe."

She slipped her arms around him too and said into the fur of his coat, "And you are mine—my very best friend. Take care, Bogey."

"Look after yourself."

"You look after yourself."

"Don't do anything foolish."

"Bogey. Come on. I can't breathe."

He let go. They shared a shy grin.

"Good luck, Lina," said Tuyaara, gently stroking the horse's nose. "We won't be far behind. You can count on us."

Michil put his arm around Dolan and they both nodded at her solemnly, as if to agree with their sister. Lina felt a pressure on her arm. Natalya was touching her. *"Nevertell."*

Svetlana lifted her chin and flicked her hair over her shoulders. "Focus, Lina. Imagine yourself into a part of the camp you can picture the best—and that's where you will go. The better you know where you're going, and the less time you spend beneath the cape, the less risk there is of becoming trapped in the nothing world. You must have experienced this when you first used it. But I believe you can do this now."

Lina nodded. "Thanks. I'll do everything I can to save Mama."

"I don't doubt it. But, as Bogdan said, don't do anything foolish. Wait until you hear us coming before you act."

Lina took a deep breath and centered herself. She felt inside her pocket for the scrap of cape, pulled it out, and held it in both hands. It started to stretch—to give. In an instant, she'd pictured one of the places she knew best—one that wouldn't be swarming with guards.

The greenhouse.

In the next second, Lina couldn't see. All she could hear was a rushing sound, like flying—or falling. She panicked, flailing her arms and jerking her legs. All sense of anything solid beneath her had completely gone.

Until the ground came up under her feet and the musty smell of warm, damp soil hit her. She blinked until the world came into focus. Lina was back at the camp.

# 46

The greenhouse was as Lina remembered—except for one detail. All the plants were gone. Only empty pots and seed trays betrayed the fact that any had ever been there. That is, until her eyes adjusted, and she was able to take in the sight of the floor.

Uprooted plants lay all around, weak white roots dangling from clods of dark earth. Torn and trampled leaves shriveled into themselves, as if trying to escape. Soil had been ground into the flagstones by heavy boots. When Lina took the vegetables, she'd left the greenhouse in a decent state. She hadn't had the heart to destroy it, not totally. Since then, this place had been the site of an explosion of rage. Only one man could have done this. Commandant Zima.

Lina remembered his violent temper with sick dread.

She'd seen it with her own eyes. How a plant had only to grow wrong or suffer in some way—have dry leaves or incurable rot—and he'd rip it up and shred it in front of her, as if it had caused him some terrible injury.

She didn't dare allow herself to remember how his rages had played out with people.

Looking at all those empty pots, ready and waiting to be planted, Lina felt a tingle in her fingers: the urge to make something grow. She remembered the way she'd felt on top of the mountains in the sunshine. The way she'd soaked up the warmth, like energy.

She remembered Svetlana's words: *"Cold magic gives insight and crosses boundaries. Warm magic is growth and creates boundaries."*

"Focus on what I wish to achieve and why—not the feeling of power itself." Lina repeated what Svetlana had told her, moved a little ways down the aisle, and took a couple of stranded seeds from the floor. She put one in her pocket and held the other between her fingers. It looked like rye. It had been the wrong moment before, but she could do this now. She knew it. The question was: How far could she push her abilities?

Footsteps scraped on the gravel outside. The sound of a hard sole, which could only mean a guard. Lina dropped the seed. She had to get out of there. But how? She glanced around. No escape. Could she hide instead? What about the piece of cape? Could she use it to transport herself to another part of the camp?

It lay in the aisle, between her and the door. She ran, dropped, and scrabbled for it.

Too late. A key turned in the lock and the greenhouse door screeched open. The sudden blast of icy air from the doorway carried the cape over her shoulder and away. She froze on her knees in the center of the aisle.

Commandant Zima filled the doorway.

# 47

Slowly, Lina stood up. Commandant Zima's glare made all her limbs feel heavy and stuck. For several seconds, he didn't move a muscle. Then his nostrils flared with fury. "You," he spat. "How?"

Zima paced toward her at a frightening speed. Lina flinched, but her legs still felt glued down. She was so frightened she couldn't move, let alone run. She could only hope he didn't shoot her on the spot or tear at her like one of the plants.

He stopped just a few feet away. "Can it be true?" He spoke quietly and slowly, scanning her face. She felt conscious of her new clothes. "You—little Lina—are back?" A softness came into his voice, which came out in a kind of sigh—almost like he was pleased to see her. Relieved, even. It didn't last long. As if remembering who he was, he pulled himself up to his full height and snapped, "You stole from me. You ruined the officers' banquet. If you *knew* the embarrassment I've had to face . . . Did you and Katya think it was funny? I assume she did help you. Have you come back now to laugh at me some more?" Dark circles cupped his bulging eyes. The anger in them and the redness rising up his neck made her shudder. His cruelty was made worse somehow by his gentle tone from a moment before.

"No, C-Commandant," Lina stuttered. "Not funny." She couldn't stop trembling. His gaze on her was terrifying.

"Were you mocking me as you planned it? Laughing behind my back?"

"No, Commandant."

He pulled his mouth into a thin, joyless line. Were those tears in his eyes? "Your mother's in the *karker*, and it's killing her. Of course, she won't ask for mercy. I would let her out, you know. All she has to do is ask, but she's too proud. Always too proud." Those were definitely tears. He wiped them away with the back of his sleeve. Lina knew then: He would always blame other people for the things he did.

Her fear curdled into rage in an instant, and then it exploded. "You're right—she *is* proud. She would never ask for help from someone like you!"

Lina's mother had done everything she could to keep Lina safe. To help the people who came to her in the

279

# 48

A murmur went up among the men and women assembled in the square.

Lina didn't feel real anymore. It was as though she were soaring high above, looking down on herself, on Zima, and on all the people who outnumbered the guards—ten to one at least. What was it Svetlana and Bogdan had said? Don't do anything foolish. Wait until you hear us coming before you act.

Too late for that.

"I can do magic now," said Lina with pride, "just like my grandmother. If you don't know about her, you should. She turns people into ghosts." As if answering her, the peach pit grew warmer. Lina spoke loudly—she was addressing the crowd, not the commandant. She scanned every face until she found Keskil's. "People call her the Man Hunter," she said.

"The Man Hunter?" The crowd turned to look at Keskil, who'd spoken. "I've heard these stories before. Everyone in Siberia knows and fears the Man Hunter."

"Well, she'll be here any moment with my friends"—Lina turned back to the commandant—"and a hundred or more ghost wolves to liberate this camp. How do you think I got back here and am wearing these clothes? How do you think I survived, when no others ever have? Keskil, Tuyaara is with them. She's coming for you!"

Commandant Zima laughed. The sound was cutting. "Folktales. Stories and gossip from the mouths of dim-witted peasants; that's all it is. You're nothing but a liar. You've no doubt been hiding in a foxhole somewhere."

Lina pulled the rye seed she'd taken from the green-house out of her pocket. "I'll prove it to you, then. Just watch. I'll show you what I can do." She held the seed at arm's length, inside her fist. *Focus.* Her hand tingled and grew warm. Something living nudged at her palm, she was sure of it. She parted her fingers.

Nothing.

The rye seed remained exactly the same as before.

The commandant had watched with a look of horror. Now he laughed again. His eyes glistened and he wiped them on his coat sleeve. "Enough of your nonsense."

"Commandant," called one of the guards.

The corners of Zima's mouth twitched with irritation. "What is it?" For a moment, he took his eyes off Lina—and froze.

Lina dared to look as well. The prisoners had broken their lines and come closer.

"Get back, you animals," hollered Zima.

No one moved.

"Get back, I said. Guards!"

The guards looked around, worried and confused. It was only supposed to be a simple morning assembly, after all—business as usual, before they took the prisoners to the mess hall and then on to the mine. Lina had witnessed thousands of mornings like this one. There was never any trouble—not before breakfast. The guards weren't used to this.

Lina seized the moment. "What if they don't get back in line? You can't shoot us all."

More low murmuring buzzed around the square, like a swarm of bees. More prisoners edged forward. Where Lina stood with Zima, it was starting to feel crowded.

"Come now," called out one of the braver guards, some distance away. Perhaps it was that very distance that made him brave. "Your motherland requires you to work in the mines. This is where you belong now. You are lucky to have been granted your lives—but that right can be taken away too."

Lina glanced back at Commandant Zima to see what he would do or say next. All the attention—all the pressure—had shifted off her and onto him. He must've felt the shift too, because his face was a mask of fury. Could it be that he'd realized what serious trouble he might be in?

He raised his pistol and aimed it into the crowd.

"Go ahead, Zima," came the voice of one of the prisoners. "Waste your bullets. What will you do when they're gone?"

Another voice shouted, "You'd need reinforcements to take us all on. And how far away are they, out here? A week by train, at least . . ."

Lina smiled. Something was happening. Something invisible but very real. Suddenly, the people weren't prisoners anymore.

Commandant Zima felt it too. Lina could tell. He knew he didn't stand a chance.

When he turned back to Lina, though, his face was set with new determination. The hand holding the pistol was still trembling with anger. Lina winced and took a step back.

And then a howl rang out. Followed by a whole chorus of howls.

"Wolves," someone shouted. "Inside the camp!"

Chaos broke loose.

# 49

The prisoners and guards fled. People ran between Lina and the commandant, knocking his pistol out of his hand. Lina took her chance. She darted away—in the direction of the *karker*.

As she ran, she glanced toward the wire. A haze of ice crystals billowed there, kicked up by the commotion. Then, through the sparkling mist, lights emerged, more than she could even count, seemingly floating in thin air. Lina realized what they were: oil lamps. The shadows!

Among them, three gaunt figures emerged. One tall. One thin. One small. Alexei, Old Gleb, and Vadim. They were like skeletons, walking in a dream.

But where were Bogdan, Tuyaara, and her brothers? Svetlana? Lina hoped they were safe.

Lina dodged around a man and then crawled between

the legs of one of the guards. She *had* to keep moving or she'd be in danger of getting trampled in the panic. All she could think about was reaching the *karker*. Freeing her mother. She had no idea how, though.

There were fewer people away from the square, and as she ran past the block that had once been Bogdan's sleeping quarters, Lina could see the entrance to the *karker* just a short sprint away. From here it looked unguarded. She made a dash for it . . .

Straight into what felt like a wall. She fell to the floor and found herself staring at Commandant Zima's polished leather boots.

"You really thought it would be that easy?" Commandant Zima reached down and grabbed a handful of her hair, right at the scalp. It burned. Lina cried out in pain and swung her leg. By chance, she caught him on the shin.

Now it was his turn to cry out in pain.

"You were supposed to be *better* than the rest of them here," hissed Zima. "My child. A respectful, obedient daughter." For the first time ever, he sounded wounded. But it didn't take long for the edge to come back into his voice. "When you were born, I was so happy. But if I'd known you'd be so ungrateful, I'd have taken you from Katya and left you out in the snow."

Lina felt sick. The rumors were true. The commandant was her father. Tears stung her eyes. After all this time, she finally knew the truth. And the truth couldn't have been worse.

The peach pit began to pulse with sharp bursts of heat—one, two, three—and then again, just as it had before their confrontation with Svetlana after they'd escaped from the train. Was it trying to tell her something? It was growing hotter and hotter.

Zima was still talking. "Look at you." He wrinkled his nose in disgust. "My own flesh and blood. This small, pathetic creature, groveling on the ground. Now you know how it feels to be humiliated."

Wave upon wave of numbness crashed over Lina. Her mind felt detached from her body, as though she were watching herself in a daze. How could this man be her father?

Lina tried to block out the commandant's words—and the fact that he'd just admitted to being her father. The peach pit was her only concern now. If she could make it grow, she might be able to shock and maybe even frighten Zima, and that might give her enough time to get away from him. But the seed in the square hadn't grown. Perhaps planting it in the ground would give it the best chance to grow. She dug down with her foot.

She needed to distract him from what she was doing. "Your child or not," she said, "I'm the same person I ever was. It doesn't change anything. It doesn't change who I am." She'd almost finished digging. "I'm not a 'creature' either. I'm a human being, like you are. Just because you wear a uniform, that doesn't make you better or more important than me—or any of us."

The hole was ready. "And another thing." Lina scowled up at Commandant Zima—her father. "I'm not groveling." She dug under her tunic and tugged the necklace. Its string snapped. The tiny beads tumbled away and scattered across the floor. The peach pit rolled across the ground in its lopsided way. Lina reached for it.

Zima's boot came down hard on her hand.

"What have you got there?" he said. He crushed her hand harder with his boot. Lina cried out and let go. Zima scrutinized it from above. "Ah. A pit of some sort. That's unusual. Where did you get it?" Without pausing for an answer, he took his boot off her hand—and brought the heel of it down hard on the peach pit.

Lina heard it crack. When he lifted his boot, she could see a deep split. Zima brought his heel down again. And again. The peach pit splintered into fragments, which he ground into the snow.

Lina could only watch as her peach pit was destroyed.

# 50

L ina's hand was bluish-white. She was having trouble
moving it. Her eyes watered when she tried. Nothing was as bad as the pain in her heart, though.
When she'd declared to the crowd that she could do
magic, she'd believed in herself. She'd felt like she could
do anything.

Now, the truth hit her hard. She wasn't anywhere near
as powerful as her grandmother. Against Commandant
Zima, she was helpless. He seemed to read her mind. "Did
you really believe all that rubbish you spouted, back in
the square?" he said. "Did you really think you could take
me on with *parlor tricks*?"

Zima laughed. Lina winced. Was it her turn, now, to be
crushed by his boot?

"Your mother will spend her last hours in the *karker*,"

he stated. "We'll have this little riot put down by the afternoon. Such a shame . . . You amounted to nothing in the end. And there I was, with such high hopes."

On the ground, where it had rolled, lay the larger bead with its note inside. The note from Svetlana—to Lina's grandfather. As she watched, the moth crawled out, as if to see the devastation for itself. It opened up its little frayed wings, testing them for flight.

Lina's eyes widened. Where fragments of the peach pit had been, now there were pockmarks in the snow. Had the pieces melted through it?

They must still be warm. Even in fragments, the pit still had its power. To grow? She'd find out.

Lina felt a burning, electric heat in her heart. It traveled through her blood. Her whole body tingled. Nothing would go back to the way it was. She wouldn't let it. She couldn't. She closed her eyes and remembered being in the Ural Mountains with Svetlana and Bogdan, on their long journey back to the camp. The way the high altitude and the sun had made her feel. She was filled to bursting with power. Now, to release it.

Lina dug her fingers under the snow. "Grow," she urged. *"Grow!"*

Everything that was left of the peach pit grew.

# 51

Commandant Zima leaped backward. Where the fragments of the peach pit had been, hundreds of tiny green shoots pushed their way out of the ground, clawing at his boots like baby hands. They thickened out in an instant, driving sharp branches toward him, covered in papery green leaves.

Lina barely noticed Commandant Zima backing away. She was drawing strength along millions of roots and pushing out more branches, until trees, ripe with peaches, began to spring up all around her. Her thoughts fluttered in thousands of leaves.

Without a word or another glance at Lina—his own daughter—the commandant turned and fled. Lina was alone.

"I thought we told you *not* to do anything foolish,"

boomed a voice from behind her. Lina knew who it was before she even turned. She'd recognize that voice anywhere.

Svetlana—with Bogdan next to her.

Lina pulled her thoughts back into herself. It felt like tugging on thousands of tiny ropes, which all gave way at the same time. She fell back onto the ground, in the shade of a crescent of peach trees, branches bending and creaking with fruit. Bogdan helped her up. She took his hand and smiled. "Turned into the 'attack and attack' technique again, didn't it?" she said breathlessly. He just grinned and shook his head.

Svetlana's stern face, usually like a carved block of ice, trembled with emotion.

Lina left Bogdan beneath the rustling leaves and stumbled to her grandmother. Her head still hurt, and the blood was only just returning to the hand Commandant Zima had crushed. Svetlana stayed very still as Lina came closer.

Lina didn't know what she was going to do until she got close. Then her feelings overwhelmed her. She threw her arms around Svetlana's waist and buried her head in her woolen coat. Svetlana went rigid with surprise. Then she softened.

Lina smiled. "Thank you for coming, Babushka. And for keeping me and Bogey out of trouble."

A crackle of gunfire went off. The guards were fighting back.

Lina tensed. "Aren't Tuyaara and her brothers out there? And Natalya?" She couldn't sense Natalya as she usually could, and she guessed she must be leading the other shadows.

Svetlana pushed Lina away, gently but firmly. "Yes, they are. But you must go and rescue your mother," she said. "Bogdan and I can deal with this."

Bogdan peered around the peach trees he'd been marveling at, startled. "Er—can we?"

Lina nodded. She was certain that they could.

Lina sprinted down the tunnel toward the *karker*. The narrow passageway sloped at a shocking rate and was dark and dank, with a smell like old leaves and filth. Her mother had spent days in this awful place. How could anyone put another human being somewhere like this?

The pounding and splashing of Lina's feet echoed off the walls. Finally she reached a locked door at the end of the tunnel. She could only just make it out in the gloom.

"Mamochka?"

"Lina!" Her mother's dirt-flecked face appeared at the bars in the door. She reached her trembling fingers through as far as they would go, so she could just about stroke Lina's hair. "Lina, you're alive?" her voice rasped. "But what on earth are you doing back?"

Lina grasped her mother's fingers, ignoring the pain in her own bad hand, and hugged them. For a moment, she couldn't speak—or find the words, even if she'd wanted to.

"Come on, my little one. Pull yourself together and get me out, will you? What's going on out there?"

"You . . ."

Lina whirled around to see the guard, Danill, blocking the tunnel. He looked scared, and he was breathing fast. "It's really you, Lina. But how? All that chaos out there—is that your doing?"

Lina stood straight. "Yes," she said. "Me and my friends, We're liberating the camp. It won't be long now before the guards are totally overthrown. So it'll be best for you—for all of us—if you let Mamochka go free. Now is your chance to get out of this place too, Danill. You must want that."

Danill hesitated.

Katya pressed her face up against the bars. "Stop dithering and give her the keys, Danill." Even in her weakened state, Katya hadn't lost her sharpness.

Danill glanced over his shoulder, and when he turned back, he looked calmer somehow. "She's a good person, your mama," he said to Lina. "Even if she is always rude to me." He fumbled with something on his belt, then passed it to her: the key. He turned to Lina's mother and said, "You've always deserved better than this place, Katya. We all have."

With that, Danill fled.

Lina jammed the rusty key into the lock. The mechanism groaned and then clunked. She yanked open the door.

Free from the cell, Lina's mother stumbled straight into her. It was supposed to be a warm, loving embrace, but it felt more like being run over by a tank. Lina didn't mind. She squeezed back as tight as she could. "Mama," she wheezed, "I found her."

"What? Found who?" It took a lot of energy for her to speak, Lina could tell.

"My grandmother. I found her. She's here."

Katya shook her head and made a noise that was half amusement, half disbelief. "Lina, you couldn't have." When Lina's expression didn't change, Katya's eyes widened. "But how? How did you manage to find her? And so quickly? After all this time here, I'd started to lose hope that I'd live to see her again."

Lina smiled. "She was already looking for us."

# 52

Back outside, Tuyaara, Michil, and Dolan had joined Bogdan and Svetlana. They were all collecting peaches.

Lina smiled. "Bogey? What's happening?"

He grinned over his shoulder at her—a big, wide, lopsided beam. "Hurry up, Lina. We need your help. We've got to take these to the square. Svetlana says the peaches you grew are so powerful that they'll turn into more trees as soon as they touch the ground. If we're quick, we can put a barrier between the guards and the rest of us—make it harder for them to use their weapons." He handed her some fruit.

Behind Lina, Katya emerged from the tunnel, blinking in the light. She'd told Lina to go on ahead while she caught her breath. Svetlana froze at the sight of her.

Then she reached for her daughter and cupped her face in her palms. "My *malyshka*," she said. Tears rose in Katya's eyes. She and Svetlana clutched each other and didn't let go.

Lina's voice was thick when she next spoke. "Mama, you stay with Svetlana while she picks more peaches. Make sure no one sneaks up on her."

"Are you joking, Lina?" said Katya. She drew back from Svetlana and quickly wiped her face. Already there was energy in her voice and color in her cheeks, as if she had drawn strength from her mother. "As much as we have to catch up on, there are more urgent things to do right now. I'm coming with you."

Svetlana nodded. "I will join you there."

Havoc still reigned in the square. People were running everywhere, but no one seemed to know what from—the guards, the dogs, the invisible wolves, or the three escapees who seemed to have returned from the dead.

More gunfire crackled from one of the towers. The guards were firing in panic. Who knew what—or who—they were even aiming for?

Lina lobbed several of the peaches as far as she could. Bogdan did the same. Tuyaara and her brothers joined them, their arms filled with peaches. Lina couldn't help admiring Tuyaara on the ice horse, her silky hair flowing in the breeze. She really was incredible.

Right away, green shoots rose up from where the peaches had landed—they grew thick and strong in an instant, unharmed by the trampling feet and the crush.

Screams went up in the crowd as the trees continued to grow. Then, an eerie silence fell. Everyone was mesmerized by what they saw. The shoots became sprigs, which became branches, which became towering trees— monstrously, abnormally tall.

On the other side of the square, Svetlana appeared, surrounded by a cluster of lights. She handed out peaches to the stunned prisoners: peaches for throwing, no doubt, so that more trees would grow. Lina cast the rest of her fruit into the crowd too.

Leaves were forming on the trees, followed by a shock of delicate white flowers that hung in the branches like snow. The petals fell, catching in everyone's hair. Guards and prisoners were staring, openmouthed, at them.

Lina held out her hand and caught some of the petals before they blew away. When she next looked up, fruit weighed heavy on the branches. Cheers and calls of excitement went up. Some prisoners were trying to climb up the trunks to reach the fruit.

"Look," said Katya, pointing. Her voice was dark.

Several of the guards had gotten tangled up in branches that seemed to be reaching out for them. They were whisked off the ground, screaming, and trapped up high in tightening tree limbs.

As Lina watched, the guards tangled up in the trees disappeared. Vanished, completely. The branches closed in on nothing, becoming empty, jagged coils. Only the odd scrap of torn cloth, a single boot, or the mist of breath remained. Where had they gone? To the nothing world?

"Keskil!" Lina turned at the sound of Tuyaara's voice.

A guard who'd been taken into a tree had hold of Keskil's arm and was pulling him closer to the snatching branches.

Tuyaara shouted again and galloped toward Keskil. The crowd leaped out of her way, opening a path in front of her. She wrapped an arm around Keskil's waist and dragged him back. The guard who'd grabbed him froze at the sight of the ice horse and its frosty, snorting breath and let go. A moment later, he vanished into thin air.

Keskil clambered onto the back of Tuyaara's horse without a second glance. It was Tuyaara he was mesmerized by.

Then Lina noticed a crowd gathering in a circle around something. She strained to see.

Commandant Zima. Some prisoners had caught him and were pushing him toward the center of the square.

Boos rang out—and calls of "Kill him!"

Lina's mother shook her head. "Never lose yourself to a mob," she said quietly, as if speaking only to herself.

This had gone far enough. "No. Stop!" shouted Lina. *Don't become him,* she wanted to say. *Don't taint yourselves with blood.* But her voice paled against all the shouting. No one but Bogdan and her mother heard.

"Hey!" Bogdan tried. "Just think about this, all right? He's not a threat now. You don't need to do that." His voice was louder, but it too got lost in the clamor.

"Kill him!" called the crowd. It became a chant—the voices harmonized and spoke as one. Became deafening. The circle around Zima closed in.

Panic gripped Lina. "No."

Katya pulled at her daughter's arm. "You don't want to see this," she said, trying to lead Lina away.

Tears streamed down Lina's face. This wasn't why she'd freed the prisoners. She wrenched her arm out of her mother's grasp. "No, stop!" Lina screamed again. She fought her way through the crowd gathered around the commandant until she was close enough to pull some of them away from him.

"Stop!" she said again. "Hurting him now, for revenge . . . It achieves nothing."

A few people backed away, and Zima reappeared with a gasp of breath, arms flailing. His hair and clothes had been tugged and torn. His skin was drained of all its color. And yet, Lina could already see the fear and humiliation in his eyes changing into anger. Before he could act on it, though, he staggered backward, his legs still unsteady. Straight into a peach tree.

The branches grasped his pistol arm and wove up the

length of it, holding him fast. "Lina?" he said, his voice soft. "Little Lina. I—" The tree clutched him tighter, drawing him in.

Lina cried out. She wanted to reach out to him, to make everything slow down and just stop. She heard her mother run to her as if in slow motion, felt Katya lift her to carry her away, but Lina was transfixed by what was happening to her father. Nobody could do a thing. Not her. Not Bogdan. Not Tuyaara.

The commandant was already gone.

# 53

The first Lina knew about where she was or what was happening was when her mother heaved her into a snowbank. "Aargh, my back." Katya straightened and clutched at the base of her spine. "I never thought I'd be carrying you at twelve."

Bogdan crouched next to Lina and held her hand. "You OK, my friend?"

Lina was not OK. She couldn't stop shaking. Every small sound caught her attention. Bogdan himself looked twitchy. They were by the wire fence, a little ways from the square, and they could still hear the shouts of the prisoners and the guards.

"*Nevertell.*" Natalya must have left the other shadows to join them. Lina appreciated her presence.

Svetlana came around the corner toward them.

"What happened?" Bogdan asked her. "What was that? Why did the guards disappear in the trees?"

Svetlana narrowed her eyes. "A Vanishing. I thought it might occur. The guards have been pushed out to the edges of this world. To the mist. We may never find them." Lina looked away, but she could feel Svetlana studying her closely. "However," she said, "know at least that the guards and the commandant are somewhere, and they are alive."

Lina didn't know what to think, or feel—about any of it.

Svetlana paused for a moment, then went on. "Lina. I have a surprise that might be of some comfort to you."

She stepped aside to allow Old Gleb to approach. Lina gasped. He let out a big belly laugh and slapped his thigh. "Kid," he said. "You're one sight for sore eyes, you are!"

Lina hugged him tight. "And the others?" she asked.

"They're fine," said Gleb. "Or, as fine as they *ever* were." He bent toward Lina's face and kissed her cheek. "You know, I had a dream you were with me," he said. His dark eyes glimmered, reflecting the snow. "It's hard to explain because I don't understand what happened, but . . . all through that long nightmare, it felt like you were looking out for me. My lucky star."

Later, Lina sat with her mother while Bogdan and Svetlana built a fire. Lina could just make out the hazy shape of

Natalya at the corners of her vision. Tuyaara and her brothers were with Keskil somewhere. They'd all stayed out of the square as the sky darkened and night fell, although from where they were, they could see the glow of many other small fires. Angry cries had given way to laughter and singing. It sounded like a big party—the first of its kind that Lina had ever known. Not that long after her birthday too.

Svetlana had called her wolves back and brought the guard dogs under control. She seemed to have a way with the dogs. They were sound asleep in one of the guard complexes now, having been fed from the kitchen and given fresh water to drink.

Every so often, Bogdan would duck out of his fire-building duties to scout around, and he'd come back with a report. People were organizing themselves, he said. Some had taken over the kitchen, rationed the food, and were dishing out meals. Others, directed by Tuyaara, her brothers, and Keskil, had climbed into the trees and were throwing down peaches for others to eat. There would be no more Vanishing now that the fighting had stopped—Svetlana had reassured them of that.

Friends of Katya's were collecting the pits from the peaches that had been eaten and taking them to the greenhouse to be planted. While the peaches on the trees replaced themselves with new peaches right away, the pits themselves no longer became trees immediately. "All enchantments have their limits," Svetlana explained.

These peach pits would need proper nurturing if they were to grow. Lina knew her skills would be needed in the coming months. If this place was to be a haven now, instead of a prison, that is.

Lina wanted that.

As the evening wore on, Lina remained with Bogdan by the newly built fire as he tucked into the hot peach stew and warm black bread that had been handed around to everyone. Lina sipped her own. She'd never tasted anything like it. It was delicious—sharp and sweet and spicy, all at once. Instinctively she checked for Natalya and quickly found her: a small silhouette, admiring the fire.

Lina's mother still sat on her other side, with Tuyaara wrapped up in blankets next to Keskil—both beside Bogdan. Tuyaara's brothers milled around, as did Svetlana, who was still keeping busy. Perhaps so she didn't collapse with exhaustion. Tuyaara had already been talking about how they could protect others from harm—using the peach forest as a kind of hidden sanctuary. It could definitely work. Tuyaara, Lina, and Bogdan would have a lot of ideas to discuss.

Lina soaked it all in, determined to remember this happiness. It didn't matter that they weren't in Moscow, in her imaginary apartment block. This was what she'd always dreamed of.

Katya squeezed her shoulders, and Lina nestled into her warmth. Her moth friend scuttled around on her fingers, its delicate brown wings folded over itself. She'd recovered the bead with the note earlier. To her amazement, the moth had still been with it.

"Did you love the command—I mean, my father?" Lina asked her mother.

"Once," said Katya. "He was different when I first came here. He wasn't in charge then—the power and resentment hadn't gone to his head. Zima was once just someone who didn't want to be here, the same as me. He did love you, Lina. In his way."

"But he wouldn't let Grandfather work in the greenhouse. And he killed Valentin. And he was cruel to us and to everyone else. He let us nearly starve!"

Katya frowned and looked away without giving an answer. There was a lot that Lina didn't understand. But she did know how complicated people could be. Perhaps she'd figure it out more over time.

Katya sniffed. "You became something good to focus on, in this place. The only thing, really." She ruffled Lina's hair and twisted the tips into spikes. She was clearly enjoying playing with it again.

"All the years you had it, did you know that the peach pit was magical?" asked Lina.

Her mother shrugged. "Not exactly. Your grandfather gave it to me when he started getting ill. I knew it got warm in the cold, and hot when there was danger, but that was about it. I kept it with me at the hospital for when patients were really struggling. I used to wrap you up in a blanket with it when you were a baby to ward off the cold."

Katya squinted into the distance. Firelight danced on her face. "Svetlana says this place isn't really here anymore—that the officers who were coming for Zima's ruined banquet won't find us," she said, turning back to Lina and glancing at the moth in her daughter's palm. "She says no one can find us, unless we want them to, because it's 'tethered by the life force of the sorceress and the guardian.' Do you have any idea what she's going on about? I thought *she* was the sorceress. I always told you she had great power, didn't I?"

Lina smiled and studied her tiny moth friend. She knew. *Lina* was the sorceress. Her moth friend, the closest creature to her when she'd made the peach pit grow, beginning the transformation of the camp, was now the guardian of this place. Already the tiny moth was growing stronger. One day, perhaps, it would be as powerful as Svetlana's giant fish, Pechal.

She'd decided to name it Nadezhda. It meant *hope*.

# 54

In the days after the liberation of the camp, many took all the bread and peaches they could carry and set out in search of long-lost family and friends. Despite the transformation of the place, many couldn't wait to get out. It had caused them so much suffering, after all.

Some were forced out. Former guards who hadn't been caught up in the peach trees. Prisoners who'd bullied or terrorized the others. These people were given a choice: to live by the new rules here or have no part of it. Above all, Lina wanted this to be a place where people had what they needed—food, warmth, shelter—and felt they could thrive, in peace. Lina had pinned her hopes on finding such a place in Moscow, ready-made. But when she'd seen the city through Natalya's eyes, she'd found that the dangers she'd hoped to escape lurked there too.

The arrests went on. The danger was real. What Lina had created, here at the camp, was what she'd always wanted to find elsewhere. This was home now. A proper one.

All the weapons in the camp were thrown into the *karker*, and the *karker* was sealed off forever.

Vadim, Alexei, and Old Gleb were among those who left. After their ordeal, Alexei didn't want to return to life as a butcher. From what Lina understood, he hoped to work in an old friend's bakery in Bulgaria, and Vadim had asked to be his assistant. Both men would leave their fearsome reputations behind. "They both say," Old Gleb explained, "that, when we were like shadows, they had waking nightmares about everything they'd ever done—that they had . . . *visitations*. I reckon they're looking to live a little differently from now on."

Old Gleb wanted to find his sons.

"Good luck, old man," said Lina, squeezing him tight.

"You too, little miss." He gave her a pat on the back. "You've got a good thing going on here. I reckon if there's anyone who can make a success of it, it's you."

She watched him leave with tears in her eyes. She felt Natalya's arm slip around hers to offer comfort. But the truth was that those like Gleb—the ones who left—would never find their way back. Not without help. If they turned to glance over their shoulder as they walked away, for one last glimpse, they would see nothing but mist.

Bogdan said he would stay—at least for the time being. Lina was glad. She dreaded him leaving more than anything.

Word from Svetlana was that the Great Leader, Stalin, was getting old and ill and, in time, when he died, many political prisoners might even be pardoned. If they were still alive, there was a chance Bogdan's parents might be freed. She hoped, above all, he would one day find both his parents alive and well. And when the time came to look for them, as long as everything was running smoothly here in the forest, she secretly thought about going with him. If he didn't let her, she might just sneak along anyway.

One night, as Lina tended to the plants in the greenhouse, she felt the atmosphere change. Right away, she knew that Svetlana was behind her. "Hello, Babushka," she said. "Have you come to check on my progress?" Lina had not seen much of her grandmother since the liberation of the camp. That journey to save Lina's mother had almost crushed Svetlana. She'd spent weeks sleeping.

"I've come to take you somewhere," said Svetlana. "Don't worry, you have done enough work to keep people fed while you're gone, and I will return you to your greenhouse afterward. Nadezhda will watch over them, with Katya and Bogdan. We will need the shadow child, Natalya, with us."

"*Nevertell*," came Natalya's whisper. She was never far from Lina's side these days.

Svetlana wrapped them up in her cape.

They traveled through the tundra—sometimes using Svetlana's cape, sometimes with Lina and Natalya riding on the back of Svetlana in her giant falcon form. There was no great rush this time. Not like before.

It was a different experience from when Lina had crossed this land with Bogdan. For a start, they weren't being chased. Secondly, spring had come. Bright wild flowers—yellow, orange, purple—bloomed from under sparkling frost. The rivers ran, carrying chunks of ice. Ravens barked at them from the trees and argued among themselves over pine cones in the retreating snow.

In the cool of the forests, they heard the padding of paws at times and caught glimpses of curious wolf faces, all white and gray, peering at them through the trees—before the animals loped away to safety.

For a time, they stopped at Svetlana's tower. Here, Lina sensed Natalya drift from her side toward the gardens. Lina guessed she wanted to walk among the plants. She'd seemed to enjoy doing that in Lina's greenhouse too.

Lina ran her fingers along the icy, translucent walls with their blue tinge and stared at all the flecks of silver and gold deep inside. She spent time in the luscious court-yard, gathering inspiration for what she could grow at the former camp. Her home. They even paid a visit to Pechal, who seemed much smaller and less frightening to Lina now. It helped that he wasn't trying to drown her.

Svetlana herself looked smaller these days too. Lina wasn't sure if it was because she was less afraid of her, or if she'd *actually* shrunk—perhaps because she wasn't storing such an unhealthy amount of cold magic inside her now. Her mother had used to say she was petite.

"Can I ask you something?" said Lina as they prepared to leave the tower. She shifted awkwardly. Though Svetlana wasn't quite as frightening as she used to be, she could still give a piercing glare. Lina cleared her throat. "You used to talk about all humans being bad—"

"They are," snapped Svetlana, and then narrowed her eyes at Lina. "Mostly."

"But you loved my grandfather so much you searched for him for years . . ."

"I've told you," Svetlana muttered, "he was different. He was everything." A distant look came into her eyes. When she continued, it was more to herself than to Lina. "I would have carried on searching for him until I'd turned everyone alive into ghosts. If that's what it had taken to find him. I would have shown them how you earn a title like Man Hunter."

Lina's voice came out weak and hoarse when she next spoke. "But how could you believe all humans are terrible when you were in love with one—when your children are at least *part* human?"

She knew what Bogdan would say. *Leave it, Lina. There's no reasoning with her kind of hatred.* Perhaps so.

Svetlana's look softened. "In truth," she said, "I knew I'd gone too far with the wolves. But I excused it to myself by saying those people bound by them were getting a second chance. That they would be helping to make amends for the deeds of their kind, by aiding me. Searching with the wolves and reporting back—as they did. And I needed them. How would I have had a chance of finding Anri and my children otherwise?

"Not returning home for so long changed something in me. That much is true. I fear I lost myself too, out in the wastes." She sighed. "I have started to release them, my wolf-bound. I've made it my business to find their families, to explain—and to do what I can to help them. That will be my new focus—as well as finding the next targets of the secret police and spiriting as many of them as I can to your peach forest for safety."

Lina nodded, and then she frowned. "But why did you do it in the first place? All those people you had wolf-bound? Like Natalya? What did they ever do?"

"It may be hard for you to understand, being part of their world," said Svetlana. "But I felt strongly, in my heart, that humans—all humans—had done this terrible thing to my family. And to me, personally. So I summoned my wolf spirits to help me search for Anri and my children. It felt like the only way. The only way."

"Babushka," said Lina. "There's something else I don't understand. Why couldn't you find us, all those years we spent in the camp? With your powers, and the cape, I would've thought . . ." Lina trailed off as Svetlana turned away. Both of them were silent for some time.

"I put an enchantment on them." Svetlana spoke so quietly that Lina had to lean in to hear her.

"An enchantment? What do you mean?"

Finally Svetlana looked at her again. "I put an enchantment on Anri and the children—so that they couldn't be found. Not unless someone already knew exactly where to look. I thought it was necessary. I felt I understood the threats posed by humans more than Anri did. But when they went missing, when they were betrayed . . . it meant *I* couldn't find them either."

Lina understood now. That had to be why Svetlana had needed her to summon her mother's image in the water mirror.

Over the rest of their journey, Lina studied Svetlana's face in the moments she thought her grandmother wasn't looking. She had to have felt partly responsible when her family disappeared. Had her anger and bitterness at losing them been even more destructive, her hatred of humans even stronger, because, in part, she actually blamed herself? Lina might never be sure.

# 55

Finally they reached Moscow.

Lina had seen photographs of the capital city, of course—the vast roads and the tall, square buildings with their walls of windows. The marches and parades.

Now that they were here in the city, though, she could only think of her mother and all those she'd left behind in the safety of the forest. She wondered if everybody else was thinking of someone too. Up the stairs of those colossal apartment blocks, behind the outward show of patriotism they presented in the parades, was half this city really mourning the loved ones who'd been taken to camps? The missing? Those never heard from again?

Lina knew "the missing" well. She'd spent her whole life surrounded by them.

Despite it being early when they arrived, cars and buses

already careened down the wide snow-cleared roads, honking and swerving in a system she didn't understand. It gave Lina the sweats. Any second, she expected a crash. How could they go so fast and not hit one another? And yet, they all seemed to know where they were heading—as if by design. Lina could barely fathom the intricate workings of such a vast city and its people. It was comforting to feel a pressure on her arm as they walked the streets, knowing that Natalya held her tightly.

Children with red scarves toggled around their shoulders walked to school, their cheeks and noses bright in the chilly spring air—though compared to what Lina had been used to, it practically felt warm. Lines of men and women waited patiently outside shops for their bread, their meat, their milk. Crane-topped towers, almost lost to mist, looked down over it all. Lina shuddered at the sight of those. They resembled the guard towers.

Lina, Natalya, and Svetlana walked for what felt like hours until they came to a grand pavilion, its pillars stretching up to the sky. The All-Union Agricultural Exhibition. In it were Lina's grandfather's famous gardens.

Svetlana spirited them through the barriers because the gardens were closed. They'd been shut down, she told Lina, after the war.

Even so, walking between the grand white pillars of the entrance was like crossing into another world. A kind of paradise, frozen in time. Straight in front of them stood a fountain as high as any building, which Lina guessed used to gush water from the enormous, intricate golden petals at the center. All around the edge stood life-size statues of people facing outward—each one of them glinting gold.

"Look at that, Natalya!" said Lina. She'd made a habit of referring to her often while she worked in the green-house, tending the plants. To let her know she was thinking of her.

"It's called the Stone Flower," said Svetlana. "Named after the old folktale."

Lina didn't know the story. But the fountain definitely looked like something out of a fairy tale.

The gardens were vast. All around were pavilions adorned with decorations just like grand temples—painted bright white and dedicated to particular things that the Soviet Union made or did, like pig farming, geology, or mechanization. Flax sheafs and grapevines were molded from plaster and decorated walls and ceilings. Giant fig-ures of bulls bore up the roof of the Meat Pavilion on top of great white pillars.

The Soviet hammer and sickle appeared everywhere too—and so did the five-pointed star she'd seen on the train. Statues of people towered far above them, bear-ing larger-than-life sheaves of wheat and waving huge flags. Their smiles, like the distant look in their eyes, forever fixed.

Lina could barely believe that it had been humans who made this place and not gods—or magical beings like Svetlana. Then they came to the pavilion for childhood, with its many statues of children on plinths. "Who are all these people, do you think? And why do they have their own statues?" asked Lina.

Svetlana frowned a little and her mouth tightened. "They were children who reported their parents to the authorities," she said. "For 'un-Soviet' behavior. Come. Let us carry on."

The other pavilions represented all the regions that made up the Soviet Union. It was the one for Georgia that they were looking for—that Lina's grandfather had worked on. Lina didn't know what to expect when they got there or what they would do once they'd found it. But she felt drawn there by some kind of force.

What they found was another vast, temple-like pavilion. This one had pillars stretching impossibly high, ending in elaborate decorations: wings—and grand arches covered in delicate petal motifs.

The gardens were overgrown and withered. Even so, if she looked hard enough, Lina got a sense of what it must once have been like, of what her grandfather had tried to create. A sheltered sanctuary of green, partly concealed by the angle of the pavilion, which seemed to gather the garden into itself and stand guard around it.

In their prime, the trees of all different sizes would have

brought dappled shade of all shapes, and borne fruits like offerings to outstretched hands. The grass would have softened every step, and low, berry-peppered bushes would have brought color and treats from below. A paradise.

Perhaps it could still be one.

Lina felt an aching heat in her palms, like a kind of yearning: electricity, coiled and ready to whip-crack. She ran her hand over the bushes, no more than a thatch of sticks now, just as she had in her dream aboard the train.

Greenness spread out from her touch. A sound like rushing water echoed around them: the sound of every plant, growing. Soon the entire garden burgeoned with berries and leaves. It was just as she'd imagined.

"I wanted you to see this place," said Svetlana, smiling, when Lina had finished. "It is a part of me. A part of you."

Lina breathed deeply. The air smelled different here. She closed her eyes and imagined being a plant, soaking in the sun through her upturned face—and her outstretched hands and arms. She thought of her grandfather and wondered how it was possible for her to feel so close to a person she'd never met—someone who was already gone before she was born. In a way, he'd helped shape her entire life from the start. Inspired this whole adventure.

"Now that you are beginning to master your powers, I will make you your own cape, using this," said Svetlana, holding out the small rectangular corner of cape that Lina had torn off so long ago. Svetlana must have retrieved it from the greenhouse. Lina had forgotten about it. "That way, you can travel more easily and visit here whenever you please. And I'll help you learn to use it safely, of course. I'll help you learn to control all of your abilities over time, so that you can use them without harm."

"Thank you," said Lina. "For all of it. But don't you want to use that scrap of cape to mend yours?"

Svetlana looked at the tattered end of her own cape and raised an eyebrow. "No," she said. "The missing piece reminds me of you, when I'm away. It helps me to remember what I've done. And how I must make amends."

Lina nodded. She could sense something in the air. Feel it lingering along every dappled path, every shaded nook, and down by the water of the fountains and ponds. It felt a little like being close to Svetlana's shadows. Except it wasn't that.

It was more like memories, so strong they wanted to burst through the air and be relived, over and over again. As if the memories themselves missed being real.

*"Nevertell . . ."*

Lina and Svetlana looked to the empty space where the whisper had come from.

Svetlana lifted her chin. "That was the other reason I brought you here. Natalya has something to show us."

# 56

G o on, child," said Svetlana. "I can help you."

Svetlana reached out her hand slowly, palm up. With her head turned to the side, out of the corner of her eye, Lina saw the outline of Natalya take hold of Svetlana's hand. Svetlana instructed Lina to relax. "Let yourself be taken with her."

She did.

The world around Lina drifted and swayed, like a reflection in water that had been disturbed. The walls and the steps beneath her melted into gray gloom and became hard to distinguish from snow—or sky. She recognized this feeling—from when Natalya had shown her the memories. The classroom. Svetlana and the roses. She breathed out and allowed it to happen. Then everything snapped back into focus in an instant.

From beyond the arches of the Georgia pavilion, deep inside it, came voices.

"Come," said Svetlana. What they walked into was a room filled with rows of desks. Lina glanced behind her. Her grandfather's garden had vanished. Instead, large rectangular windows looked out onto an open space with lush grass. Red roses grew around a tree at the center.

"I've seen this before! Natalya showed me," said Lina. "First in your hut and then when we were on the train." She stared at Svetlana. "She saw you from her classroom window. This classroom. She watched you do magic."

Svetlana nodded.

At each desk in the room sat a child, all dressed exactly the same. At the desk beside Lina sat a pink-cheeked little girl with brown pigtails. It was Natalya, just as she'd seen her beneath Svetlana's cape. Natalya watched the teacher at the front of the class with her wide blue-green eyes, but her attention kept drifting to the window. She'd drink in the outside world for long moments. It seemed to Lina that she only glanced back to make sure the teacher thought she was paying attention. A dreamer.

The shadow of Natalya still held Svetlana's hand, surveying the vision with them both. As they all watched, the Natalya at her desk looked to the window and gasped. Her eyes grew a bit wider. Lina didn't have to look around to know that she would see Svetlana outside—the memory of her—raise a rose from its bud in seconds, just to kill it.

The real Svetlana lifted her chin and squinted straight ahead. "When I came back from one of my trips to the mountains, I found them gone. My entire family, missing—and I had no way of finding them. I only knew they had been betrayed by other humans, since that's what *some* humans do. Supposed friends, entrusted with their location in the city . . . I searched for them. All this time, I've been searching."

"And you had Natalya wolf-bound. Why? Just because she'd seen your magic?"

"I saw enemies everywhere. I knew Anri had spoken in classrooms about his work. Even taken the schoolchildren for trips to see the gardens. It would have been just like him to tell them too much—about magic. I thought that's why Natalya came to me, sneaking around, watching. I thought that she'd betrayed us to the authorities. This child became the first of my wolf-bound shadows."

"She'd seen something magical," Lina said to herself. "She thought *you* were magical. And she only wanted to see if you could be real."

They were silent for a very long time. The children in Natalya's memory went on scribbling at their desks.

Lina cleared her throat, and when she spoke, her voice was soft. "Svetlana. My grandfather *was* arrested for speaking of real magic to children. But Mama said he'd also joked with friends that the Great Leader was telling them all a fairy-tale lie, when the reality of his 'great achievements' was very different. Mama always said that he was denounced by a colleague, and when the secret police came, they just decided to take my mother and uncle away too. That had nothing to do with Natalya. She was as much a victim as him. Or you. Or anyone."

Svetlana gazed down at the simple vision of the girl at the desk but directed her words to the shadow at her side. "Natalya, if this is true, then I am truly sorry. You came to me hoping for something wonderful—and I gave you horror."

A single tear flicked off the end of Svetlana's long black eyelashes and landed on her cheek. It seemed to reflect everything—the whole world in miniature. She smudged away the tear with her finger.

Shadow-Natalya left Svetlana's side and tugged urgently at Lina's sleeve. Apparently she had something else to show her. Lina looked around the classroom. A poster in bold black, white, and red caught her eye. It was taped to the classroom door, and it said:

NEVER TELL CHILDREN ABOUT THINGS THEY CANNOT SEE.

Lina gaped. "Never tell," she said to herself. "*Nevertell*. Svetlana, what does it mean?"

"It means fairy stories. Folktales. Ghosts and spirits. People like us. It means 'Don't imagine,' I suppose.

Imagining tends to give people inconvenient ideas, and those with power don't like to be inconvenienced."

Lina nodded and folded her arms. "Ideas like escaping from a labor camp or crossing all of Siberia. Where would we be without ideas?"

"Before I met Anri, I lived alone in the mountains to protect myself from this sort of curiosity," said Svetlana. "I've seen how it can destroy the object of its fascination—or fear. I don't know which is worse. Humans kill what they think is most terrifying and what is most precious—you cannot deny it."

"Not Natalya," said Lina. "Not me or Bogdan or Tuyaara." So much of what Svetlana said was true, but together they could do better. *People* could do better. She believed it so much that it burned.

Svetlana walked around to stand in front of Natalya's desk and folded her arms across her stomach. "Right before I bound her, she swore she'd never tell . . ." Svetlana broke off and put her hand across her own mouth.

"Would you like to leave now?" Svetlana asked shadow Natalya. "It will mean no more of this half existence. It will mean peace." Her eyes glistened.

Natalya's shadow nodded.

Svetlana stood up straight in an instant, snapped the heels of her boots together, and raised her chin high. "In that case, I release you."

Natalya let out a long sigh, like a sudden gust of wind.

Lina reached out for her. "Goodbye, my friend!" she said. "And thank you. Thank you for everything."

Natalya's silhouette fell to the floor like a heap of abandoned clothes, which then too disappeared. The vision faded. Lina and Svetlana were back inside the grand Georgia pavilion. This time, they were alone.

# EPILOGUE

In the depths of Siberia, in the harshest cold, a forest grows. It's a forest like no other in this part of the world, because it's made up of peach trees. The fruit from these trees is self-replenishing. Pick one to eat and, by the time you're done, a new peach will have grown.

No one here knows hunger. At least, not anymore.

Once, the forest was a labor camp. Lina was born there. Her father was a vicious commandant who treated the prisoners with cruelty, while demanding respect in return. But respect isn't what grew in their hearts.

In the forest, they now have happiness and safety.

There are growers, harvesters, cooks—and everything in between. Including a teacher—Tuyaara. She splits her time between studying in Yakutsk, seeing her family, and being with her love, Keskil, in the peach forest.

They have Nadezhda the moth too. She flies around the forest's perimeter, keeping watch, but always comes back to Lina. Already she's grown to be the size of Lina's palm. It's the magic, making her bigger and prolonging her life.

True to her word, Svetlana and a network of informers seek those most in danger of arrest. She visits the peach forest rarely, but when she does, it is with important news from the outside, or with people in desperate need of protection. Lina enjoys her visits. Her favorite times are when they can all be together—Katya, Svetlana, Bogdan, and brave Tuyaara with her Keskil—to share a meal around a campfire and tell one another their stories.

# ACKNOWLEDGMENTS

A huge, visible-from-space THANK YOU in flashing lights to:

My agent, Bryony Woods, for taking a chance on me in the first place and for being utterly fantastic.

Every other professional who's worked on this book to make it what it is, including Sandra Dieckmann and Rovina Cai for their beautiful artwork. And the whole team at Walker—especially Annalie Grainger and Emily McDonnell for their amazing editing.

The Literary Consultancy for the Free Read, and the WoMentoring Project, which set me on course to getting my agent. Mslexia, which longlisted *Nevertell* in its Children's Novel Competition, and novelist Rosemary Dun, for teaching me what I needed to learn.

Everyone who believed in me and shares my excitement

about this book. And, quite frankly, anyone who's put up with me this far—Charlotte Godfrey, Clare McMillan, and Siobhan Cole being prime examples. Not to mention those who took time out of their busy lives to give me feedback on parts of this story: Sarah Louise Robinson, Thom Axon, Susan Angoy, and Rachel Knightley, that's you! Amazing writers, every one.

All those who helped in other ways. Alvaro Sánchez López and Firuz Ozari, as well as Herself and her marvelous blog, Kiddingherself.com, for the insight. Ayar Kuo for the inspirational photography. The editors of *Inside the Rainbow,* in the pages of which I learned of "Never tell a child about things he cannot see." Authors Sarah Baker, for coffee, chats, and writerly advice, and Stefan Mohamed—who was generous enough to read my first attempt at a novel.

To LW, PJ, Mandii, Codex, Holly, Kate, Flo, and Ken. I give praise to Britney every day for your friendship, solidarity, and humor, which has kept me sane.

My parents, Simon and Lisa Orton, for bringing me up around books and for always nurturing my passion for writing. And my parents-in-law, Linda Wilding and Jon and Jane Pullara, for all their encouragement along the way. All the rest of my family, who are just awesome. In particular, Nan Axon, who was a sheer force of nature.

Matt Pullara for always being such a rock. And Isaac Pullara for being an inspiration.

**KATHARINE ORTON** has an English degree and a master's in creative writing. She worked for Barefoot Books in Bath, England, before leaving to focus on her writing and her young family. She signed with her agent after taking part in the UK's WoMentoring Project, which pairs female writers with professional literary women. *Nevertell* is Katharine Orton's first novel. She lives in Bristol, England.